Chapter 1: Could it get any worse?

"We need to talk."

"This can't be good." Jessica sighed.

"No! It's fine. It's good. Really."

"Well, out with it!"

"Jessica, you're my sister and I love you."

"But?"

"No but! No. It's good, really. Now that your parole is finished, we thought it would be better for you to start over in a new place. Somewhere away from Philadelphia. Best for you."

"Best for me? You mean best for the family."

"Of course not! That's not what I meant at all."

"If I leave, Mom and Dad can tell people I'm doing volunteer work in Africa, like they did while I was in prison."

"They never... forget them. This is for you." She placed her hand on Jessica's arm.

"What did you mean by away from here? Harrisburg? Pittsburgh?"

"That would be fine. Or maybe a bit farther."

"Such as?"

"California."

"California? You do want to get rid of me. Why don't you send me to Alaska, for fuck's sake?"

"Don't be silly. You would have to drive through Canada to get to Alaska and, with your criminal past, they would never let you across the border."

"My criminal past? You make me sound like Al Capone. Everyone knows

I was framed!"

"We all believe you..." She avoided eye contact with Jessica.

"Why don't you hire me as your nanny? I love your kids. I've been looking after them for six months, and doing a kick-ass job."

"Yes, ah, you've been great with the kids, it's just..."

"What?"

"I know it's not your fault. You picked it up in prison."

"Picked up what in prison? You make it sound like I got the clap!"

"Nothing like that! Don't be gross! No, it's, well, you swear a lot."

"I don't swear that much. Hardly at all. In fact, I never swear. I don't know what you're talking about."

"Jeremy told Todd to put away his toys the other night and he told Jeremy to 'f' off!"

"Your husband is too thin skinned. Besides, Todd probably picked that up on the street."

"He's four! He doesn't go on the street. He only goes with his Aunty Jess."

"I'll bet he picked it up from the boy next door. That kid is a real potty mouth."

"He's a year old for Christ's sake! Now you got me doing it."

"How am I supposed to get to California? Did you think of that?"

"Jeremy has fixed up the old–"

"Oh, not that shitty Gremlin! Is he out of his fucking mind?"

"He's a good mechanic. He says the car will get you there without any problems."

"What about money? How am I supposed to drive across the country with no money?"

She stood up and held out an envelope. "There is five hundred dollars in here."

"Five hundred? You expect me to make it to California with only five hundred dollars? That won't even pay the gas."

"You were a stock broker."

"What the fuck has that got to do with anything?"

"You worked with money. You must know how to be frugal."

"Frugal? And what do Mom and Dad think about you shipping me off to the west coast?"

"This money comes from them."

"Fuck."

"It's for the best, Jessica. You can start over. No one will know about your past."

"Yeah, well, I'm not a charity case!" She grabbed the envelope, startling her sister. "But I'll take this money because you owe it to me for looking after your snotty, brat kids! And Todd is lucky he had his aunt to teach him some real words because his fucking politically correct father never will!"

"Keys are in the car," Jessica's sister called after her as she stomped up the stairs.

Jessica stuffed her meager possessions in a back-pack, went out to the car, threw herself in, and tore out of the driveway.

Seven days later, she was standing on the Las Vegas strip, holding a sign that read "willing to do nothing for money." Apparently, humor does not work for panhandlers because her cup remained empty. When she spied a policeman approaching, she decided to call it a night and retire to the comfort of her car.

He was nervous. Meeting an editor at 10:00 in the morning was never good. He paced around the suite and continually checked his watch. At 9:59 there was a knock on the door. He peered through the peephole.

"Come in, Trish," he said as he swung the door open.

"Wilson. Good to see you again. Well, one hopes?"

"As well as can be expected. Drink?"

"Too early for me. But you're welcome to..."

"Please, sit." *Could this get any more awkward?*

"Thank you. I suppose you know why I'm here."

8

"My proposal."

"Yes. Among other reasons."

What the heck does that mean? Wilson wondered.

"Wilson, you have been a beloved and respected author for many years, and we are honored to have been your publisher. Your books have entertained and informed countless children."

"That's kind of you to say. Of course, it hasn't exactly hurt your bottom line, right?"

Trish stared at him as a long pause followed his attempt to lighten the mood. Wilson shifted uncomfortably on the sofa.

"We do find that your recent proposal to write an action thriller along the lines of the Jason Bourne novel is a bit of a stretch from your usual work."

"I used that novel as an example. My book would be completely different. Only the genre would be the same."

"Frankly, Wilson, your proposal seemed clichéd and uninteresting. And some of your characters seem, what's the word I'm looking for; bizarre."

"But I would..." Wilson slumped back.

"People who write works like that have lived the life. Ex-soldiers or former MI-5 operatives. You're a children's author whose life-experience involves studying farm animals to convert into Willikers characters. Face it, Wilson, you will never be able to write an action novel. The fact is, you're not the type of man to get involved in anything adventurous or dangerous. You are, and I say this with all due respect, wimpish. No offense."

"None taken," he replied, just above a whisper.

"And there is another thing I need to talk to you about. Your book signing this evening will be your last."

"My last? I don't understand. I have seven more appearances remaining on the tour."

"We're giving them to John Baroque for his new novel."

"Baroque? You can't be serious?"

"The decision has been made. Coincidentally, and you're going to love this,

John's book is an action thriller! Isn't that rich?"

"Yes. Rich." *Could this get any worse?*

"Have you read John's book?"

"Haven't had the pleasure."

"It is wonderful! Very similar to what you proposed, if you had the tal... I mean, experience, to write an action thriller. He was a marine."

"What kind of a ridiculous name is 'Baroque' anyway?"

"It's his pen name. He wishes to protect his privacy."

"Is that why the advertising poster shows him shirtless?"

"Isn't that a wonderful photo?"

Wilson sighed. "Perhaps you're right, Trish. I should concentrate on improving the Willikers. Write something new and fresh."

"Yes. About that."

"What is it?"

"It's good! Nothing to worry about. We feel the Willikers have run their course and plan to retire them."

"But I have a contract for three more books!"

"Yes, well, there is a clause in your contract stating we have the option to pull out of the agreement if sales do not reach a certain level. We have a warehouse full of copies of your last book, and stacks from the one before. But this is good. You can retire. Travel more. Enjoy your golden years."

"My golden years? I'm barely middle-aged!"

"Really? You should consider joining a gym. Anyway, must run."

"What about the book signing this evening?"

"On as scheduled. Think of it as your swan song."

"I will make this a great event tonight. At least I can go out with dignity."

"Dignity? Perhaps if you had quit two years ago, I mean, yes, go out with dignity. It is all you have left. No offense."

"None taken."

"Goodbye, Wilson."

"Trish. Always a pleasure."

"Don't get up. I'll see myself out."

Wilson remained slumped on the sofa watching her depart.

"I was wrong. It could get worse!"

"Oh great! A wall. Stupid GPS app. Now I'm going to be late. Maybe if I recalculate I'll find it." As Wilson fumbled with his phone, he got a text.

Hi sweeety! Hope the tore goes wel. I'm movng out. It's over! Bye. Angel.

"Moving out? She's breaking up with me by text?" He typed *What do you mean? You're leaving me?* He hit send and stood staring at the screen. Nothing. Time seemed to stand still as he waited for a reply. Something. Anything!

"Hey mister! Let me see your hands!" a woman shouted from behind him.

Then another text appeared. *I'm taking the dog. Lovs.*

"She's taking my dog!?"

"Hands! Now!"

Wilson continued to stare at the screen. "Perhaps you could help me," he called over his shoulder. "I'm trying to get to the Regent Bookstore."

"What?"

"The Regent Bookstore?" Wilson turned around. Looking at her tattered clothes and disheveled hair, he continued, "Never mind. You don't look the type to frequent bookstores."

"What's that supposed to mean?"

"Nothing. Give me a sec to reprogram this thing."

"Hey, mister! I have a gun! Let me see your hands!"

Another text came on Wilson's phone. "Finally, a response from Angel."

Book signing cancelled. Sheri.

Cancelled? Because I'm late? Wilson.

Children burning effigy of you in front. Don't come here! Sheri.

Wilson stared at the screen.

"Ah, excuse me. Could we get on with this?"

Wilson didn't move.

"Are you okay? You're not having a stroke or something, are you?"

"What? Oh, I forgot about you."

"Still here. Still want your wallet."

"My wallet?"

"Yes. This is a stick-up, dumbnuts."

"There's no need to be rude."

"Can we get on with this?" the woman asked.

"I'm not having the best day. My book signing got cancelled because children are burning an effigy of me in front of the bookstore. And this is the second time in a week!"

"Yeah, well, we all got problems."

"Oh yes, and I suppose your day is worse."

"I'm living in my car and haven't eaten in two days. How's that?"

"Maybe you are worse off than me."

"I'm more pathetic than you, yay me!" she said sarcastically. "Now, can we continue with the business at hand? It's getting dark and I need to get back to my car before they tow it away."

A police siren could be heard in the background.

"Look, throw that gun in the trash where it belongs and let's get out of here before I have to spend my evening in a police station explaining how some lunatic woman tried to kill me. And if you haven't eaten in two days, I will buy you dinner. But first, throw away that gun!"

"You're some piece of work, you know that?" She threw the gun into a garbage can at the end of the alley and they hurried out onto the street.

"I passed a little diner a ways back. We'll go there if it's okay with you?" he asked.

"Anywhere is fine with me."

They continued along the street and turned left at the corner. After a block they entered a diner. The woman went to the last booth and slid into the seat followed by Wilson who sat across from her.

"Get you something to drink?" the waitress asked cheerily.

"Just water," he replied.

"Diet cola."

After the waitress left, he said, "I'm Wilson, Wilson James. And you are?"

She hesitated. "Cari. Just Cari, okay?"

"Fine by me. Tell me, Cari, if that is your real name, how did you end up in an alley with a gun, attempting to mug me?"

"You don't think I could do it, do you?"

"Do what?"

"Mug you. I felt sorry for you because you seem like such a dope."

"I'm sure you make an excellent robber."

"Don't patronize me! I was a Wall Street broker before the collapse in 2008. I can do anything I put my mind to and don't you forget it! I was, ah, I was only trying to get you to buy me dinner. That's it. And it worked perfectly. Just like I planned."

"Wall Street broker to mugger in five years. Impressive."

"Patronizing again."

Wilson's attention was diverted to a small television over the counter to his right.

"Police now have a suspect in the brutal murder of Wall Street executive Ralph D. Brentwood from New York," the news commentator began. "In town for a convention, Brentwood was found dead earlier today in his hotel suite by a maid. Police say he died of a single gunshot and this woman, seen here in a police sketch, was seen running from the room. She has tentatively been identified as Jessica Stone, also from New York, a former colleague of Brentwood's. Ms. Stone was convicted in 2010 of embezzlement and fraud and served two years in federal penitentiary for her crimes. Her present location is unknown, but if anyone sees her, do not approach as she is considered armed and dangerous. Contact police immediately."

Wilson turned his head and stared at her. "Is it Cari? Or Jessica?"

"What? No! I don't know what you're talking about. I look nothing like that woman in the sketch."

13

"There is a resemblance."

"There's no resemblance!"

"Then you wouldn't mind if I call 911 and let the police sort this out?"

"Doesn't bother me in the least."

He took out his phone and began dialing.

"911, what is your emergency?" the operator asked.

Cari grabbed the phone. "Sorry, wrong number," and hung up. "Don't look at me like that. There is a simple explanation."

"Do you want to tell me now, or should we wait a while so you have time to think it up?"

"I resent that! I haven't lied to you. I live in my car and haven't eaten in two days. That's the truth."

The waitress returned with their drinks. "Ready to order?"

"I'll have a double cheeseburger, large fries, and onion rings," Cari told the waitress.

"Just a hamburger and small fries for me."

"Be ready in no time." The waitress smiled and left.

"And your name?" he continued.

"Ah," she hesitated. "Cari is my middle name. Yes, that's it. Cari is my middle name."

"What is the real story?"

She shifted in her seat and looked around the diner. They were the only patrons.

"Okay, here's the God honest truth. I do know Ralph. Did know Ralph. We worked together and were close at one time."

"Why did you kill him?"

"I didn't kill him!" Cari shouted, trying to hide her face when the waitress looked toward her. She leaned across the table and continued in a low voice, "I was at Ralph's hotel room this morning. When I arrived the door was ajar, I walked in, and found him lying dead near the bathroom door. I thought I heard someone in the bedroom, the gun was on the floor next to him, and I panicked

MANY PIGS IN MANHATTAN

and grabbed it. I thought the killer was in there. Then I ran out of the room."

"That's the gun you tried to kill me with?"

"Man, you're a baby! I didn't try to kill you and I didn't kill Ralph. He was already dead when I arrived. Aren't you listening?"

This woman is delusional! Didn't try to kill me? She pointed a gun at me and wanted to steal my wallet, Wilson thought.

"Here you go." The waitress interrupted them as she set down their plates of food. "If you need anything just yell," she added, scurrying away.

"Looks great!" Cari said as she eyed her plate. "Tell me about you. What's your story?"

Wilson raised an eyebrow. "As soon as you're finished eating, I'm leaving. That's my story."

They ate in silence. The way Cari wolfed down her food gave him little doubt about what she had told him. At least part of it.

"Finished?" he asked.

Cari nodded. "Thanks."

He got up and headed to the cash register. After paying, he returned to the table to leave a tip and saw Cari had left. When he stepped outside the diner she whistled and motioned him over.

"Are you going to mug me again?"

"Get over yourself! I just wanted to thank you again for dinner and for believing me."

"Who said I believe you?"

"It was implied in your tone."

"Implied in my... Look, forget it. No harm done. I would say it was nice meeting you but..." He shrugged, looking anywhere but here.

"Yeah, likewise. Anyway, thanks again for dinner." She moved close and hugged him then pulled back. "See you around."

"Not likely," Wilson said, and turned to hail a cab.

When he had settled in the back seat he glanced around, but she was gone. What a strange day. Strange and disheartening. The cab arrived at his hotel after a short ride. Wilson pulled out a roll of bills to pay the driver, entered the hotel, and went straight to the elevator. He stepped in and pushed number seven. He fumbled in his pockets, searching each one twice for his key card. "I can't believe this!" He threw his hands up in despair. It really kept piling up today. He punched the button for the lobby to get a new key.

A young woman was typing on a computer at the desk.

"Good evening." He smiled at her. "I'm Wilson James, room 716. I left my key in the room."

"No problem, Mr. James. I can print you a new one right away," the clerk replied. "My daughter loves your books."

"Thank you."

"Except the last two. She doesn't want to read them anymore."

"Out grew them?" he asked optimistically.

"No, ah, well, she didn't like, I mean..." the woman trailed off. Wilson's shoulders slumped. "Oh, I'm sorry! I shouldn't have said anything, but they're expensive and I'm a single mother. It's tough when you spend hard-earned money for your child on something that isn't very goo—that she doesn't, ah..."

"It's okay. Here, let me refund you." He started to pull out cash for her.

"Oh no, Mr. James. That's not what I meant. No, it's fine. Really. Here's your key. Enjoy the rest of your stay."

Embarrassed, Wilson took the card and hurried to the comfortable solitude of the elevator.

This day gets better and better, he thought as the elevator rose. The doors opened and he walked, head lowered, to his room.

"No need to stay in Vegas. Might as well pack and head for the airport. Maybe I can catch a redeye out tonight. Then what?"

Wilson shuffled across the living room of the suite and into the bedroom, where he filled his suitcase from the drawers of the dresser. He was in the bathroom gathering up his toiletries when the door to the room opened and closed.

Funny time for maid service. "Hello! Who's there?" he asked as he walked out of the bathroom. "You! How did you get in here?"

Cari stood just inside the suite door. "Funny story, I didn't think you would open the door if I knocked, so when I hugged you outside the diner I accidentally ended up with your keycard. You shouldn't leave it in the envelope marked with the room number."

"Accidentally?"

"Oh, and at the same time I accidentally got your wallet." Cari held it up.

"My wallet!" Wilson shouted, snatching it from her. "And I suppose you accidentally got my money and credit cards!"

"I'm not a criminal!" Cari glared at him.

"We'll see." He was searching through his wallet and counting the money.

"I did borrow twenty dollars though."

"Borrowed?"

"That's right, borrowed. You'll get it back. Want me to sign an IOU?"

"Wouldn't be worth the paper it's written on," he muttered.

She sneered at him. "I keep telling you I am innocent."

"You just happened to be in that guy's room right after he was murdered?"

"No, I didn't just happen to be there," she replied.

"Are you saying you did it?"

"No! When I heard Ralph was in town I tried to meet with him. I found out which hotel he was staying at and kept leaving messages for him. I even waited around the lobby one time but got kicked out by security. Then, last night someone put a note on the windshield of my car saying that Ralph wanted to meet with me at a specific time in his room. That's why I was there this morning."

"Hold on. Are you saying that someone lured you to that room immediately after Ralph was killed?"

"You believe me now, don't you?"

"I wouldn't go that far, but it does sound suspicious."

"I'm being framed."

"It is convenient a witness spotted you."

Cari's eyes lit up. "You do believe me."

"It doesn't matter what I believe. Anyway, I'm leaving tonight. The room is all paid for two more nights. You might as well use it. But don't steal anything!"

"Where are you going?"

"Home."

"Where's home?"

"Not Las Vegas. Goodbye Cari, or Jessica, or whoever you are. It has been interesting."

Wilson walked out the door and took the elevator down to the street. He slumped into the backseat of a taxi and closed his eyes. The news came on the radio. "There has been a new development in the homicide of New York investment broker Ralph Brentwood. Late this evening the gun used in his murder was recovered from a trash can in an alley off 9th Avenue. Initial reports from the police confirm the fingerprints on the gun belong to Jessica Stone of New York. Stone was Brentwood's former colleague and lover and served time in federal prison for felony fraud. A close friend of Brentwood's, Miles Jacoby, stated that Stone had been stalking Brentwood and threatening to kill him and had been forcibly removed from the hotel in which he was staying the day before the murder. Stone is five foot eight, one hundred and forty pounds, with light brown, shoulder-length hair and green eyes. Police have issued an all-points bulletin for her arrest and are watching all avenues of departure from Las Vegas."

Cari stepped out of the shower when there was a knock at the door. She wrapped a towel around herself, hurried out, and peered through the eyepiece. She opened the door and smiled. "Couldn't stay away could–"

"Who is Miles Jacoby?" Wilson asked.

"A two-bit pain in the ass. Why?"

"Did you see him anywhere in Vegas?"

"No, but if I had it would have been attached to Ralph's ass. He's the biggest suck-up. Where did you hear about him?"

"On the radio in the cab to the airport. Jacoby told a reporter you were stalking Brentwood and threatened to kill him."

Cari scowled. "I did no such thing! I only wanted him to help me find a job. When I got out I tried to see him but Miles always ran interference."

"What would Jacoby gain from Brentwood's death?"

"He would become a managing partner in the firm."

"What is he now?"

"Ralph's assistant."

"There's your motive. If we go to the police–" Wilson turned toward the door.

"No!" Cari backed away. "I can't chance it! I was framed once by them and if I turn myself in the same thing will happen again, only this time I'll be put away for the rest of my life!"

Wilson walked over and sat on the couch. She sat down beside him.

"Do you believe me?" she asked, peering sideways at him.

He looked at her.

She wrapped her arms around herself. "Stop staring! You're freaking me out."

He continued to sit in silence. She slid to the end of the sofa.

"Ever heard of John Baroque?"

"I would remember a name like that!"

"He's a twenty something debut author who wrote my novel." Wilson sighed.

"Not following."

"For several years I have been doing research on an action thriller, like the Jason Bourne novel. Are you familiar with the Jason Bourne films?"

"What woman isn't familiar with Matt Damon?"

"I pitched my idea to the publisher but she turned it down. And then, all of a sudden, this Baroque guy has an action thriller published! Coincidence? I think not."

"Was he a soldier or something?"

"Marine."

"What about you? Were you in the military?"

"No."

"Police?"

"No."

"FBI? CIA? Boy scouts?"

"What's your point?"

"Climb mountains? Ride rapids?"

Wilson rolled his eyes. "No."

"You're fucked! You got to have experience to write something like that, if it's going to be believable."

"My editor said the same thing. Without the vulgarity. But, as I was riding to the airport, I had an epiphany. You." He smiled at her.

"You sure you're not having a stroke?"

"You're right!" He stood up and began to pace. "Nothing exciting has happened to me until now. I want to write a book based on you."

"You want to write about me?"

"Yes. Not only what has happened to you, but your miraculous escape. Picture it: the heroine flees an unjust system because she is being framed for a heinous crime." He turned to the window, raising his hands and spreading them wide, as if picturing the story.

"You want to profit from my misery. Is that it?"

"No I— listen. I have a small place in the mountains on the island of Crete. I use it to get away from the publicity and reporters, at least I did when they were interested in me. No one knows about it. All I have to do is get you from here to there."

"Oh, I see exactly what you mean!" Cari said angrily as she stood and wrapped the towel tighter around herself. "I may have made some mistakes but I'm no whore!"

"Whore? What? Oh, no. That's not what I meant! God, no. Ewww!" Wilson frowned, shuddering.

"What do you mean, 'ewww'? You would be lucky to have me! What are you, gay or something?"

"No, I'm not gay. I want to help you! I'm not asking for anything in return."

"Except using me as a guinea pig to save your pathetic career."

"I don't see anyone else lining up to help you!" He glared at her, crossing his arms over his chest.

"Yeah, well, I can help myself," she muttered, turning toward the window.

"With what? This room for two nights and twenty bucks?"

"I was doing fine before you showed up."

Wilson scoffed. "Robbing tourists in alleys? Oh wait, you weren't successful at that either."

"You don't have to rub it in! I'm not having the best day." She began to cry.

"Oh, look, I'm sorry. I didn't mean to make you cry." He took a tentative step toward her, his hand outstretched.

She turned and looked at him. "Fuck, you men are easy. A few fake tears and you'll do anything for us."

"Yeah well... I... oh shut up!"

"You don't get to be a top broker on Wall Street by being weak or stupid. Or survive two years in prison." Cari sighed. "But the fact is, if Miles is behind this frame, I'm fucked and then some. He'll be sure to put me away. He always hated me."

"You're interested?" Wilson perked up, his voice an octave too high. He cleared his throat.

"As you said, what other choice do I have? So, what's this big plan to get me to Greece?"

"Well I..." He hesitated. "The thing is..."

She stared at him. "You haven't got a clue, have you?"

He rubbed the back of his neck, avoiding eye contact. "That's not exactly true."

"Well, what is it?"

"I'm working on it. This is new to me. Smuggling people." He shrugged.

"Not a clue. I'll be in the bathroom if you come up with something brilliant."

She stalked off to get dressed, shutting the door behind her with a snap.

She was right about that, he didn't have a plan. But this could be the inspiration he needed. If he could get her to Greece and into hiding it would provide the perfect plot. The details would fall into place. All he needed was a plan.

"Anything yet?" Cari asked, emerging from the bathroom.

Wilson looked her up and down. "You're wearing different clothes."

"That's what I used the twenty for. Went to a shrift shop. What's our next move? We're a long way from Crete."

"First, we need to get out of Vegas."

"Came up with that all by yourself, did you?" Cari smirked.

"Being a smart-ass isn't helping. And besides, I don't hear anything from you."

"Hey, this is your book. I'm just a minor character in it."

"No, you're the main character."

"Really? I'm the female Jason Bourne?"

"That's right. For getting out of Las Vegas we can't use public transportation because they'll be watching everything and they know what you look like. Wait! That's it! First thing we do is change your appearance."

"How so?" she asked, looking apprehensive.

"Remember in the first film, Bourne changes his girlfriend's hair by cutting and dyeing it."

"I'm your girlfriend? Is that the way it's going to be?" Cari asked in an angry tone.

"What? No, that's not what I meant."

"Fuck, you're easy." She shook her head.

"What?"

"I'm kidding! Don't you have a sense of humor?"

"I have a great sense of humor, when something is 'funny.' And you shouldn't swear."

"What are you, some kind of prude? Don't tell me you're a Republican, for fuck's sake!"

"I'm not a prude! Nor a–"

"Kidding! It's like shooting fish in a barrel. You wouldn't last a week in prison."

"I have no intention of going to prison and even if I did, I would last fine, thank you very much."

"A children's author with no sense of humor. Yeah, you'd do great."

"It's getting late. Let's get some sleep. First thing in the morning I'll go and get the supplies. Then, I'll rent a car and we'll head out."

"Head out where?"

"Somewhere we can find a flight to Greece," he said, looking around the room. "You can take the bed and I'll sleep on the couch."

"You're an okay guy, for such a baby," Cari teased. "By the way, what are your children's books about?"

"I created the Willikers," he told her, fluffing up the sofa cushions.

"The Willikers?! Are you kidding? They are everywhere! Cartoons, movies, even cups at fast-food joints. You must be worth a fortune! And you bitch because I borrowed a lousy twenty bucks." She scowled at him.

"I'm okay financially, but I have to support two ex-wives who have expensive taste. And I made a lot of bad investments."

"You need advice from me. I could make you a fortune." She threw him a pillow from the bedroom.

Wilson caught it and lay on the couch, punching the pillow once to make a spot for his head. "I'll take you up on that when we're in Greece. Especially if this book doesn't pan out."

"Well, goodnight." She turned off the light.

"Goodnight Cari."

"And thanks. Even if you don't believe me yet."

Cari settled into bed and lay staring at the ceiling. *I can't believe it,* she thought. *I've found the perfect man. Or should I say, the perfect patsy! It will be easy to manipulate him. But I need to be patient. When the time is right I can roll him and take the car. Sis was half right; I need to start over, but not in California. Especially now.*

Wilson stretched out on the couch. *This will be great! I'll have the perfect plot for my novel. All I have to do is get the two of us to Crete.* He turned onto his side and looked at the light shining in under the door. *Who am I kidding? I can never do this. And if I get caught...* He was shaking. *Trish was right. I'm no adventurer. I should sneak out now, but I told Cari I would help. I know! I'll convince her to turn herself in. That's it! I can go with her to the police. They'll be grateful I convinced her to surrender. I'll even hire a good lawyer for her. Yes, that's the solution. Better to leave the adventure stuff to Baroque. At least I won't end up in jail. I wouldn't do well in prison.*

The next morning Wilson was up early. When he returned from getting donuts, Cari was still sleeping. He opened his laptop and navigated to his publisher's website.

"I don't believe this! All Baroque! Not a word about my book. No wonder it's not selling. What has he got that I don't have? Look at him. He doesn't have the intelligence to write a novel. I'll bet he used a ghost writer. He's got nothing going for himself. But he does look good without a shirt."

"Who looks good without a shirt?" Cari asked as she entered the living room.

"Uh..."

"Let's see!" She spun his laptop around. "Oh, you're right. He does look good without a shirt! John Baroque. That is such a cool name."

"Give me that!" Wilson snapped, spinning the laptop back around.

"Do you often sit around talking to yourself and looking at half-naked men?"

"I wasn't. You wouldn't understand."

"Is that the guy you were talking about?"

"Yes."

"Wow! I can see why his book is selling. Look at him. Ruggedly handsome, brimming with confidence. He's got it all! I'd buy a copy. Think he would sign it for me?"

24

"Could we not talk about him? And I'm the one helping you."

"He could 'help me' any time! Could you get in touch with him? I'm sure he could come up with a plan to get me to Greece."

"That's it! I'm doing it!"

"Doing what?"

"Getting you to Greece!"

"I thought we settled this last night?"

"Oh, yes. We did. I'm reaffirming my commitment."

"Are you always this high strung?"

"Sorry. It's— never mind. How did you sleep?"

"It was wonderful. Certainly better than the back seat of my car."

"I went out and got donuts for breakfast." He pointed to the box. "How did you end up living in your car?"

Cari took a donut and went to the coffee maker. "When I got out of prison I stayed with my sister for a while and worked for her, babysitting her two kids. I tried to find work around where they lived in Philadelphia, but got nothing. Then, I decided to travel across country looking for work after my parole was finished. Her husband had this old Gremlin in the back, and it ran, so I asked them for it. I worked my way to Arizona and saw a story about this convention in Vegas. Ralph was the keynote speaker and I decided to take a chance and try to see him about a job."

"Sounds rough." *I wonder if she was framed? My book would be better if she was. And why did she end up homeless? Her family should have helped her more, unless...*

"It has been," she answered, looking at the floor. The more dejected she looked, the more he'd give her.

"Maybe you can start a new life in Greece."

"Sure, maybe." *This is going to be easier than I thought.* "What now?"

"After we eat I'll cut your hair, then I'll go out and pick up some hair coloring and clothes for you. And I'll reserve a car for tomorrow morning."

I can't believe I'm going to let this guy cut my hair! I'll probably end up looking like a Muppet! I sure hope this is worth it, Cari thought.

"Where are we going?" Cari asked, stuffing a donut in her mouth. "Do you have a plan yet?"

"Here's what I've got so far: we leave by car and head to Phoenix."

"What's in Phoenix?"

"An airport and a guy I know who can make a false passport and driver's license for you."

"You know a guy like that?" Cari was ecstatic. *He's getting me a passport! This guy is such a sap! Maybe it is worth a Muppet haircut.*

"I've been doing research on this book for ten years and during that time I met some interesting characters, including this guy in Phoenix."

"Ten years? How much have you written? How do I fit into it?"

"Well, I haven't exactly, ah, I haven't started writing anything yet. But I'm thinking about it a lot."

"Do you have writers' block?"

"Come on, let's cut your hair," Wilson said, standing quickly and heading to the bathroom.

"That's it! You have writers' block. If you haven't written anything, how could that Baroque guy steal it?" Cari asked.

"Can we not talk about him?" Wilson yelled from the bathroom.

Cari grabbed a pair of scissors and walked up to the bathroom door. "How many books has he written?"

"This is his first."

"Wow! He must be good. Or you suck." Cari smirked.

"Remind me again why I'm helping you?"

"To salvage your pathetic career. You should thank me for the inspiration. Of course, you realize what will happen to you if you're caught?"

"I don't plan to get caught."

"I spent two years in federal prison and you know what I learned from the other inmates?" Cari looked at him seriously. "First, everyone in there is innocent. Second, no one ever plans to get caught."

He clenched his fists. "Do you ever stop talking?"

"You could begin with the mugging in that alley. Write about that," she suggested.

Wilson rolled his eyes. "I guess you don't."

There was a knock on the door.

"Must be housekeeping. Hide in the bedroom while I get rid of them. And be quiet," Wilson told her.

After Cari left he went to the door and peered through the eyepiece. A man in a suit was standing there. His stomach dropped. Definitely not housekeeping.

"Who is it?" Wilson called through the door.

"Detective Harrison of the Las Vegas police. Are you Mr. James?"

"Yes. What is this about?"

"Would you mind letting me in, Mr. James?"

"Show me your badge."

The detective held his police badge up to the glass. Wilson swallowed hard and unbolted the door.

"What is this about?" Wilson asked again.

"May I come in?" the detective asked.

"Certainly," he responded, stepping out of the way. "Please, have a seat. Could I get you anything?"

"No, thank you," the detective replied as he sat on the couch. Wilson glanced around the room to see if any trace of Cari remained.

"Have you heard about that murder yesterday of the New York businessman?" the detective asked him.

"Yes I have, Detective. Brentwood, isn't it?" He had to play it cool, not look nervous.

"That's the fellow. I'm here because the suspect in the case, Jessica Stone, formally of New York, was reported as being seen in this hotel. We checked surveillance footage on the camera in the elevator and found she came up to the seventh floor, but we don't know which room she entered. Myself and my partner are interviewing all the guests on this floor."

"I saw a sketch of the woman on the news last night and can assure you I have not seen her. From what I heard she shot this guy in cold blood." He tried to look frightened. Or appalled, he wasn't sure which.

"I can't discuss details of the case, but she is considered extremely dangerous. She apparently knew her victim. It wasn't random. We want to assure the public there isn't any danger but she shouldn't be approached. Unless you try something heroic, like capturing her," he added with a slight grin.

Wilson raised his hands. "I would not get anywhere near this woman."

"Are you alone, Mr. James?"

The question spooked Wilson. "Yes, I'm in town alone."

"No, I meant in this room."

"Yes, I'm alone, unfortunately." He laughed nervously. "It's my last night, unless I get lucky at the bar..."

The detective stood and handed him his business card. "This is my info if you think of anything, or happen to spot her."

"Don't worry, Detective, if I see her you'll be the first to know." He smiled in an attempt to be reassuring and confident.

When Detective Harrison stepped over the threshold, he turned and faced Wilson. "What are your plans, Mr. James? The front desk says you are checking out tomorrow."

"Yes, I'm heading to Phoenix."

"For what purpose?"

"I'm appearing at a book signing."

"Returning to Vegas?"

"No. Heading home afterwards. Or possibly taking a vacation before starting another book."

"Thank you for your time. Oh, one last thing. How can I get in touch with you after you leave?"

Wilson reached into his pocket and pulled out a card. "Here, this is my publisher. She knows where I am most of the time."

"Phoenix?"

"That's right."

"Again, thank you."

"Any time." Wilson waved as the detective walked away. He shook from head to toe, closing the door quickly and leaning his forehead against it. He was going to be in so much trouble if he got caught. Was this going to be worth it? Maybe he could write a different book, come up with a new idea.

"Fuck!" Cari exclaimed coming out of the bedroom. Wilson jumped.

"Did you hear?" he asked, turning toward her.

"Most of it. They saw me here." She bit her nails and put a hand on her hip.

"Yes. Apparently someone recognized you in the lobby last night and the camera on the elevator caught you getting off on this floor."

"Do you think he suspects you?" Cari asked.

"I don't know. He acted kind of strange, as if he knew more than he was letting on." *If my years of watching cop shows is worth anything.*

"Could be bluffing." She shrugged. "They do that sometimes, pretend they know something to get you to incriminate yourself. Don't worry, they probably have nothing on you or they would have taken you in for questioning."

"We should leave early tomorrow morning," Wilson said.

Cari ran her fingers through her hair. "Even with the change, how am I going to get out of here? They might be watching the hotel for a few days."

"I've got it!" Wilson exclaimed, a manic gleam in his eye. "It's something Bourne would do."

Cari looked at him, frowning. "I'm not climbing down the exterior of the building from the seventh floor!"

"No, that's not what I was thinking. Though that is a good–"

"No way!" she interrupted his imaginative musings.

"Okay," he placated. "My idea is to disguise you like a man."

Cari tilted her head. "A man?"

"Yes. Fake beard, short hair, men's shoes, the whole bit. You go out front and get a cab. Go to the motel on Tropicana and I'll be waiting there for you in the rental car. Then we head out of town. I'll leave a half hour before you to be sure I'm not followed."

"I hate to admit it, but that's not bad. Where are we going to get the disguise?"

"The phone book. Good old-fashioned detective work. We search the phone book for costume stores then, when I go get the car, I make a detour to the store, and before you know it, you'll be a guy." He clapped his hands together. "Let's get started. We have a lot to do today."

Wilson was pleased with himself. Cari was right, this was a brilliant plan. *Suck on that, Baroque! I'm going to have a best seller in no time.*

Chapter 2: The Bookman

By that evening they were prepared. Cari, with Wilson's help, had cut her hair short and dyed it black. He had found a full beard and moustache to match, and picked up some clothes and shoes from the thrift shop.

Staring at the finished product he exclaimed, "It's amazing! No one will recognize you now."

"I must admit it looks good. Jason would be proud of you." Cari spun in the mirror, taking in her new appearance. It felt good to not be herself for once.

"We should get some sleep then head out–" Wilson began.

"No, we should leave now."

"Now? But I thought we agreed–"

"I have a bad feeling about this!" Cari looked at him and chewed a nail. "Let's do it now. You go ahead to the car and I'll walk out through the lobby, turn left, and go down the street. If there is no one following me I'll meet you in front of the thrift shop. Okay?"

"I'm a little nervous," Wilson confessed.

"It'll be alright," Cari assured him. "Go to the garage and get the car."

"What if someone is following either one of us?"

"Drive around for a while and try to lose them then go to the diner where we ate last night. Got it?"

"I've got it." But his confidence was wavering.

"I'm going down the stairs. You take the elevator. Good luck."

"Good luck, Cari."

She put a hand on his arm. "In case something goes wrong, I appreciate what you've done."

"Save your thanks until we're standing on Crete!" he said, waving her off. Cari smiled and walked out the door.

A few minutes later, Wilson grabbed his suitcase and left the room. It was 9:30 p.m. His knees shook as he waited for the elevator. He sighed with relief when the doors opened and it was empty. He pushed the button for the underground parking garage and leaned back against the wall. It was a quick ride and when the doors opened the garage appeared deserted. He hurried to his spot and threw the suitcase into the trunk. When the car started, he began to relax. It seemed likely, at least to him, his plan might succeed.

The down arrow light went out as the elevator left the garage and climbed two floors to the lobby. When the doors opened, Detective Harrison stepped onto the empty carriage and pushed number seven. His instincts from many years of police work told him something wasn't quite right with Mr. Wilson James, children's author. He had to speak to him again before James left to see if there was anything behind his uneasy feelings.

Wilson drove out of the garage and stopped at the street. He didn't spot anyone. He pulled out slowly then gunned the engine. He stole constant glances at the rearview mirror, but all seemed well. In a few minutes, he neared the thrift store and could see Cari standing by the doorway. He pulled over and had barely stopped before she jumped in the car.

"I told you! Nothing to it," she beamed.

"We're still a long way from Crete."

"Maybe so, but we're a little closer than we were." *Optimism is key,* she thought. *Gotta keep him feeling confident.*

Wilson turned onto Tropicana and headed east toward the outskirts of the city. Traffic was light and within twenty minutes he could see the lights of Las Vegas fading in the mirror. Relief flooded over him. Maybe this was actually going to work.

"So, what's the next step?" Cari asked.

He shrugged. "I thought we would stop in Flagstaff to figure out our next move. I need to contact someone in Phoenix about getting papers for you."

"How are you going to get these papers? They must cost a lot?"

"Probably a few thousand," Wilson estimated. "I've done business with these people before. I can get a better deal."

Cari raised an eyebrow. Maybe Mr. James was more adventurous than she thought. "What do you mean you've done business with them before? Are you telling me I'm not the first person you've smuggled out of the country?"

"No, it's nothing like that. You see, when I married my second wife she was only interested in my money. She turned into a real witch and started having affairs. Didn't even try to hide them from me. I created another life to escape. At first it was only in my mind, but as time went on it became more and more real. I identified with my fictional character and planned all kinds of daring adventures for myself, my fictional self. I even acquired fake papers for my alter ego. Then I went so far as to plan the perfect murder."

"The perfect murder?" *I should have got him to take care of my 'problem.'*

"That's right. I was going to commit the perfect crime and write about it under an alias."

"But you said she is your 'ex', not your deceased wife."

Wilson chuckled. "There was one fatal flaw in my plan."

"Which was?"

"There was no way I could do such a thing. Sometimes just thinking about it made me throw up." He grimaced, gripping the wheel tighter.

"You're kidding?"

"No. My ex started to think I was dying because every time I got near her, I would barf."

Cari burst out laughing. "Oh, that is too funny."

34

"Not everybody is as cold blooded as you," he replied angrily.

"Hey, I haven't done anything," she said, raising her hands.

"Except kill your boss," Wilson pointed out.

"Ex-boss," she corrected, then glared at him. "And I didn't kill him!"

"That's not what the police think."

"If I were a cold-blooded killer, I would have shot you in that alley. And all for a lousy sixty bucks!" Cari crossed her arms.

"Sorry my death wouldn't have been more profitable for you."

"Apology accepted. What did you use the phony papers for?"

"I never used them. Well, the bank card a few times."

"Jason Bourke!" Cari blurted out.

"How do you know that name? I mean, no."

"I went through your wallet, remember? There is a driver's license and bank card with the name Jason Bourke." *I'm beginning to think I have underestimated you.*

Wilson nodded. "That's the imaginary me, yes."

"Jason Bourke, original. You really are serious about this Jason Bourne thing aren't you?"

"Drop it."

"What's the bank card for?"

"I always knew I couldn't kill her, no matter how much I hated her." *If only I had the courage to do such a thing.* He glanced at Cari. *Maybe if I was more like her.* "I opened a secret bank account under the name Jason Bourke and siphoned funds into it so she wouldn't get everything in the divorce."

"What did she get?"

"Half of everything including future royalties for ten years."

Cari grimaced. "How long ago was that?"

"Five years. It was after that when my work began to suffer. I write a book a year but the last five haven't sold well. And the last two lost money." Wilson stared straight ahead, dejected. He hated that his books hadn't done well. Writing was his life. He knew it was time for a change from the children's book scene, but he couldn't convince anyone his other writing was worth it. Cari was his one chance, he had to make this work.

"Sounds like a classic case of depression coupled with the fact you sabotage your own work. I had a lot of free time in prison and studied psychology."

Wilson's phone vibrated loudly in his pocket. They both jumped at the sound.

"Who would call me at this hour?" he mused.

Cari shrugged. "Let it go to voice-mail."

"It's my publisher," he said, looking at the screen. The phone stopped vibrating and he let out an audible puff of air. It dinged. "There's a voicemail. You listen, I can't do it."

He held the phone out to Cari, a grimace across his face. She took it and played the voicemail, holding it tight to her ear.

"What does she want?"

"She says you must call that detective in Vegas."

"Darn! I told you there was something strange about the way he acted. He must suspect me." He ran his fingers through his hair and slammed his hands on the steering wheel.

"What now, Jason?" Cari raised an eyebrow.

"We'll stop in Flagstaff and I will call Baby-Boy."

"Baby-Boy? That's your guy's name? Baby-Boy?" She laughed.

"Yes, that's his name." Wilson scowled. "And you don't want to let him hear you laughing at it."

"Oh, I'm so scared of Baby-Boy," Cari cooed, wiggling her fingers.

"These are some tough guys we're dealing with. Watch your step and let me do the talking. They know and trust me." He puffed out his chest. Who was she to judge his connections? At least he had them. If she was as resourceful, she wouldn't be living out of her car.

"Tell me, is this Baby-Boy single?"

"You're a riot, you know?" Wilson smiled. She was so mercurial. And certainly not like any woman he had ever known.

"How long to Flag?" she asked.

"Another three hours."

"Okay, I'm going to get some sleep. Want to be well rested when we I meet Baby-Boy." She laughed again and put her feet on the dashboard, snuggling in to sleep.

When they arrived in Flagstaff, he exited onto Butler and drove into the parking lot of a motel. Cari was still asleep when he returned with the key and drove around to the back.

"Are we here?" she asked groggily.

"Yes. Come on. I've got the key. One room with two beds."

She rubbed her eyes. "What time is it?"

"About 2:30 a.m."

He grabbed his suitcase from the trunk and they found their room.

It was daylight when Wilson came back to the room.

"Where have you been?" Cari asked at his return.

"I went out to find a burner phone." He held up a small flip phone that looked like it was from the 1990s.

"A what?"

"A burner phone. It's what they call these disposable phones. Use them a few times then throw them away. Don't you watch CSI?"

"Not a TV girl."

"I watch all the cop dramas."

"That's where you get your info?" she asked, a quizzical look on her face.

"There and the internet."

"Oh God, this is worse than I thought!" She slapped a hand to her forehead. How had she landed with this guy? They were so going to get caught and she would be in jail again. For life this time. She couldn't let that happen.

"I got us this far, right?"

"You're my hero. I'm going to take a shower." She sauntered off to the

37

bathroom, trying to look unconcerned.

"I'm going to see if I can get Baby-Boy over the phone." Wilson shook his head as she laughed again at the mention of the name.

When she came out of the bathroom, Wilson was in animated conversation on his new phone.

"Let me write that down, Baby-Boy. That address is on West Washington?... Okay... How much?... How much!?... They better be the best for that price... Yeah, I know you guys are... Okay... Female, five eight, black hair, green eyes... back east somewhere... Hang on. How old are you?" Wilson asked Cari.

"Thirty two."

He looked her up and down. "Baby-Boy, she's thirty eight."

"Hey! Thirty five!" she corrected him, glaring.

"I'm five foot eleven–"

"Oh, come on! You're five nine tops," Cari interrupted him. "If you get to be five eleven, I get to be thirty two."

Wilson waved her off. "Brown hair, blue eyes, 150 pounds. Got everything?... Thanks." He hung up the phone.

"What's the deal?" Cari asked.

"Everything's good. We head to Phoenix and stop at the photographer first. Next, it's on to Eloy to pick up the finished product. Everybody works separately. Less chance of getting caught."

"And you trust them?"

"Yes. You've seen their work."

"How much is it?"

"Five thousand."

Cari froze, eyes wide. "Dollars?"

"No, pesos. Of course, dollars."

Wow! He is unbelievable! Maybe I should consider going to Greece. If he's this big of a sucker, take it as far as I can. My prison sisters would be so proud of me. And jealous!

"You seem deep in thought?" He stared at her.

"Ah, I was just thinking about how much I'm going to owe you."

Wilson smirked. "I'll send you a bill."

"What are you going to do about that cop?"

"Right, forgot about him. Maybe when we get to Phoenix I'll call and see what he wants. I haven't done anything wrong. He can't have me arrested."

"What do you mean you haven't done anything wrong? Are you that naive? Or stupid? You are harboring a fugitive in a murder case. Plus, you took me across state lines. You could get ten years for that. Maybe more! And they might try to connect you with me and thus to the murder." Wilson went white, his face a mask of fear. *Shit! Wrong thing to say! Must fix this!* "Of course, I would tell them we weren't together until after the murder. No need to worry about that. And I'm sure your alter ego could talk his way out of the other problems. I know Baroque could easily get out of it."

He bristled at the mention of his competitor's name. "I doubt he would be capable of any such feat. All muscle, no brain cells."

"He sure has muscles—I mean, you're right. I'm glad you're the one helping me."

"There is one small problem," Wilson said, regaining his composure.

She sat down on her bed and looked up at him. "Only one? And it's small?"

"I checked online before we left and there are no direct flights from Phoenix to Athens and, what's worse, all have two stops."

"What's the problem with that?" Cari asked.

"The first stop is in the US, the second, somewhere in Europe, depending on the airline. I don't want to take a chance on changing planes in the US. There is less chance of being spotted in Europe."

"Makes sense. What's the next nearest airport we could go to?"

"Dallas."

"In Texas?"

"Unless they moved the city."

Cari glared at him. "No! We're not going to Texas!"

"What have you got against Texas?"

"We are NOT going to Texas, or across Texas, or anywhere near Texas!" she shouted, breathing heavy.

"Okay, okay. Calm down. We will miss Texas. Let me see. How about Atlanta?" he asked, perusing a map on his phone.

"Atlanta works. As long as we don't go through Texas." She smoothed out her shirt, composing herself.

"It will add some time and distance, but we can go around. We better head out now. The sooner we get there the sooner we get the papers."

"What about that cop? You going to call him back?"

"I'll have to. There are more messages from my publisher. There's this place north of Phoenix, it's called Deer Valley. There is a park there. We'll stop and I'll call him. He already knows I'm going to Phoenix and besides, if I call from here, he might want me to return and we're only four hours away. Calling from Phoenix gives us more time."

"I hope you watch a lot of television."

"It takes me two months to write and illustrate one of my books, and two weeks to promote it. The rest of the year I have nothing to do. So yes, I watch a lot of crime drama. There's no need to worry."

She shook her head and walked toward the door. *What have I got myself into this time?*

They stopped south of Flagstaff for breakfast then continued straight through to Deer Valley. He pulled off the freeway and drove to the outskirts of the city.

"What is this place?" Cari asked, looking around.

"The Deer Valley Nature Conservancy, or something like that. It's Indian petroglyphs and a museum. We can visit it if you want after I make the call."

She gawked at him. "Why not? Maybe we could visit some museums and art galleries while we're in town."

"There's no need to be sarcastic," he told her, frowning. He pulled into the parking lot, took out his phone, and dialed the number. "Yes, hello. Could I speak to Detective Harrison, please... Wilson James... Thank you." After a few minutes, he heard the officer's voice on the other end of the line.

"Good morning, Detective Harrison, you've been trying to reach me?... Yes, that's correct, I'm in Deer Valley north of Phoenix... Early this morning around 4:00, I think... You did?... At what time?... 9:45... I'm sorry, Detective, but I'm a very heavy sleeper. I didn't hear you knocking... What's that?... Oh, you did. I see. And you found what?... Jessica Stone's fingerprints in the room... I see... Return immediately... That is not a problem I'll—stop that! No! Help! I've been kidnaped, help!" Wilson hung up the phone.

"What the hell was that about?" Cari asked.

"They searched the room this morning and found your fingerprints all over. Darn! We should have wiped it down." He snapped his fingers.

"What was that about kidnaped?"

"I had to say something, right?" Wilson shrugged. "I couldn't deny you were there so I made it appear you have kidnaped me. That should buy us some time."

"Kidnaped you? You fucking idiot! It isn't bad enough what they think I've done and now I've kidnaped you? They will be positive I'm guilty now. You fucking idiot!" Cari put her head in her hands. Her heart was pounding as if she had just run miles, her palms sweaty. This guy was going to get them in so much trouble. She should've just stayed living in her car while she had it good.

Wilson looked sheepish. "It's not that bad."

"Not that bad? I'm wanted for a murder I didn't commit and now for kidnaping a fucking idiot!"

"Stop yelling at me before you draw attention to us. Besides, this buys us time."

I may have underestimated his level of stupidity! "What about the car?" Cari asked.

"What about it?"

"They will find out, if they haven't already, that you rented this car and now, thanks to your brilliant idea, they think you're in danger. We'll be picked up in no time."

"Hadn't thought of that." Wilson scratched his chin, looking rather less concerned than Cari wanted him to be.

"What a surprise! Do you have any clue what you're doing?"

"I resent that! We're on our way to get false papers, thanks to me. And once we have them, I will rent a car under my assumed name and we're free and clear to Atlanta. So there, I'm not doing that bad after all, thank you very much. All we have to do is get through Phoenix. Once we have the papers we'll be golden. Trust me, Jason Bourke knows what he's doing."

"I'm so screwed!" She put her head in her hands.

"That's the spirit! Off we go to the photographer and a new life." Wilson put the car in reverse and began to back out of the parking space.

He's a lunatic, she thought. *Maybe I should tell him about Texas.*

"Darn!" He slammed on the breaks.

"What now?" she asked.

"I'll bet their going to ping my phone."

"Excuse me? What does that mean?"

"You really need to watch more CSI. The police can track where you are by pinging your cell phone. We must destroy my phone." He picked it up, twirling it around in his hands as if it were a rare, intriguing fossil.

"Why don't we throw it away?"

"Someone might find it. I know, we'll run over it!"

Definitely a lunatic! she thought. *Wonder how I could get in contact with Baroque?*

He drove back into the parking space, stepped out of the car, placed his phone behind the tire, and returned to the driver's seat. He backed up, drove ahead, backed up, and drove ahead again.

"That ought to do it." He got out and picked up the many pieces of his phone and carried them over to a nearby trash can. "That's better. Now they won't be able to track us."

"All they have is our car description and license plate." Cari scowled.

"You're a real downer sometimes, you know that?" Wilson told her.

42

"You're not the one facing a murder charge. Oh, and thanks to you, a kidnaping charge!" She glared at him, cursing herself again for getting involved with this idiot.

"And I keep telling you, I'm going to get you out of this."

She folded her arms over her chest. "You better." *Or you may end up like Brentwood.*

"Trust me. Off to the photographer." He pulled out of the parking space again.

"Is he making the papers too?" Cari asked as they took a left out of the park.

"No. After I pay him, he will send the pictures over the internet to Baby-Boy who makes the papers. Then Rattler assembles them."

"Where do we pick them up?"

Wilson shrugged. "Don't know. The photographer will tell us where."

"This is getting more complicated than any Bourne film."

"I know. Isn't it great? This book is going to be so good." His eyes lit up like a child on Christmas.

It wasn't long before they were back on the freeway headed south. Wilson mulled over the plan once again. It seemed pretty fool-proof to him. Once they got their new identities, everything would be simple.

"Oh no," he said.

"What?" Cari tensed, sitting up straight as an arrow in her seat.

"Stay down in the seat." Wilson pushed on her shoulder. "A patrol car just pulled up behind us."

The blood drained from Cari's face. She scooted down as low as she could. "Were you speeding? That's how a lot of criminals get caught, you know, by breaking some minor infraction and getting stopped."

"I wasn't speeding. I was five miles under the limit." Wilson's knuckles were white on the steering wheel.

Cari snuck a glance in the side mirror. "He's staying right behind us. Slow down a bit. Maybe he'll go by."

As Wilson eased off the gas the trooper slowed accordingly, staying behind them.

"Here's the plan," Cari advised him. "When his lights come on don't stop on the freeway. Pull off the first exit you come to and stop on a side street. Get out of the car to distract him and I'm going to make a run for it."

He looked skeptical. "When the suspect runs, they always get caught."

"Don't tell me, CSI?" Cari rolled her eyes.

"That's right. Wait, his right blinker is on." Wilson watched the patrol car in the rearview mirror. "Stay down. He's taking this exit. There he goes. He wasn't planning to stop us. He was getting off the freeway."

Cari let out a sigh of relief. "How much farther?"

"Not long. Maybe ten minutes. We stay on I-10 to the exit for Washington. Baby-Boy said it's only a few blocks to the place. It's on the north side."

Cari smiled every time he mentioned Baby-Boy. It seemed ridiculous that a forger would choose such a silly name.

"Do you have a special underworld name?" she asked him.

He nodded smugly. "As a matter of fact, I do."

"Well, what is it?

"I'm known as the Bookman." He smirked.

She burst out laughing. "You made that up."

Face reddening, Wilson cleared his throat. "No, they made it up. Everybody uses a false name in the business."

"In the business. You sound like a pro alright. But I have a hard time picturing you as a bad-ass gangster."

"Watch and learn. Here's our exit."

They pulled off the freeway and stopped at a red light, then proceeded west a few blocks. Wilson pulled up to an inconspicuous white house on the corner and parked around the back.

"Let me do the talking," Wilson told her as they walked to the door.

He rang the bell and the door opened a crack.

"Yes?" a deep voice asked. His green eye and a hint of his five o'clock shadow could be seen through the crack in the door.

"The Bookman." A dog could be heard barking inside.

"Just a minute." The man closed the door. "Put the dog in the bedroom. Got customers," they heard him yell from inside. "This way," he motioned when the door reopened.

They followed him down a narrow hall into a room on the right. The blinds were closed and the room dark. He flicked on a light to reveal several studio lights, tripods, and two cameras.

"Got it?" the man asked.

Wilson pulled two envelopes from his inside coat pocket. "Is Baby-Boy here?"

"No. He'll be by later. Went to Rattler's place. Leave his with me."

"That's the envelope marked BB. The other's yours."

"What's your handle?" Cari asked him.

"What?" the man asked.

"She wants to know your name. You'll have to excuse her. A newbie."

The man looked at her. "Frank."

"Happy now?" Wilson asked sarcastically. Cari made a face at him.

"Sit over there on that stool. One at a time. Take your coat off."

Wilson sat first for what took all of five seconds then Frank said "next" and Cari took his place.

"Done."

"Done? That's it?" Cari asked.

"That's it. Rattler will have the images before you walk out the door. By the time you get to her place the papers will be ready. Oh, I got to give you directions. Here," Frank handed Wilson a scrap of paper. "Door's that way," he pointed. "Doris, you can let the dog out!"

"I think we should be going," Wilson told Cari. He really didn't want to meet the dog.

"Right behind you," Cari agreed.

She slammed the door shut after they were safely outside and they hurried into the car.

"Read me the directions," Wilson said as he backed out of the drive and pulled up to the red light.

"Let's see. This handwriting is kinda hard to read. 'South on 10 to Eloy. Exit onto service road to south end of town. Left on East Park Link Drive. Five miles to crook in road. North is big butt'."

"North is big butt? What the heck does that mean? Let me see that." He snatched the paper from her.

"Right there, big butt. We turn at the big butt."

"There's an 'e' on the end. It's butte."

"I don't know what a 'butte' is."

"Well, it's not a butt, I can tell you that."

"What is it?"

"It's a rock formation that rises up from the desert. I'll show you when we get there."

"How am I supposed to watch for it if I don't know what it is?" Cari asked with a look of frustration.

"Tell you what, when you see a giant butt, let me know."

"I'm riding with one."

He made a face at her. "Read the rest of the instructions."

"Let's see, where was I. 'North is a butte', with an 'e.' 'Pull-off on left. Take dirt road north. Past butte for six miles. Gate on left side. Walk past gate. Don't drive or will be shot.' Oh I don't believe it! We're supposed to find this place? And he's going to shoot at us?"

"Not if we walk. And it's she."

"Rattler is a she?"

"More or less."

"What's that mean?"

"You'll find out."

"How long will it take to get there?"

"Maybe an hour."

"And it hasn't crossed your mind they're sending us to who knows where for nothing?"

These people made Cari more uncomfortable than the women in prison.

The whole thing felt shady. *I guess it is shady*, she thought.

"If we don't get the merchandise, Rattler doesn't get paid. And besides, I told you, I've done business with these people before. They're trustworthy."

"If you say so."

"I do. Want to listen to the radio?"

"Why not." Cari played with the buttons until a song came on.

"This is KBB, the sound of the south with a news update. It seems a murder in Las Vegas now has a Phoenix connection. The fugitive accused of the deed is headed this way. Last known whereabouts of one Jessica Stone was in Deer Valley earlier today. Stone is five foot eight, 140 pounds—"

"Hey! 130 buddy!" Cari shouted at the radio

"With shoulder length light brown hair and green eyes. She is considered armed and dangerous. Do not approach. If you see her call 911 immediately. She is said to have a male hostage as yet unidentified."

She turned off the radio. "They make me sound like Bonnie of Bonnie and Clyde."

"Look at the bright side," Wilson said.

"There's a bright side?"

"They didn't mention the car. That means they haven't found where I rented it yet. This gives us more time to get the papers, ditch this car, and rent another under my new name."

"I guess that is sort of good."

"At least it's not bad." *Though it could be better.*

They rode in silence and watched for police cars but all was quiet. Wilson breathed a sigh of relief when they reached Eloy and pulled onto the service road. They soon came to their turn and headed east into the desert.

"We shouldn't see any cops out this way," Wilson assured her.

"Doesn't look like we're going to see anything out this way." The sand and sage brush went on for miles in a flat, endless tract. Cari could see the heat rising from the ground in waves, making the horizon blurry. She imagined being stuck out there with nothing but the sun and sand for company and shivered at the thought. *Would definitely be better than prison, though.*

"Ever been in this area?" Wilson's question pulled her from her reverie.

"No. When I came cross country I was farther north. I didn't even make it to Phoenix."

"It must be rough trying to find a job."

"I found the perfect job doing the books at this small mom and pop business, but when they found out I was an ex-con, goodbye job."

"I thought people weren't allowed to discriminate against ex-cons?"

"They're not. They make excuses like it has already been filled, or we had an unexpected downturn and the job isn't available any longer. Laws are fine, but there's always a way around them." She sighed, shoulders slumping. Life had certainly been hard since she got out of prison. How could the system have failed her like it did? And it was all about to happen again!

"I haven't been happy with the results from my stock portfolios. Maybe when you get to Greece you wouldn't mind managing them for me?" Wilson asked.

Cari stared at him. "Are you serious, or is this a pity offer?"

"Are you in any position to turn it down? Don't forget, you still owe me twenty dollars."

"I'll think about it."

"That's big of you."

"Is that it?" Cari asked.

"Is what it?"

"The butte, with an 'e.' Look over there. Is that it?" Cari pointed at a rise of land in the distance.

"Must be. And there's the pullout and beside it the road. You see, I told you there was nothing to worry about."

"Only some nutcase woman with a gun."

"Been there, done that."

She caught herself before laughing. "Not even close to being funny!"

Wilson turned onto a narrow dirt road and they headed north into the desert.

Soon after passing the butte (with an e) they came to a dry wash.

"That doesn't look too good," Cari said.

"The trick is to drive fast," Wilson said, pushing on the accelerator. The little car sped up and bounced through the wash without a problem. "Just like that."

"Bourne couldn't have done it any better."

Wilson sat a little straighter in the seat. The second wash was smaller than the first and they zipped through without incident. About a mile on they came to a wide and deep wash that had a trickle of water running in the center.

"This one doesn't look so easy to get over," Cari observed.

"We should check it out to see where the best place is to cross." Wilson stopped the car and got out.

"You aren't seriously thinking of trying to cross this, are you?" she asked as they stood on the bank. She squinted into the water, as if waiting for a fish to come up and tell them it was safe.

"See over there?" He was pointing to their left. "Those are vehicle tracks. It looks okay. Don't worry. We'll be fine."

"Didn't someone say that at the Alamo?"

"Just get in the car."

Cari eyed the wash, wringing her hands. "I think I'll walk across and meet you on the other side."

"Suit yourself, but watch out for the quicksand."

She froze. "Quicksand? Are you kidding?"

"Sometimes along these washes, especially if there's water, you'll find patches of quicksand," Wilson said.

"How do you expect to drive across if there is quicksand?"

"Simple. I follow the tracks. If they made it, I can."

"Fine, but, so help me, if we get sucked into quicksand there will be another murder."

Wonder what that means? Wilson thought. *Is she kidding again?*

They returned to the car and he drove toward the tracks. Wilson backed up from the bank and looked at Cari.

"Ready?" he asked her.

"Does it matter?"

"Not a bit." He pushed hard on the accelerator and the car jumped forward.

They dropped into the wash and moved smoothly on the hard-packed surface. Spray flew as the front tires pushed through the water and they emerged unscathed on the other side. A much wider expanse of the wash appeared ahead. They drove into the second section and at first continued at a fast pace but then the car began to slow.

"Don't slow down!" Cari ordered, her voice shrill.

"I'm not! The gas pedal is pushed to the floor!" he countered. The car began to twist and finally came to a complete stop. "Don't worry. I'll get us out. I've been stuck before."

She glared at him as he shifted from forward to reverse and back again. The car wouldn't budge.

"Now what?" Cari snapped.

"We can't be very far from Rattler's trailer. We'll walk there and have her come back to pull us out. Simple."

"You're simple," Cari complained as she unbuckled her seatbelt and stepped out of the car. "Man, I can hardly walk in this stuff. You sure we're not in quicksand?"

"No, it's too dry. And besides, the car isn't sinking. It'll be fine. Rattler will pull us out. We're old friends."

I may have seriously overestimated him! For someone who claims to have done this before, he doesn't seem to know what he's doing. Jason Bourne, he ain't! Cari thought as she struggled through the sand. It was mid-afternoon and the fall sun beat down on them. They had walked for nearly an hour when they spotted a gate on the left of the road.

"That must be the road to her trailer. This isn't too bad," Wilson tried to reassure her.

She clutched at her throat. "It would be better if we had some water."

"We can get water at her place. Besides, she might shoot us!"

"I beginning to regret not shooting you in that alley."

"I'm growing on you. Admit it," Wilson chided her.

"Suppose she'd lend me a gun?"

They walked for a few minutes when a shot rang out.

"Where's Baroque when we need him!?" Cari shouted as she ducked for cover.

"After all I've done for you?" Wilson asked, glaring at her.

Chapter 3: Blondie

"Off my land, Federales!" a female voice shouted from the distance.

"Rattler! It's me. Bookman," Wilson shouted from his protective half-crouch.

"Bookman? Is that you?" a voice replied.

"Yes, it's me. We're here to pick up the package."

"Who's the bitch?"

"Bitch?" Cari responded.

"Shhh. Don't antagonize her. It's nothing personal," he shot at Cari. "She's with me, the second package," Wilson called back to Rattler.

"Come up!"

"Come on, let's go," Wilson told Cari.

"I'm walking behind you."

"Now you know how I felt in that alley."

"Ha ha."

Rattler extended her hand to Wilson when they met. "Been a long time."

"Quite a while. This is the Broker," he introduced Cari. Rattler ignored her.

Rattler was a stocky woman with long grey hair. Her face was creased with wrinkles from a lifetime of living under the Arizona sun. Her eyes were dark and piercing and belied a great intelligence. "Come on down to the trailer."

They followed her over a small hill where they could see a rusty camper in the distance.

"Where's your dog?" Wilson asked.

"Federales got him. Came in the night and took him. Must of tranquillized him cause he never said a word."

"Who are the Federales?" Cari whispered in his ear.

"I think they're the Mexican equivalent of the FBI."

"The Mexicans are after her?"

"Come on in, Bookman," Rattler said when they had reached the trailer. "And you too, Blondie."

"Blondie?" Cari asked in surprise.

"Don't antagonize," Wilson cautioned her again.

"Sit yourselves down. Don't mind the mess. Can I get you anything?" Rattler asked.

The inside of the trailer was cramped and dark. Piles of newspapers littered the floor and empty Tequila bottles filled an overflowing garbage bin. Cari noticed several rifles leaning in a corner.

"A bottle of water would be great," Wilson said.

Rattler went into the fridge and pulled out two bottles. "Here you go." She smiled handing Wilson one bottle. "Five bucks," she said, thrusting the other toward Cari.

"Five bucks?!"

"Five bucks, Blondie! You got a hearing problem? Cough up!" Rattler glared at her, leaning forward slightly. Her body hummed with aggression.

"I've got it. She doesn't have any money." Wilson began to pull out his wallet.

"Never mind. Your credit's good here. How is she paying for the papers?" Rattler asked in a friendly tone, ignoring Cari.

"I'm carrying her."

"Alright then. Drink up and I'll get them." Rattler disappeared into the back of the trailer.

"Why does she keep calling me Blondie?" Cari whispered after she had left. "I have black hair."

"Don't antagonize her."

"Have a look at these," Rattler told Wilson, handing him a brown envelope.

He opened it and slid out the contents; an American passport and Vermont

54

driver's license. Opening the passport, he read the name, "Allen Waterman, born July 23, 1970."

"I shaved a few years off. You don't look your age," Rattler said pleasantly.

"Perfect." He smiled at her.

"They'll get you through anywhere. Top of the line."

"And, um, do you have mine?" Cari asked tentatively.

"Here." Rattler threw a second envelope in front of her.

Cari slid out the contents and opened the passport. "Rose Denise, born May 10, 1972! That makes me 42! Seven years older than I am!"

Rattler stared at her for a moment then sneered, "It suits you."

Wilson grabbed Cari's arm and shook his head.

"Perfect," Cari growled through clenched teeth.

"I see you're walking. Could I interest you in a pickup? Four-wheel drive. Runs perfect. Three hundred bucks." Rattler sounded like a used car salesman.

Wilson shook his head. "No, we're good, but that does remind me. We got stuck in a wash a few miles back. Could you pull us out?"

"Twenty bucks." She shrugged.

"That's fine. And here." He handed her an envelope.

"Thanks. They okay?"

"Another satisfied customer. But we need to get going."

"Sure, come on. We'll take Chuck. He'll get you out. You too Blondie!" she snapped.

"What is her problem?" Cari whispered to Wilson, who ignored her.

They went outside and around to the back of the trailer. There stood a pickup mounted on enormous tires that raised the running boards nearly three feet off the ground.

"Is this the one you want to sell?" Wilson asked, looking the truck up and down like a woman in a pretty dress.

"Oh no, not Chuck. That one over there." Rattler pointed to a similar truck but with smaller tires and much more rust. "That's the one for sale. Runs perfect. Climb in. Need a stool, Blondie?"

"No, I'm fine," Cari replied as she struggled up into the cab.

"Yes, need a stool, Blondie?" Wilson quipped.

"Shut up!" Cari replied as she slid into the middle.

"Good to go?" Rattler asked as Wilson settled in.

He nodded. "Good to go."

She fired up the truck and they were surrounded by a deafening roar. Cari covered her ears as they tore out of the driveway and bounced across the desert. When they neared the gate, Wilson asked Rattler if she wanted him to open it, but she never heard him, and drove through the ditch on one side. What had taken them over an hour to walk, she drove in a few minutes. Rattler spotted the car in the sand, drove around in back of it, and stopped.

"There's some chains in the back. Grab one, will ye, Bookman?" Rattler asked him.

Wilson and Cari jumped out of the truck and went to the back. He opened the tailgate and slid out an enormous chain he could barely lift.

"You think she loaded that in herself?" Cari asked.

"What do you think?" Wilson raised an eyebrow and grunted under the chain's weight.

"I think I wouldn't want to be a Federale." They both laughed as Wilson fastened the chain around the back bumper of the car and to the trailer hitch of the truck. "You best stand back. Way back," he cautioned Cari.

Moving around to the driver's side, he yelled "okay!" to Rattler who started the truck. Wilson slid into the driver's seat but, before he could start the car, he felt a terrific jolt and heard a crunching noise as the car lurched backwards a short distance. He hurried out and saw the rear bumper being dragged behind the truck while the rest of the car remained stuck. Rattler stopped and got out of the truck. She unhitched the chain, picked up the bumper, and carried it to Wilson.

"You might want to hang onto this. I got some duct tape in the truck to re-attach it after I get you out. Best hook to something more solid this time." She handed him the bumper and went back to the truck. "Guide me back."

Wilson noticed Cari looking at him with a smirk on her face.

"Shut up!"

"I didn't say a word," she said, as he struggled to put the bumper in the backseat of the car.

"Guide her back, okay Blondie?"

Cari focused her attention on Rattler who had started the truck and was reversing at a fairly high speed. "Back up!" she yelled over the roar of the engine. "Slow down! Hold it! That's close enough. No! Stop!" she screamed. This was followed by the sound of metal on metal as the trailer hitch of the truck caught the trunk cover and peeled it back like opening a tin can. When the back window shattered, Rattler stopped.

"Close enough?" Rattler called back.

"Move ahead just a bit," Cari replied.

Again, the sound of screeching metal as she pulled ahead. Rattler got out and came around back. "Scratched the paint a might," she observed. "I'll hook on the rear axle this time. She'll come out or die trying!"

Rattler grabbed the chain and crawled under the car as Wilson stood staring in disbelief.

"I guess that uses up your security deposit," Cari mused.

Wilson glared at her and gritted his teeth.

"Okay, we're good to go," Rattler called as she headed for the truck cab.

Wilson hurried into the car and started it. Putting it in reverse, he gunned the motor at the same time the chain tightened. The car began to move backwards, but was sinking deeper in the sand when there was a terrible jolt. The back of the car dropped. He turned off the ignition and sat with his head resting on the steering wheel.

"How bad is it?" he called back to Cari.

"Not that bad. Oh, except for the fact the rear axle is lying about twenty feet behind the back of the car. Other than that, everything is good," she replied cheerily.

He stuck his head out the window and scowled at her. "You're a real pain sometimes, you know that, Blondie?"

"Don't make 'em like they used to," Rattler observed as she looked at the destroyed car.

Wilson got out and went to the back of the vehicle to assess the damage. "Still got that truck for sale?"

"Yep, five hundred."

"I thought you said three?"

"Supply and demand!" Rattler replied, as she smiled at him and winked.

"Fine. Is cash okay?"

"Suits me. And it's forty for pulling you out."

"Forty? But you destroyed the car!"

"I got to give you a ride back to the trailer. Cash is fine." Rattler held out her hand.

"That truck runs perfect?"

"Like a new one."

"Alright, here." Wilson counted out five hundred and forty dollars.

"Nice doing business with you." Rattler grabbed the cash and shoved it into her pocket. "One thing about the truck. Doesn't start too good."

"You said it runs perfect?" Wilson asked.

"Does, once you get it started. But he's a bear to start. Got to have two people. You'll be fine, you got Blondie." She jutted her chin in Cari's direction.

"Yes, I got Blondie," Wilson sighed.

"Lucky you," Cari added.

They climbed up into the truck for another bone-jarring ride through the desert back to the trailer. When Rattler stopped they jumped out and went over to inspect their "new" truck. Large holes were rusted through the sides and the back bumper was missing. A license plate was tied on the tailgate with wire.

"Pink slip is in the glove box. Grab it for me, Blondie," Rattler ordered.

Cari pulled open the door and reached in for the glove box cover. When she pulled, it came off in her hand. She threw the cover behind the seat and fished around for the registration, found it, and brought it to Rattler who was standing by the hood. She took out a pen, signed it, and handed it to Wilson who signed Allen Waterman.

"He's a bit temperamental to start. Push the gas pedal to the floor. The second guy has to reach under the hood, pull the choke open, and hold it until the truck starts, then let go right quick before it catches on fire. Got it?"

"Nothing to it. Got it?" Wilson looked at Cari.

"Only thing is you get kind of greasy under the hood. Bookman, you get in the cab and Blondie can climb under the hood."

"Works for me." Wilson smiled at Cari.

"I hate you!" Cari replied as she walked by him to the front of the truck.

Wilson got in and held the gas pedal down. "Okay," he shouted.

"You see this thing here?" Rattler was pointing under the raised hood. "You got to hold it like this." She pulled back on the choke mechanism.

"I see what you mean." Cari nodded.

"Reach in there and pull it. When the truck starts, let go. Got it?"

"It's somewhat complicated, but I think I can handle it."

"Start it, Bookman!" Rattler hollered.

Wilson turned the key and the engine slowly turned over a few times then suddenly burst to life. Cari shrieked and jumped back as a short flame erupted from where her hand had been.

"See, nothing to it." Rattler laughed. She slammed down the hood. "Good luck, Bookman. Stop in next time you're down this way."

"Thanks for everything, Rattler, and I will. Blondie told me how much she enjoyed the visit and hopes to make it back again!"

"Tell her to come alone next time!" Rattler shot back.

As Wilson laughed, Rattler leaned in the window and whispered in his ear, "Watch out for that one." She nodded toward Cari who was getting in the cab.

"It stinks in here! And it's filthy!" Cari said.

"You'll get used to the smell by the time we reach Atlanta."

"What did she say? A little pillow talk?" She smirked.

"Ah, she wished us luck."

"You mean, she wished 'you' luck." Cari stared at Wilson. *He's lying! Wish I knew what she said.*

She rolled down the window but before it was open the handle came off in her hand.

"Hey! This is a new vehicle! Careful!" Wilson admonished her.

"I got grease all over my hands." She held them up for him to see.

"There's a rag on the floor under the edge of the seat."

She picked up the rag, shrieked, and threw it out the window. "There was a scorpion in it!"

"You didn't hurt him, did you?"

"Hurt him? He's poisonous!"

"Only if he stings you. He won't hurt you if you don't hurt him," Wilson said in a condescending tone.

"Wonderful! I'll remember that if there's a rattlesnake behind the seat!" she spat.

"Could be. This hasn't been driven in a while by the looks of it."

"Do we have gas?"

"Yes and no."

"What does that mean?"

"The gage is on empty, which means we have none, unless it doesn't work. Then we're fine."

"Prison is looking better and better!"

"Ready?" Wilson asked her.

"Does it matter?"

"Not in the least!" With that he put the truck in gear and gunned the motor. It roared into action, sputtered, and died.

"Guess the gage works," Cari told him.

"Probably because it hasn't run for a while. Under the hood, Blondie, and we'll try it again."

"Shut up!" Cari climbed out of the truck and lifted the hood. "Okay!"

He turned the key and the engine jumped back to life.

"See, just some cobwebs to clear out then it'll be fine."

"Cobwebs? Probably from a Black Widow the way my luck's going."

"They have Black Widows in this area."

"You're such a ray of sunshine," Cari said as she slammed the door shut.

"Atlanta here we come," Wilson sang out joyfully. This time the truck lurched forward, backfired, and sped away.

"Where are we headed?" Cari asked.

"Northeast across the desert until we come to a highway. Then north. This has turned into a lucky break for us."

"Lucky? You've got to be kidding."

"No. Think about it. When they find the car, they will think we were heading south to Mexico."

"I suppose that is possible," she said.

Cari sniffed the air and grimaced. "The stink is getting worse in here. It smells like a skunk died."

"That's not dead skunk. It's exhaust fumes. There must be a hole in the floor. Look around and see if you can find it."

"You want me to poke around under the seat? Are you crazy? My theory of a rattlesnake in here isn't that farfetched!"

"Don't be a baby. If there is one, push him out the hole in the floor."

Cari stared at him and thought, *he is a fucking lunatic!* She grimaced as her hand moved gingerly under the seat. "Found it!"

Wilson jumped. "The rattlesnake?"

"The hole, smart-ass. Most of the floor is gone and the seat isn't holding on by much."

"We should be fine as long as we keep the windows open and drive fast." He was speeding along cutting down small trees and sage brush.

"Did you ever think—look out!"

He hit the brakes but it was too late. They went over an embankment and landed in a dry wash.

"You okay?" he asked, gripping the steering wheel tightly.

"Fine. You?"

"Good. But the truck stalled again," Wilson informed her.

"Oh, isn't that just peachy!" Cari jumped out of the cab and slammed the door behind her.

The truck started on the first try.

"You're getting good," he said when she returned.

"Maybe I can become the warden's mechanic when I'm sent back to prison."

"That's the spirit!"

Cari looked at him and shook her head.

He put the truck in gear but they didn't move.

"Don't tell me we're stuck again," Cari snapped, looking out the window into the mud.

"This has four-wheel drive. I put it into gear and we're off." He began looking around the dash for the gear shift.

"What about that?" She pointed to a bent handle under the dash on the center console.

He pulled the lever then pushed on the gas pedal and they were moving again. He looked at her and smiled.

"How are we going to get out of this?" she asked.

"We'll drive until we find a place where the bank is lower."

"Look in the mirror. There's a piece of the truck back where we landed," Cari told him.

Wilson glanced in the side mirror and shrugged. "Still going. It can't be that important."

"That is so comforting," she replied sarcastically.

They went a short distance before Wilson saw a low spot along the bank and pulled up and out on the opposite side. When he attempted to take the truck out of four-wheel drive, the gear handle broke off in his hand. "Ever heard the expression, you get what you pay for?"

"I'm getting your help for free, right?" Cari smirked.

"Smart-ass!"

"What are these mountains?" she asked.

"Don't know the name, but Rattler said to keep them on our right and we would come out on the road to Florence. We'll stop there for the night. Should be a motel and maybe we can find a used car dealer to pick up something better."

Cari patted the seat. "Better than this? You wouldn't trade this, would you? He's like a member of the family."

They continued bouncing across the desert until finally they could see traffic on a highway in the distance.

"Look at that," Wilson pointed at the cars. "I told you I knew where we were going."

"Great! But what about that?"

"What?" Wilson asked as they came over a small ridge.

"That–" The screech of metal being pierced came from the side of the truck. "Fence!" Cari added.

Wilson looked sheepish. "I thought there was a gate there."

"There certainly is now!"

He stopped the truck and got out to survey the damage.

"Not too bad. A few scratches that's all."

Cari hopped out to look for herself. "Scrapped off some of the rust. But what about the fence dragging behind us?"

Wilson went around to the back and crawled under the truck bed, but could not untangle the mess. "Got any wire cutters?"

"Oh damn, I left them in my other pants."

"The sarcasm really isn't helping."

"Now what?" Cari threw up her hands.

"We continue on. Look," he pointed, "the highway is right there. Get in, unless you plan to walk."

They returned to the truck and drove off. As they neared the road Wilson spotted a gate and headed for it.

"You want me to open that or are you going to drive through again?" Cari asked.

He scowled. "Just open the gate."

Cari jumped out and pulled the gate back. After he drove through, she motioned him on farther and farther until the wire dragging behind cleared the opening. He was out on the highway when he stopped. They pulled away and could hear the wire jingling along on the pavement.

"Soothing, isn't it?" she asked him.

"Shut up!"

"Harrison, the captain wants to see you in his office."

Detective Harrison stood and walked toward the office. He was six foot three, long and lanky with a shock of thick white hair. Two months from retirement, he was still a handsome man and one of the best detectives in the city. It was why he had this case.

"Sit down, Harrison. Bring me up to date on the Brentwood murder," The captain ordered when Harrison entered.

"Our main suspect is still Jessica Stone, but she has disappeared for the moment, though the Arizona State police are on the trail of their car as we speak."

"Their car?"

"Yes sir. There appears to be someone else involved, though we don't know how at this time."

"That writer?"

"Wilson James, yes. So far, I haven't been able to find any connection between the two. There is ten years age difference and they seem to be from different origins. It is bizarre, but there must be a connection."

"What's their connection concerning this case?"

"Even more strange. At first, I thought he might be helping her, then I got that weird call from him claiming to be a kidnap victim."

The captain looked at him, eyebrows raised. "You're not buying that?"

"Not really." Harrison shrugged. "I think he's trying to put us off the trail."

"Why do you think he's helping her?"

"Wish I knew."

"Any idea where they went?"

"He rented a car the day before they left Vegas and I managed to track down the company. They checked the GPS and found the car in the desert south of Phoenix. Troopers headed there but couldn't get to it and had to call in off-road vehicles. They're going to contact me as soon as they find it."

"Heading to Mexico?"

"It appears that way. I sent their pictures to Mexican border crossings from the coast to the gulf. If they try to cross we'll get them. I also alerted our border guards and officers in case they attempt to cross illegally."

"What about the case? You think she's good for it?" the captain asked.

"It looks like a slam dunk." Harrison's voice was flat.

"I've seen that look before. But?"

"But it doesn't make sense to me. I've been going over the case files from her conviction and it seems the Feds might have been a bit hasty in their prosecution of her."

The captain shifted in his chair. "Tread carefully, Harrison. The Feds won't like it one bit if you try to overturn their conviction."

"I'm not, Cap, but it does make me question this case."

"How so?"

"Motive. If Brentwood did frame her on the securities fraud it would be a motive. If she was guilty then where's the motive? If anything, he should have been pissed at her, not the other way around. And I don't like this Jacoby guy."

"You think he might be good for it?"

"Problem is he has a solid alibi. We're trying to dislodge it but, so far, no luck. Of course, he could have hired someone. And he had plenty of motive."

"What was it?"

"From what I've been able to learn, this guy has been a loyal employee of Brentwood's for many years but he never gets promoted. Everyone rises past him, including Stone, and he remains an assistant. Now, with Brentwood dead, he inherits the company and is the big dog."

"What's the company worth?"

"Around a hundred million. They nearly went bankrupt in 2009 but got a huge bailout from the government."

"That's a lot of motive. Keep on him, but don't let that girl get away. Or the writer. I've got a few questions I want to ask that fellow."

"I'll let you know as soon as I get something." He stood and turned toward the door.

"You always did like the strange ones, Harrison. Guess you got one this time."

Cari parted the curtain and stared out at the street. It was early morning and little was stirring outside. She glanced to her right, saw the rust-bucket pickup sitting there, and burst out laughing.

I can't believe we made it here in that thing. Can't even take off with it if I wanted to leave this idiot! Patience, Jessica. He'll trade it for something better, something that needs only one person to start.

She jumped at a knock on her wall. Wilson was in the next room and apparently awake. She went over and pounded on her side. A single rap replied, then she heard the door of his room open and close, and watched his shadow pass the window. She pulled open the door before he could knock.

"Good morning sunshine. Sleep well?" He leaned against the door jamb, smiling.

"You're in a cheery mood this morning," she observed as he entered the room and sat on the bed.

"I found this tourist place down the road and bought a small atlas and have been plotting our route. The guy said there isn't any place selling used cars in town and our best bet is in Globe. We need to work our way northeast because *someone*, who shall remain nameless, doesn't want to travel across Texas. Anyway, we'll head to Albuquerque then across the high plains into Oklahoma and see from there. I think ol' Ben will get us to Globe."

"Ol' Ben?" Cari asked smiling at him.

"I named our truck."

"I see." She looked at him as he stared at the atlas and pointed out the route.

"We should grab something to eat at a takeout restaurant. And we need gas."

"How do you know?" Car asked. "The gauge doesn't work, remember?"

"Instinct."

"Oh God."

"You ready?" Wilson asked.

"Yes. Think we could do some shopping in Globe? I'm getting tired of wearing the same clothes and rinsing my socks and underwear in the sink. And I'm taking a towel to wipe my hands on after starting the truck."

"Don't complain. You volunteered for that part."

"Volunteered? Your girlfriend threatened me. What choice did I have?"

"We're just friends."

"With benefits?"

"Okay, now I lost my appetite." He grimaced, holding his stomach, and walked out of her room to the truck.

As she shut the door behind him, she burst out laughing. *What is it about him?* In a few minutes, she was outside lifting the hood in preparation of starting Ol' Ben.

"Okay!" she yelled.

He turned the ignition and the truck came to life.

"I got something for you," Wilson informed her as she slid into the seat and shut the door.

"A present? For me? You shouldn't have." She batted her eyelashes.

"Here." He handed her a large pair of sunglasses and a wide-brimmed floppy hat. "You need to conceal your identity."

"God, how big do you think my head is?" The hat sat on her ears and the glasses covered most of her face. Wilson burst out laughing.

"As if this doesn't look suspicious! And what did you get? Oh, nice. You get the cowboy hat. You look cool and I look like a Hamptons' wife reject!"

"Stealing towels is illegal," he pointed at the motel towel lying on her lap.

"I'm facing life for murder and, thanks to you, kidnaping, and you're worried about a towel?"

"Could get ten days for that."

She rolled her eyes. "They can add it to my two life sentences. Can we go?"

He backed the truck out into the yard and pulled up to the street. A short distance along, he stopped at a gas station and shut off the truck.

"Morning," the attendant greeted him. "Fill it up?"

"I didn't know anyone did that anymore," Wilson said, searching for the gas cap.

"One of the last. Where's your cap?" the attendant asked, joining the search.

"Not sure. Haven't had this long. Just bought it."

The attendant looked at the truck. "Whatever you paid, mister, you got beat."

"It's a classic."

"A classic what?"

"Haven't figured that out yet. Find the filler?"

"Yep. It's under the box and has a rag stuffed in it."

"Don't lose that rag. Parts are hard to come by for this model."

The attendant cast him a glance as he crawled under the back to the filler pipe. He made it to twenty-two dollars before the fuel began to leak out of the tank.

"That's all she'll hold, mister. It's pissing out the tank."

"That's fine. Only going to Globe."

The attendant chucked the rag into the pipe and crawled out. "That isn't too safe," he said, pointing at the rag.

"I plan to fix it up when I get to Globe."

"Good luck with that." The attendant shook his head in disbelief.

"Keep it," Wilson said as he handed the attendant thirty dollars. "For your trouble."

"Thanks, mister. Have a good one."

"Oh, I will."

When he got back into the cab and slammed the door shut, it bounced open.

Several attempts resulted in the same.

"Now what?" Cari asked.

"It appears my door latch is broken. Got any wire or string on you?"

"Of course. I always carry wire with me!"

"You're not a morning person, are you? Be right back," he said, and jumped out of the truck. Wilson went into the garage and emerged triumphantly holding a piece of wire. He got in and fastened the door shut. "Like a new one!"

"You really think this is getting us to Globe?"

"Don't say that! You'll hurt Ben's feelings." Wilson rubbed the dash affectionately.

Cari smiled despite herself, then quickly rearranged her face into a scowl. *Stick to the plan!*

They pulled up to a local drive-thru, stocked up on breakfast, and continued to follow the highway north to US 60. They turned right, and sped off in the direction of Globe. They had only been on the road for a short time when patrol car lights appeared behind them.

"Oh damn, the cops!" Cari exclaimed.

Wilson pulled the truck onto the side of the road and sat idling. The officer pulled in behind and exited his car carrying something in his hand.

"Morning, officer. What seems to be the problem?" Wilson asked.

"You lost this back there," he replied, holding up their license plate. "Lucky I saw it come off."

"Wire must have broke." Wilson pinched the bridge of his nose, feigning frustration.

"I could give you a ticket for this but," the officer stepped back and looked at the truck, "it would appear you got enough problems."

"That's mighty kind of you, officer. Me and the missus are obliged." He took the plate from the officer and handed it to Cari. "Here hon. Hustle your little butt back there and re-wire this." Turning to the officer again, "got to keep 'em busy and out of trouble, right?"

"You folks have a nice day," the officer replied.

"You too, officer."

Cari hurried around back and re-fastened the plate while keeping her head low then returned to the cab. The police car pulled around them and left.

"What the hell was that? 'Mighty kind of you, officer'?" Cari admonished him.

"I'm just trying to fit in. You know, pretend we're locals."

"A local from where? This is Arizona not Arkansas. We're not the Dukes of Hazard!"

Wilson frowned. "Definitely not a morning person."

"And why did I have to fix the plate?"

"My door won't open, remember?"

"At least you don't have to worry about falling out!"

"You're so dramatic about everything. You should have studied Buddhism instead of psychology in prison."

"I'm saving that for the next time. Which won't be too long the way things are going!"

"Hey Cap." Harrison knocked on his door. "They found the car."

The captain put down the report he was reading. "Come in. And?"

"It's strange. They fished it out of a ravine at the foot of some mountains south of Eloy, Arizona. The car is totaled."

"Any sign of the suspects?"

"Nothing. Did pull her prints and another set off the steering wheel that match those found in James' room. No blood in the car but it's the strangest thing." Harrison leaned on the desk.

"What is?"

"The rear bumper was in the back seat."

"You're kidding?"

"No. They said it had been torn off before the car was dumped."

"How do you know it was dumped?" the captain asked.

"Tire tracks. Looks like a flatbed brought it there but no idea from where. GPS pegged it farther north but there isn't much of anything in that region except desert."

"What do you think happened?"

"Wish I knew, Cap. This keeps getting weirder and weirder. Oh, forensics went over the hotel room and it would appear she cut her hair and dyed it black. And we think she left the hotel disguised as a man."

"Did they leave together?"

"Doesn't appear so."

"Kind of shoots down the kidnap theory."

"Looks that way. I must admit, I can't figure this one out."

The captain rose and moved toward Harrison. "Keep at it. Something will turn up. It always does. You want to go to Arizona?"

"No need at the moment. But I'll keep you informed."

"Better find her before you retire or this will always haunt you."

"I intend to, Cap. I intend to." As he started to leave, he noticed a book on the captain's desk. "John Baroque. Cool name."

"It's a new action novel. He sounds like one hell of a man!"

"Maybe this Baroque guy could help me figure this out." Harrison chuckled and shut the door.

Chapter 4: I'll scratch your belly

As soon as Wilson spotted the huge sign that read "Abe's Honest Car Sales," he yelled, "That's it! That's the one."

"The one what?" Cari startled awake from a troubled sleep.

"Where I'm going to get our next ride. And you didn't think Ol' Ben would make it. Shame on you for doubting!" Wilson pulled over on the side of the street a little past the lot. "You drive up the street. I'm going to walk to the lot. That way they won't connect us to the truck in case they catch up to Rattler."

"What are we going to do with it?" Cari asked.

"I'll ask if there's a scrapyard in town where we can get rid of it."

"Don't say that too loud, you'll hurt Ben's feelings."

"You're starting to sound like me." Wilson got out and walked back to the dealer. He was looking at cars when a short, thin man with a comb-over hustled up to him.

"Hey there, Tex. Looking to buy? I got some of the best deals west of the Mississippi."

"Got anything in the $1000 range? Cash money."

"Come around back, these here are the pricier models. Some just like new. Looking for anything specific? Got a trade?"

"No to both. I want something small and reliable. Maybe got another 10,000 miles in it. It's for commuting to work for the wife. She just got a job in Superior and we live in Miami."

"That's about a twenty-mile hike. I got something over here. It's red. Does that matter?"

"That's her favorite color. How much?"

"Seven hundred. No rust. Only 290,000 miles. One owner. Just came in two days ago. My mechanics checked everything and it's ready to go. Pay and drive. Want to try it?"

"No. I'm in a hurry. Any guarantee?"

"One day."

"I'll take it."

"We'll go in and sign the transfer. Have you in it in fifteen minutes."

"Sounds good."

"Got to tell you, friend, you're my kind of customer. Knows what he wants and is ready to deal when he finds it. Didn't catch the name?" He stuck out a spindly-fingered hand.

Wilson shook it once. "Allen Waterman. Is there a scrapyard in town?"

"Follow US 60 east straight to US 70 and it's on the right near the edge of town."

The salesman had been correct; in about fifteen minutes Wilson was on his way in their new red car. He spotted the truck idling beside the street and pulled in ahead. He jumped out and jogged to Cari's window. "Here, you take the car. There's a scrapyard up ahead. Follow me."

They switched vehicles and Wilson drove to the scrapyard.

At the gate, a man approached. "Can I help you?"

"What will you give me for this?" Wilson asked.

"Drive up to the front. Go in and ask for Sheila. She'll give you some papers to fill out and as soon as we have someone available they will inspect it. Should take about two hours."

"Will you give me twenty for it?"

"Like I said–"

"Twenty, cash."

The man walked around the truck then made a phone call. "Got the papers?"

"Here, all signed." Wilson shoved them into the man's hands.

"Mr. Waterman." He dug out his wallet and counted out twenty dollars. "Here you go."

"Nice doing business with you." Wilson took the money and walked away leaving the truck idling. *Better not shut it off,* he thought as he hurried to Cari and the waiting car. "Get out quick! Turn around and head back to that gas station across from the lights. We need gas before we head north."

"What did you do?" Cari asked.

"Man, you have a suspicious mind." Wilson slammed the door and reached for his seatbelt.

"You're starting to act like me."

"No need to be insulting!"

She crossed the street and drove into the gas station.

"You fill it up and I'm going in to get us some traveling food," Wilson instructed Cari.

As Cari stood pumping gas, she caught her image reflected in the side mirror and broke out laughing. Her large hat rested precariously on the oversized sunglasses.

"This doesn't look suspicious at all," she said. She was sitting in the passenger seat when Wilson emerged with a bag of groceries and a blonde in shorts and a barely-there tank top.

"Rose, this is Kimmy. She's heading north and I offered her a ride as far as Show Low."

"Hi! I'm hitching across the US. Cool, no?" Kimmy bounced as she talked, a mega-watt smile lighting up her face.

"Hop in the back and take these. Supplies for the road," Wilson said as he handed her a small bag.

"Can I see you privately?" Cari said through clenched teeth.

He nodded, then looked at Kimmy, smiling. "Make yourself comfortable. Won't be a minute." Wilson followed Cari away from the car.

"Are you fucking stupid? I'm running for my life and you invite a stranger along with us?" Cari pointed at the car, her other hand on her hip.

"She's cool. And besides, I need more characters in the book. I can't focus on just you."

"More characters? Ever heard of imagination? I can't believe this. What if she recognizes us? She looks young enough to be reading your books."

"She's nineteen. You worry too much. She'll be good company. She likes to talk."

"Oh yeah, that's why you invited her, for her 'stimulating conversation.' It had nothing to do with the fact her big boobs are practically hanging out of that tank top." Cari stood cross-armed.

Wilson looked away. "I hadn't noticed."

"Bullshit! Let's go before I do something to you I might regret." Cari stormed back to the car.

"Any problem? I wouldn't want to cause trouble," Kimmy said leaning on the back of the front seat.

Turning to face her, Cari pointed and said, "You might want to put that away," referring to her left breast.

Kimmy giggled. "Sorry. I like to give them their freedom."

"And I'm sure they appreciate it." Cari scowled.

"Everything good?" Wilson asked as he slid into the driver's seat.

"Great," Kimmy responded.

"Let's get out of here!" Cari growled.

Wilson pulled back onto US 60 and they headed north into the mountains.

"What's your story?" Kimmy inquired.

"We're newlyweds," Wilson enthused. "I'm Allen and this lovely creature is Rose. A Rose by any other name, right Kimmy?"

She tilted her head. "I guess. What does that mean?"

Cari groaned.

"Never mind," Wilson mumbled.

"I'm a performance artist from San Francisco. I'm hitching across America to New York. That's where artists become famous. My last piece was me standing naked on Fisherman's Wharf holding a bunch of grapes between my legs. I called the piece 'ode to wine country.'"

Wilson looked at Cari, who was trying hard not to laugh.

76

"What do you do?" Kimmy continued.

"Well, I'm a failed writer and Rose is a convicted felon. We murdered her former boss in Vegas and are on the run."

Cari stared dumbfounded at Wilson. After a few moments silence Kimmy broke into hysterical laugher.

"That was great! My turn. Let's see. Oh, I know. I'm a famous actress traveling undercover doing research for a role in a Hollywood blockbuster! This is a cool game! My last ride was in a camper but the couple was boring. He was an electrician and she was a legal secretary. Boring! Okay, Rose, your turn."

"Leave me out of this." Cari peered out the side window attempting to ignore the pair.

"You'll have to forgive Rose. We're headed into the deserts of New Mexico to meet our mother ship that will take us back to our home planet."

More laughter from the back seat. "Maybe you could take me back to your planet for breeding!"

Cari groaned again.

More characters my ass! Cari thought. *I know why he invited her. Not that it bothers me. Why should it? He means nothing to me. He's only my ticket out of this mess. I'm not jealous in the least. It's good! I don't have to talk to him. I can sit here in silence. Doesn't bother me at all!*

The time flew by and after a few hours they entered Show Low.

"We're staying on US 60 east into New Mexico," Wilson advised Kimmy when they saw the sign for the town limits.

"Headed to the mother ship!" Kimmy added.

"To the mother ship!" Both broke into laughter as Cari sat in silence.

"I'm going north to Holbrook. Or maybe I'll stay in Show Low for a while. Haven't decided. You can let me out anywhere," Kimmy said.

Wilson pulled the car into a gas station and stopped. "It was nice meeting you, Kimmy."

"It was great! Best ride yet!" She smiled and climbed out of the car.

"Hear that, dear," he looked at Cari. "Best ride yet."

77

Cari stuck her tongue out at him.

"Well, thanks for the lift. Bye."

"You're welcome. Good luck," Wilson called after her.

"Newlyweds? Why did you tell her that?" Cari asked.

"Adding plot twists to the book."

She shook her head. "Let's just go."

"Okay, Blondie."

It was early evening when they reached Springerville. Wilson stopped at the first motel they came to and went in for a room.

"Full up," Wilson informed her when he returned. "Fellow says there's another down the road a bit. We'll try there."

"We can sleep in the car if necessary," Cari suggested.

He smiled at her. "Ahh, missing home?"

"Shut up. Could we eat in a restaurant instead of take-out and junk food from a grocery store?" she asked.

"If there is a place close to the motel, sure, why not? We do want to keep a low profile, though."

"Oh right, like when you invite big-breasted nineteen-year-olds along? So low profile."

"You're just jealous at having to share me."

"Jealous? You could continue to New York with her for all I care as long as you leave me the car. I got my papers. I don't even need you any longer."

"Darn, now you tell me. I wonder how long it would take me to get back to Show Low?"

"You're not funny." She stared out the window, frowning.

Wilson pulled into another motel and disappeared inside. As he looked around the lobby he came face to face with it: a large poster of John Baroque. "I don't believe it!"

"He's something, isn't he?" a woman asked from behind the counter. "We have a small book store around the corner. His book is hard to keep on the shelf but I got one stashed away if you're interested."

He scowled at the poster. "No, thank you."

She looked at Wilson. "We got some self-help books on the other side."

"Do you have a room?" he asked in disgust.

"One left."

"Fine."

He filled in the registration card and paid in cash. As he was leaving the woman asked again if he wanted the Baroque book.

"What's the matter with you?" Cari asked when he returned.

"Nothing!" he snapped, snatching his bag out of the back seat.

Cari raised an eyebrow. "Did you notice? There's a small picture of your buddy in the window."

Wilson grumbled under his breath.

"What was that?" Cari asked.

"Got the last room! Only has one bed but it's a king. Can I trust you?"

Cari laughed. "You wish. It'll be fine. We're both mature adults. Okay, I'm a mature adult. You, I'm not so sure about."

"There's a Mexican restaurant down the road. It's getting dark so we should be okay. This seems like a nice little town where people mind their own business. And he's not my buddy!"

After cleaning up, they drove to the restaurant and walked in. It was small with a bar on the left and several tables to the right. A young woman greeted them with a big smile and a "welcome." They sat in the corner and, after ordering, Wilson stared out the window, thinking.

I wonder what Rattler meant? I don't know what it is, but there's something about Cari that doesn't seem right. "What were you in prison for?" Wilson asked.

The question caught Cari off-guard. "Ah, I was in—I was framed. That's why. I told you already."

"You said you were framed, but for what? And why?" Wilson pushed.

"Ralph was into some crooked stuff before the collapse, but I was always honest. When the FCC began to investigate the firm, he ended up clean.

79

Somehow a bunch of files, files I had never seen, ended up on my computer, and the feds found them."

"How did this Jacoby guy figure in?" Wilson continued to grill her.

"I think he hacked my computer and put the files there to cover for Ralph."

"And that's all there was to it?"

Fuck, he's getting suspicious. I got to cover myself better. "No. Ralph and I started dating a few months before it all happened. I think Jacoby was jealous because him and Ralph were best friends and he felt I was stealing him away. Plus, he hated me and wanted to help his friend."

That would be a motive, Wilson thought.

"That's all there is to it," Cari said. *That should do it. Not the brightest guy.*

When they returned to the room Wilson realized how tired he was. Perhaps the strain was getting to him. Even though he appeared light-hearted and optimistic, he harbored grave doubts he could pull this off. And he was beginning to have doubts about Cari.

"Which side of the bed do you want?" Wilson called to her as she brushed her teeth in the bathroom. "Left or right?"

"Depends."

"On what?"

"Left or right facing the bed, or lying in it?"

"Left or right, what? Ah, how about this; side toward the door or side toward the window."

"Window," she replied, exiting the bathroom.

"Okay. But remember, stay on your side!"

"Yeah, yeah. Goodnight." Cari waved him off, collapsing into bed.

"Goodnight."

Though exhausted Cari lay there in the dark unable to sleep. After a while she whispered, "you awake?"

"Yes," he whispered back.

"I'm curious about your place in Crete."

"It's way up in the mountains along the north shore. There's a road that goes over the mountains to an interior plain and near the top is a museum and tourist shop. A narrow dirt road goes by and winds around the hill to a Y. To the left, the road rises a little farther, then levels off. About two kilometers on is my place. It's a small year-round house with a spectacular view and lots of land. I have a tenant farmer who lives rent free and takes care of the place for me when I'm gone. I never have to worry about it, and no one knows I own it. It's perfect for you to hold up at."

"Why did you buy it?" she asked.

"To escape from the world."

She sighed. "That's what I could use."

"We all could. Once in a while."

"It sounds perfect. Goodnight Wilson." She rolled over to face the window.

I think one more day should do it. I wonder how much money he has on him? He keeps getting money from bank machines. I need to figure a way to get that roll and the keys. Tomorrow night, I'm gone. His place in Crete sounds nice, though. And he's not a bad guy, even if he is wimpish—Stop it Jessica! Stick to the plan! Use him and don't get involved. If I hadn't got involved with Ralph, those guys would never have figured out what I was doing. That cost me two years. If I blow this, it'll be twenty-five to life! She shuddered at the thought.

Wilson was walking down a long corridor when a door suddenly slammed shut behind Cari. The room was cold and damp and she pleaded with him to help her. Then she was laughing. Cari was on the outside. He grabbed the bars but the door wouldn't budge. The stench of fear filled his nostrils. He tried to scream and was startled awake. Wilson was shaking and covered in sweat. He pushed his legs out of the bed and went slowly to the table. A small light dimly illuminated the room. It was still dark outside and Wilson could just make out Cari's form lying under the sheets.

He went into the bathroom, closed the door, and flicked on the light. His reflection in the mirror was pale and drawn.

What have I got myself into? I want to show up Baroque and Trish, but is this worth it? I could leave now. Sneak out before she wakes up. But what would happen to her? I think she's probably sweet under that gruff exterior. She's certainly way ahead of Angel! That woman is as thick as a post. Don't know what I saw in her. Okay, if I'm being honest, I saw the same thing I did with my other two wives. And what did that get me? Cari is completely different. Ugh! Don't be a sap! I need to figure a way out of this.

He washed his face and went to the table.

"What're you doing?" Cari asked groggily.

"Morning. Studying the atlas. I think if we take turns driving we could go right through to Atlanta in about three days."

"That's fine with me. The sooner the better." She sat up in bed. *He doesn't sound too enthusiastic.* "We'll stock up before leaving town. We won't have to stop except for gas."

"And bathroom breaks," Cari added.

"That's what sage brush beside the road is for." Wilson looked at her skeptically.

"You don't think I could do that?" Cari asked.

"Do what?"

"Pee outside. It's because I'm a city girl, isn't it?"

Wilson chuckled. "You did get freaked out by a scorpion so no, I don't think you could."

"I spent two years in prison where the toilet is in the middle of the room. If you're shy you get over it real fast!"

"If it makes you feel more at home you can leave the bathroom door open," he said, returning to the atlas.

She made a face at him, went into the bathroom, and shut the door.

After leaving the motel they picked up groceries and Cari managed to find a hat that fit and better looking sunglasses. Once the car was gassed-up, they continued east in a jovial mood.

"We're not going to Albuquerque," Wilson began as they pulled out of town. "We'll stay south and stick to the back roads, avoiding the interstates where possible. It's pretty barren territory and I don't expect to see any cops. We stay east to Logan then turn north. From there, we work our way to Oklahoma, thus, avoiding Texas."

"Sounds good," she replied, studying the atlas. "How long to the state border?"

"We should be in Logan in about five hours. It's 7:30 a.m. now. By 1:00 for sure. After that another couple of hours to the border."

She yawned and rubbed her eyes. "I think I'll catch some sleep. Didn't sleep well last night."

"You were tossing and turning most of the night."

"Sorry. I guess the stress is catching up to me." She shrugged.

"Rest now. You can drive later."

"Harrison? Where's Harrison?" the captain called out into the squad room.

"Here Cap. Just got off the phone." He raised a hand.

"What's this I hear about a break in the case? They've been spotted in Albuquerque? We best contact the state police immediately."

"Afraid not, Cap. It seems some flake named Kimmy called an Albuquerque radio station and claimed she was 'hitching across America' and got a ride with a couple from Globe to Show Low."

"What's the problem?"

"The couple had large dark eyes, strange shaped heads, and were heading into New Mexico somewhere to meet their mother ship that would take them to their home planet."

"Jesus Christ! The loonies come out as soon as the news spreads." Disgusted, the captain returned to his office.

"Always seems that way, Cap," Harrison called after him.

When Cari awoke they were in the desert southeast of Albuquerque.

"Feel better?" Wilson asked her.

She stretched. "Yes. How long did I sleep?"

"Three hours."

"God, I guess I was tired. Want me to drive?"

"Yes. I could use some sleep, especially if we're driving all night. We're on US 60. It shouldn't be too much longer before we hit US 54. Follow that to Tucumcari."

"Got it. 60 to 54 to Tucumcari. Then what?"

"Wake me."

At the small town of Logan, they turned north and stopped at a picnic ground for lunch.

"This is beautiful country, isn't it?" Cari asked no one in particular.

"Truly is." Wilson nodded, looking around.

"How far to the next town?"

"About fifty miles. I'll drive again."

"Thanks," Cari said. "Gives me a chance to watch the scenery."

They packed up and headed out once more.

"When you're in prison staring at four gray walls day in and day out, you dream about places like this. Wide open and free. This is paradise." She looked at him and smiled. "Tell me about Crete."

"It's a wonderful place. There are lots of mountains and several plains, mostly in the interior of the island. And miles of sandy beaches. The people are friendly and accommodating and in the south there are palm trees in some places. The weather is beautiful; not too hot in the summer and pleasant in winter. The mountain tops get snow and occasionally it snows at my place."

The miles passed quickly on the flat terrain as the two continued in conversation. Suddenly, the car made a strange noise.

"What was that?" Cari inquired.

"Nothing. Probably hit a stone or some–"

"There it is again!"

This time the noise was much louder and the car began to slow. Wilson pushed on the gas pedal but there was no reaction. He steered the vehicle onto the side of the road.

"I'll check under the hood." Wilson pulled the handle, walked to the front, lifted the hood, and leaned on the car. After a few minutes Cari joined him.

"Know anything about engines?" she asked.

"Every man knows about cars!" Wilson scoffed at her.

She popped her hip out and glared at him. "Do you know anything about engines?"

"Not a thing!"

She threw up her hands. "We're stranded in the middle of nowhere and the car is broken."

"It isn't broken. It is broke down."

"Oh, excuse me. I should know the correct terminology when I explain it on the stand at my trial!"

"Someone will be along any moment. If they can't fix it we'll ride to the next town and find a mechanic, or buy another car. Simple!"

"You're simple. We haven't met one car since we turned on this road."

"That's fine. We don't want to go back. We'll wait for one going the same way."

"I think there is something seriously wrong with you!" She got back into the car.

Wilson walked over, opened the door, and leaned down to talk to her. "We could walk, if you want. We can't be that far from the next town."

Cari was silent.

"Okay. We'll wait for someone to come along. The good people of New Mexico will help us. You'll see."

He leaned back on the front of the car and stared off into the distance. Within five minutes he heard a vehicle approaching from behind. He waved his arms as a minivan neared. It went by and stopped in front of them.

"See, doubter. Help is here," he proclaimed triumphantly.

Cari emerged from the car and joined him as a man with whiskers and very long hair tied in a ponytail approached. "Problem folks?"

"Yes. Thanks for stopping. It just died as we were driving along. You know about cars?"

"Not so much, but my pal Ned does. Hey Ned!" he called back to the driver of the van.

"What's up?" A scrawny man with a patchy beard stuck his head out the window.

"Car died. Probably the water pump."

"Mind if I try it?" Ned asked when he had joined them.

"Go ahead," Wilson told him.

Ned slipped in behind the wheel and called out, "Okay?"

"Yeah. Try it," the fellow with the ponytail answered.

He turned the engine over a couple times. When it didn't start, he joined the others by the front. "Definitely the water pump."

"We got one in the van?"

"Not for this model. Can probably get one in the next town," Ned said.

Two women exited the van and walked up to the group.

"We can give you a ride and you can find a mechanic," Ned offered.

"We'd be happy if you–" Wilson began before Cari cut him off.

"We should stay with the car and you could send someone back," she interjected.

"Up to you folks," long hair told them.

"You know, come to think about it, there might not be any mechanics in the next town," Ned added.

"You're right. Might have to go to Raton."

"That means it would be well after dark by the time we even find someone. You folks would have to stay out here all night."

The long haired man looked them up and down. "You shouldn't be out here all night. Best to come with us."

"We'll all get to know one another," one of the women added. "I'm Jean

MANY PIGS IN MANHATTAN

and this is Rebecca. Ned's the mechanic and this guy with the ponytail is Josh. Come on, we got plenty of room."

"I'm Allen and this is Rose," Wilson said, gesturing to Cari.

"Better lock up the car. Can't trust some people," Josh said.

Cari glared at Wilson as they walked over to the van. "I don't like this," she whispered.

"You got to learn to trust people."

"Where you folks headed?" Ned asked.

"Denver."

"No way! Us too."

"Maybe after we get to be friends we can go all the way with you nice people," Wilson said.

"Pitch in a little for gas and we're good!"

Everyone piled into the van and they sped away. The conversation was light and friendly for about twenty minutes. Suddenly, their attitude changed. Josh, who was sitting in the front passenger seat, turned around and pointed a gun at Wilson and Cari as the van slowed and pulled onto the shoulder. "We'll be asking you to empty your pockets and hand everything to our lovely wives, if you don't mind. And we want the car keys as well."

"Look, you don't want to do this. I have influential friends–" Wilson began.

"Save it, bud. Cooperate and we'll leave you beside the road. Don't, and we'll dump your bodies in the ditch. Either way works for me." Josh shrugged.

Wilson avoided Cari's scathing looks as he handed over the contents of his pockets, including the new passport and driver's license.

"How much cash is there?" Josh asked his wife.

"Around six hundred," Rebecca replied with a smile.

"That everything?"

"Nothing left," Jean answered after searching their pockets.

"Okay, get out! And you want to keep your mouths shut or we'll be back, understand?"

"Believe me, we won't go to the cops," Wilson replied.

Wilson and Cari stood in the ditch as the door closed and the van headed back in the direction they had come.

"I'll bet they know exactly what's wrong with the car and they're going back to get it. That's why they drove us to here, to give themselves time to work on it, or strip it. Well, this is certainly a setback." Wilson sighed, his shoulders slumping.

"A setback!? A setback!? You're a fucking moron! A setback? We're in the middle of the fucking desert with no food, no water, no car and, oh yeah, don't forget, no fucking papers!" Cari threw her hands in the air and paced up and down the side of the road. "One more night! That's what had I decided. How stupid could I be?"

Wilson turned to her, confused. "What do you mean, one more night?"

"Ah..."

"I told you it would be three to Atlanta."

"Ah..."

"Is there something you're not telling me?" Wilson asked. *Something Rattler figured out?*

"I meant, one more night before I would get some new clothes. At least that was what I hoped."

"Rattler was right about you."

"Rattler is a moron."

"Perhaps. But she is insightful."

Fuck! What am I going to do? I lost everything. I can never get away on my own. If he walks away now I'm screwed. "I robbed a gas station in Texas," she began. "It was late in the evening, I was broke, hadn't eaten, and my car was almost out of gas. I pulled into this station in a small town and put in some gas but had no money. There was a kid on duty alone so I pretended I had a gun in my jacket pocket and he handed over the money. Two hundred and sixty one dollars. Plus, twenty in gas. And I grabbed a bag of potato chips when I ran out. I didn't want to tell you because it is the only criminal act I ever committed and I am embarrassed and ashamed. I didn't want you to know. I was set up and took the fall for Brentwood and Jacoby. I did not kill Brentwood and now I'm being set up by Jacoby again." *Hope I didn't lay it on too thick. Now for the big finish.* "But this is my problem, not yours. I appreciate everything you've done for me and I thank you. You are very clever and I wish you well. I should have listened to you at the beginning and turned myself in. That way you wouldn't have gotten involved." She looked down at the ground.

Wilson glared at her. "Man, you're a baby."

"Excuse me?" Her head snapped up.

"A little setback and you start feeling sorry for yourself."

"Little setback? We lost everything, including our papers. What are we supposed do now?"

"For your information, Jason Bourke still has his passport, driver's license, and bank card well hidden in the bottom of my shoes! What do you think about that?"

Cari sagged with relief and smiled. "I think I'm lucky you're the one helping me, and not John Baroque."

Wilson laughed. "He's a hack!"

"Probably had a ghost writer! Has anyone checked his military record?"

"He was most likely a dish washer."

They were both laughing now, though neither knew why.

"Like hitchhiking?" Wilson asked, after he brought himself under control again.

"No!"

"But you meet some of the nicest people, like Kimmy."

"Oh God," she groaned.

"You know, it wouldn't hurt if you undid a few buttons on your blouse." Wilson touched the collar of his shirt.

"I'm not exposing myself for the sake of a ride!" She glared at him and crossed her arms over her chest.

"It couldn't hurt." He shrugged.

"I'm going to hurt you if you come up with any more asinine ideas like that."

"You sure swear a lot when you're angry."

"Better not make me angry. Wait, I hear something coming. Is it those fucking hippies again?"

"Looks like a truck of some kind," he said. "Yes, it's a pickup. Quick, three buttons should do it!"

Cari scowled, hitting his arm. Wilson had his thumb out and the truck slowed. A family of four filled the cab.

"Howdy. Our car broke down and we're trying to get to Mosquero. Headed that way?" he asked.

"Yep. We live this side of town. Happy to help you two but cab's full, though you're welcome to ride in the back with Jennifer," the woman in the passenger seat informed them.

Wilson turned to Cari and smiled.

"Oh wonderful! I hope she's wearing a halter top!" Cari said.

"No, miss, Jennifer is a pig. The boy's prize winning porker. But she won't mind some company," the woman said.

Wilson beamed.

"You're loving this, aren't you?" Cari said.

"Many pigs in Manhattan?" he asked.

She rolled her eyes. "Plenty, but they all have two legs and are male."

They walked around to the back and Wilson pulled open the tailgate. A very large sow sat up and grunted. She wasn't tied in any way.

"I don't think so! There's no way I'm getting in with that thing!" Cari said, backing away.

"How bad can it be? After all, you had to share a bed with me last night."

"True, this can't be any worse."

"Want some help up?" Wilson asked, beaming.

"If you can get up there, I can."

"Suit yourself." Wilson hopped up next to Jennifer. Cari quickly followed. He pulled the tailgate shut and settled down next to the pig.

"Better sit down. It's not safe riding on the side like that."

"I'm close enough, thank you." Cari had to grab hold as the truck lurched forward and began to speed up.

"You're a nice girl, aren't you?" Wilson cooed as he stroked the pig's neck. She grunted softly.

"You two want to be alone?" Cari asked him.

"She is the best company I've had in the past few days."

When he looked at Cari she stuck her tongue out.

"Don't pay attention to the mean lady. I'll scratch your belly," Wilson told Jennifer as she lay down again.

"What are you, some kind of Dr. Doolittle?"

"If you've read the Willikers, you know most of the characters are based on animals. I lived on various farms during my life studying them. Pigs are one of the smartest animals there is, even smarter than dogs."

"Maybe I should ask her for a plan to get to Crete."

Cari settled down into the truck and began stroking Jennifer's belly. "No one would ever believe I'm petting a pig's belly in the back of a truck somewhere in the New Mexico desert. You aren't going to include this in the book, are you?"

"People like animals. It's a good way to introduce one without sounding corny."

"Oh, come on! No one would believe this is a plausible scenario for an action adventure. Jason Bourne did not pet one pig in his films."

"Maybe he would have had less stress if he had," Wilson said.

"It is rather soothing patting her, I must admit. She seems so, I don't know, zen."

"Hard to believe she has razor sharp teeth."

"Razor sharp?" Cari's hand paused.

"I once saw a sow rip a German Shepard dog to bits defending her piglets."

Cari stopped petting her and moved as far into the corner as possible.

"Relax, she doesn't have any babies to defend. They hardly ever attack unless they're defending their babies."

"Hardly ever? That's reassuring!"

"We're coming up to our turn, guys," the driver of the truck yelled back to them. The truck slowed and pulled off onto the shoulder. Wilson and Cari jumped out and went to the driver's window.

"Thanks very much for the lift. I would offer you something, but unfortunately we're broke at the moment."

"Don't want nothing, friend. Glad to be of help. Town center is about three hundred feet further on. Go to the post office. They'll be able to help you."

"Thanks again."

"Thanks for the ride. Bye Jennifer," Cari added.

"See, that didn't work out too bad. Made a new friend," Wilson said as they walked in the direction the driver indicated.

"I suppose you can never have too many pigs for friends."

"That's the spirit. There's the post office on the left," Wilson pointed out.

"I hope our pictures aren't hanging on the wall."

"You're such a ray of sunshine! Come on."

"Can I help you?" a dark haired middle-aged man, who spoke extremely slowly, asked as they entered.

"Hello. Is there any bus service through here?" Wilson asked, while Cari cast a glance around the interior.

"'Fraid not. Need to get somewhere?"

"Yes. Our car broke down. I don't suppose there's a place in town to rent one?"

"No rental agencies here," the clerk replied.

"Know where the nearest one is?"

"That would be Las Vegas."

"Las Vegas? Are you kidding?" Cari asked, perplexed.

"Las Vegas, New Mexico, not Nevada," Wilson explained.

"Don't worry, miss, happens more than you think. You look familiar. From around here?" the clerk asked as he stared at Cari.

She looked down at the floor. "No, New York. On our honeymoon."

"Oh, isn't that nice. Congratulations." He smiled at them.

"How far to Las Vegas?" Wilson asked.

"About 70 miles."

"How can we get there?"

"Best bet would be Agnes."

"Agnes?"

"See, she got hurt and is on permanent disability, but can drive, and is the town's unofficial designated driver. You need to get somewhere, Agnes will get you there," the clerk explained.

"Sounds good. Is there a bank machine nearby?"

"Next door in the entrance to the bar."

"That's convenient."

"Want me to call Agnes for you?" the clerk asked.

"That would be great. Tell her we need to go to a car rental agency."

Wilson soon returned flush with cash again thanks to Jason Bourke, an extremely resourceful gentleman.

"Agnes will be here in five minutes," the clerk informed them.

"Thank you. We'll wait outside."

A newer model dark-blue sedan pulled up in front of the post office. Wilson couldn't help but notice the car tilted toward the driver's side. The door opened and a very large woman struggled to pull herself out. She had shoulder length brown hair, a tanned face covered in wrinkles that could not completely hide the fact she had once been beautiful, and wore a flowered dress that stretched to the ground.

"You the couple wants to go to a car rental in Vegas?" she asked.

"That would be us. Hi, I'm Allen and this is Rose."

"I'm Agnes."

"Nice to meet you," Cari shook her outstretched hand.

"I charge 25 dollars straight up then fifty cents a mile. It's 75 miles to the agency, plus I've got to drive back, so I have to charge both ways. Makes a total of one hundred, cash."

"Sounds fair," Wilson agreed as he pulled out some money.

"No, no. Pay when we get there. I only take money from satisfied customers. You ready?"

"Yes. Rose, you want to sit up front?" Wilson asked.

"No, the back's good for me." Wilson held open the door and as she walked by whispered, "you sit next to Agnes, I know how much you like big boobs!"

"Get in the car!"

They fastened their seat belts and Agnes sped out of the lot.

"How long to Vegas?" Wilson asked.

"One hour, if the cops ain't around. And they're never around out here. So, what's your story?"

"We're newlyweds," Wilson enthused.

"Newlyweds? If you want to jump in the back with the missus I'll turn up the radio and you can have at her!"

Wilson looked back at Cari. "It's okay, Agnes. I'll pass."

"Little lady kind of shy?"

"She gets a bit loud."

"Loud? Hell, I broke a few windows in my time!"

"I'll bet you did." Wilson couldn't help but smile at the thought.

"First time married?" Agnes asked.

"Third for me. First for her," Wilson replied.

"I been married seven times!"

"Seven?"

"That's right. Back in the sixties and seventies I was a line dancer in Las Vegas. The one in Nevada. The men drooled over me, I tell you."

"I bet they still do," Wilson added.

"Honey, this one's a charmer!" Agnes called back to Cari. She had a deep laugh that filled the car. Cari made a face at Wilson when he glanced at her.

"Anyway, first husband was Benjamin. Called him Benjy, you know, like the little hairy dog 'cause he had such a hairy one. Unfortunately, his secretary liked them hairy too and when I caught him screwing her, I divorced him. He had some money and I got a nice piece of change. Then I married number two, Lyell, a no good two-bit hustler. Screwed me out of my money then ran off with some floozy. Never heard from him again. We always like the bad ones, don't we, honey," she said to Cari, to no reply.

"Anyway, then came Romeo," Agnes continued.

"Romeo?" Wilson asked.

"God's honest truth. That was his name. Nicest man I ever met but blind as a bat. Had glasses an inch thick and could barely see when he wore them. We go to this fancy hotel on our honeymoon and we're on the fifth floor. He tells me 'you bend over dear Agnes and I'm going to get a running start.' I bent over and aimed her right at him. He came flying across the room, missed me completely, went out the balcony doors, and over the railing. Landed flat on his back right in front of the hotel entrance, naked and stiff as a board!"

Wilson could hear Cari laughing in the back.

"If only he'd been longer down below it might have snagged on the balcony railing and saved him. I sued the hotel and won a pretty penny.

"By husband number four I was getting a bit jaded and just wanted to be married. Found this gambler in Reno one night and told him if he hit the roulette wheel I'd screw him and if he hit twice I'd marry him. Damned if he hit three times! Never seen such luck. But his luck changed and he gambled away everything I had.

"Number five was a sweetie pie. And smart. He was a scientist and worked for the government. I loved that man. I became friends with this Russian woman and turned out she was some kind of spy or secret agent or something. She only wanted to find out what my husband was doing. When I found out he was doing her, I ratted them out to the Feds.

"By the time number six came along I was getting a lot bigger. When I was dancing I had legs down to here and boobs out to there. I was something. But by the time number six came along I was putting on the pounds. That was when I was at my biggest. I've lost a lot in the last few years. Anyway, George was a small man, about a hundred pounds, and short. He liked it when I was on top.

One night we're going at it and wasn't paying attention and first thing I know George isn't breathing no more. I tried mouth-to-mouth and called the paramedics but it was too late. I screwed poor George to death! And he was my favorite too! Fortunately, he was loaded. Set me up good financially.

"And now I'm on number seven. Lucky seven. Stanley. Stanley is a good sized man, if you know what I mean, and about 30 years younger than me. But that's okay, at least he can keep up with me. Course there's a down side to having a young lover. That's how I ended up disabled, threw out my back. You should have seen the look on that government woman's face when I explained to her how I got injured. I don't think she believed me so I told her everything in great detail. Never seen anybody's face get that red before! When I offered to bring Stanley in her office and give a demonstration, she signed them papers fast enough. Anyway, I collect disability, but it ain't much, so I drive people from one place to another. How about you folks? What's your story?"

Wilson hesitated and fortunately noticed a sign indicating the Las Vegas town limits.

"We're here already? That didn't take long," Wilson said.

"I'm pretty heavy on the gas. The agency isn't far. Be there in five minutes."

"This has been a great trip, Agnes. You're a wonderful traveling companion," Cari added.

"If you're up this way again, look me up."

"Maybe we can come to your next wedding," Wilson said, a twinkle in his eye.

Agnes burst out laughing. "You're alright. If things don't work out for you give me a call. I don't figure Stanley can survive this much longer!"

Agnes pulled the car to a stop in front of the car rental agency. Wilson handed her the money and a tip.

"Thank you, sweetie. Anytime you need it," Agnes told him.

"Bye Agnes," Cari called as she exited the car.

After Agnes had pulled away Wilson looked at Cari. "She meant a ride when she said any time I need it, right?"

"That's not what I thought!" Cari laughed.

"Oh God!" Wilson went into the building.

When he came out Cari was leaning against the wall watching traffic. They walked around to the back of the building and found a small black sedan.

"You should get a sports car next time. Maybe a Ferrari," Cari told him.

"A Ferrari? That wouldn't be inconspicuous."

"Inconspicuous? Like inviting Kimmy along?" Cari asked.

"She was—it's not like—never mind."

"I'll bet Baroque doesn't have a spitfire wit like that." Cari looked at him and smiled.

"Shut up!"

"What's the plan now?" she asked.

"We keep going east." Wilson opened the passenger door for her.

"What about my papers? I can't get out of the country without a passport."

"I know a guy in Atlanta who can supply us. They may not be the quality of Baby-Boy's, but they are still very good."

"How do you know people like that in Atlanta?" Cari asked suspiciously.

"I lived there for a few years with wife number two."

Cari fidgeted with her fingers. "Why do you keep telling people we're married?"

"It's a distraction."

"What do you mean?"

"Most people can only focus on one thing at a time. When I tell them we're newlyweds they forget about seeing our faces on the news last night. It's what magicians do. Why? Does the thought of being married to me bother you?"

"No. I was just–"

"You would like to be married to me?"

"No, it's—what?" Her face contorted in confusion.

"You don't want to marry me?" Wilson asked.

"What? Shut up! You're trying to confuse me." She turned away.

"See, it works. What did you think of Agnes?"

"Wonderful woman. Think her stories are true?"

"Who cares? She is going to make such a great character for the book. I'm telling you, this is writing itself."

"You can't use her as a character."

"Why not?" Wilson asked as he pulled the car out onto the highway.

"Oh, come on, no one would ever believe it."

"You do remember I'm writing a novel? It's fictional."

"I know what a novel is. You're doing this as an adventure like Bourne. You have to use realistic characters, not bizarre ones like Agnes or Rattler."

"What about the Harry Potter books? She used all kinds of weird characters."

"True, but that is another genre. For this adventure, you need realistic characters people will believe and like or hate."

"I need interesting characters. And the book is only 'based on' real events. I can add things and invent scenarios that never happened. Look at the things Bourne does. They're not all realistic."

"That's artistic license, but the characters in the work are real. And if I'm the main character I think I should have some say about the writing of the book."

"That's another thing, I'm not sure you will be the main character. I think it would be more appropriate for the genre if the lead was a man."

"A man? Oh fuck! You want to make yourself lead." Cari half turned in her seat and was glaring at him.

"That's another thing, you swear too much. Bourne never swears. I'm going to have to edit out half what you say."

"I don't swear. Only when I'm pissed at you. If you stop making me pissed off it will be fine. And you can't be serious in thinking you're the main character. An adventure needs a strong lead, someone the reader will believe could do anything. Shit, you fold like a napkin at the mere sign of trouble."

"Excuse me?" Wilson asked.

"Like those hippies. When he pulled that gun, you should have grabbed it and kicked him in the balls then trashed the other three."

"Grabbed the gun?"

"John Baroque would have."

"Baroque! I'll bet he's all talk and no action. Packaging. That's what he is. Fancy packaging with nothing inside. I wasn't afraid. I was waiting for the right moment to make my move." Wilson squeezed the steering wheel until his knuckles turned white.

"The only move you made was out the door when he told you to."

"I suppose you could have done better?"

"Damn right!"

"Then why didn't you make a move?" Wilson asked.

"You were sitting right behind him. I was in the third row seat. There was no way I could reach his gun, but if I could have I would have kicked his sorry ass!" Cari punched her hand with a fist.

"Right, like that would happen."

"I studied karate for five years and have a blue or brown, or some color belt. So yeah, I could have kicked his ass. I know I can kick yours."

"Oh please." Wilson giggled.

"I hate to say it, but you're kind of a wimp. No offense."

"Why do people say 'no offense' right after they offend you?" Wilson asked.

"Beats me. Am I still the main character?"

"I'll think about it."

"I'm not worried one way or another because you'll never write it."

"Where's Harrison?" the captain asked.

"Albuquerque, Cap."

"Albuquerque? What the hell is he doing there?"

"You were away when we got the news. There was a hit on Wilson James' credit card in a town called Tuca, no. Tucu, wait, what was it? Tucu something or other. It's in New Mexico east of Albuquerque. Harrison is flying to Albuquerque and renting a car. He should be on the ground by now if you want me to contact him."

"No, that's okay. But let me know as soon as you got any info."

"First thing, Cap."

Harrison hurried through the airport toward the exit and the shuttle to the rental cars. They told him it would take about two hours to reach Tucumcari and he was anxious. The message only stated that someone using James' credit card had been picked up at a shopping center. It seemed uncharacteristic of James to make a mistake like that because no matter what they had done, Harrison was beginning to admire the writer's abilities.

His badge got him to the front of the line and it wasn't long before he was on the interstate driving east. It was late afternoon when he arrived at the police station.

"Detective Harrison of the Las Vegas police," he told the desk sergeant as he held up his badge.

"One minute, Detective. I'll buzz the chief."

"Detective Harrison, I'm Chief Brady, welcome," he extended his hand. "Sent a message to you but you had already left Vegas. The guy we picked up isn't your man James but a low-life car thief. I talked to him but he insists he found the card in the parking lot and was trying to return it to the owner. Of course, he was buying a big screen TV at the time."

"Mind if I talk to him?" Harrison asked.

"You're welcome to, but I don't think you'll get anything out of him. He's been in and out of jail and knows how to work the system. Have a seat and I'll set it up."

"I appreciate it."

Harrison sat in the lobby for ten minutes before another officer appeared.

"Detective? Come with me, please."

Harrison rose and followed the officer to a small room in the back. A man with long hair tied in a ponytail sat behind the table.

"Name's Josh Carter. Has a long sheet," the officer informed Harrison as he handed him a folder.

Harrison sat down opposite the prisoner and glanced at the material in the file. "Mr. Carter, I'm Detective Harrison of the Las Vegas, Nevada, police. I would like to ask you a few questions about the credit card you were attempting to use."

"I told the other officers I found it. That's all I know. I was planning on returning it."

Staring at him, Harrison continued, "How did you plan to return it when you don't know who the owner is?"

"I don't know. Maybe I was going to ask at the information desk in the store." Josh shifted in his chair.

"And how was buying a big screen TV going to help you find the owner?"

"I incurred expenses looking for him and thought I deserved a reward."

"It says you were arrested with a female companion. Will she verify your story?" The detective continued to stare at Josh.

"Damn straight she will."

Harrison pulled a photograph out of an envelope he had brought and slid the picture across the table. "Ever seen this fellow?" he asked of James' photo.

"Can't say I have."

"What about her?" He showed him Jessica Stone's photo.

"Never seen her either. Who are they?"

"Murderers."

"The hell you say!"

"That's right. They killed a man in Las Vegas, Nevada. A very important man. And now you have the murderer's credit card."

"Told you, I found it." Josh tapped his fingers on the table.

"This is how I see it playing out, Josh. May I call you Josh?"

"That's my name."

"Okay Josh, this is how I see it playing out. You have a murderer's credit card and that links you to him thus connecting you to the murder." Harrison grinned ever so slightly.

"Hey, wait a minute! No damn way I had anything to do with any murder! I never been to Vegas, least not the one in Nevada." Josh sprang up from his chair.

"Doesn't matter. If you aided and abetted them, you are as guilty of this murder as they are." Harrison didn't flinch.

"What's this aided and, what was it?" Josh asked as he leaned over the table.

"It means you helped them. I bet when we check that card for fingerprints we're going to find yours and Wilson James' on it. That, my friend, links you to him and the murder. With your rap sheet, you'll never see the light of day again. Prepared to die in prison, Josh?"

"I never been to Vegas! You can't pin this on me!" he shouted.

"I want James and Stone, but if I can't have them, you'll do. I need to close this case. People want someone to take the fall and you're as good as anyone. I arrest you and I can retire."

"I want a lawyer!"

"Sorry, Josh. You revoked your right to counsel when they questioned you before and that still applies. No lawyer, Josh. All you got is me. If I walk out that door and call my captain he will start the paperwork to extradite you to Vegas. I'll be able to take you back with me." The detective sat back in his chair and smiled.

"Okay! But if I tell you everything can you make these charges go away?"

"I'll put in a word for you with the chief. But whatever you get here won't compare to what they'll do to you in Vegas."

"I don't want to rat out my, ah, friends."

"All I want is these two," Harrison pointed to the pictures. "I couldn't care less how many there were of you."

"Okay." Josh sat down. "We were heading north on 39 and we see this car on the side of the road with the hood up so we stop. My friend tries to start it and we realize it's a simple fix. We tell them the water pump is finished and could we give them a lift to the next town. They get in and a few miles down the road we clean them out and leave them beside the road then come back to get the car. That's the God honest truth, Detective. No lie." He stared at the detective with his best look of innocence.

"Was it these two in the pictures?"

Josh picked up the photos. "Hard to tell. They both wore big sunglasses and hats. He had a cowboy hat. Could be them but they looked a lot different."

"Different how?"

"He had several days beard and her hair was short and black. Could be them but I don't know for sure. That's the God honest truth, Detective."

"When was this?"

"Yesterday afternoon."

"What did they have on them?"

"I think it was around two hundred cash and a couple passports and driver licenses."

"What happened to the passports and licenses?" Harrison asked, his hopes rising.

"We destroyed them. Too hard to fence."

"What were the names on the passports?"

"Let me think, ah, Allen something and, ah, a flower."

"A flower?"

"Rose! That was it. Allen and Rose."

"Last names?"

"Don't remember. Honest!"

Harrison grabbed the photos and stood up, startling Josh.

"Are you taking me to Vegas?" Josh asked.

"No."

"But you're going to help me with these charges? Right?"

"I'll put in a good word for you." Harrison walked out of the room and back to the chief and another officer who were waiting.

"How'd it go?" the chief asked.

"It might be the ones I'm looking for. Their car broke down on highway 39 and this guy and his buddies stopped and robbed them and took their car. Where's highway 39?"

"East of here then north when you get to Logan."

"A lot of towns on that road?" Harrison asked.

"Two. What did these two do?"

"Killed a guy in Vegas in cold blood."

"Got another Bonnie and Clyde?" the officer inquired.

"We'll see. Thank you, Chief." Harrison shook the chief's hand and headed for the door.

"What about this one? Any more use to you?" the chief called as Harrison was leaving.

"None, he's all yours. Oh, one thing." The detective turned back toward him. "Josh said they took some passports but destroyed them. If that's not true and they turn up, I would greatly appreciate knowing."

"I'll put out the word around town. If we come across them you'll be the first to know," the chief said.

With that Harrison returned to his car and headed to Logan. "I'm only a day behind you, Wilson. Only a day behind."

Chapter 5: We always get them in the end

Wilson couldn't sleep and he had gone out early to fill the car with gas and pick up some food for the road. When he returned to the motel, he spotted the flashing lights of police cars in the early dawn light. He pulled into the parking lot of a fast food place and turned out his lights. From where he sat he could see their open motel room door and watched as two officers led Cari out in handcuffs.

"This is how it ends. Maybe it's for the best. I could never have pulled this off, unlike Baroque." Wilson spit out the name. "What am I supposed to do now? Maybe I'll head back to Vegas. I can get in touch with my lawyer and find out what they intend to do to me. Wonder what time it is." He flicked on the radio.

"...pork bellies are down. In other news, the Edenburg-Willows prize for excellence for a first novel has been awarded to an American, John Baroque. Love that name! The prestigious prize comes with fifty thousand dollars cash, and a first class ticket to the ceremony in England. Baroque's book has been compared to the Jason Bourne novel, though he stated that, 'my character makes Bourne look like a Catholic school girl!' The governor is expected–"

"That's it! You can steal my novel, you can corrupt my publisher, you can even take my book signings, but no one calls Jason Bourne a school girl!!!" he shouted at the radio. "I'll show you how to write an action novel!" He clenched his teeth and glared at the police cars.

"She's going to be locked up for sure. They'll never let her get away. She'll be sent back to Vegas. Wait, I know! Where did I see that sign?" Wilson asked himself.

The officers loaded Cari into the back of one of their cars and closed the door. Wilson jammed his car into drive and tore out of the parking lot. He drove along the main street until he saw a small sign with an arrow pointing left under the word "police." He cut across the street and spotted the building on the right. The car screeched to a halt by the main entrance, he shut it off, and ran into the building and up to the desk.

"I'm Wilson James! I was kidnaped in Las Vegas and managed to escape! I've been driving around town trying to find this place but I made it! I'm free!" His hands flayed in the air in a grand gesture.

The officer sitting behind the desk stared at him in astonishment. "Could you repeat that, Sir?" he was finally able to get out.

"My name is Wilson James, the writer. I was kidnaped by this lunatic woman in Las Vegas, Nevada, a few days ago. I managed to get myself free this morning and sneak out while she was still asleep."

"One minute. I'll get the chief." The officer left him and returned in short order with another man.

"Good morning, I'm Oliver Cirka, Chief of police. How may I help you?" the man extended his hand.

"I'm Wilson James–"

"From Las Vegas?"

"That's right. I was kidnaped by–"

"Jessica Stone?"

"That's right."

The chief withdrew his hand. "State police ran a joint operation with us this morning. We arrested her not more than twenty minutes ago."

"Are you serious?" a look of astonishment on his face. *Better not push it too far.*

"Yes. She's on her way here. Should arrive any minute. That's why we're in early this morning."

"I've been driving around what seemed like forever trying to find this place in the dark. I must have got out just before you guys grabbed her," Wilson said, as he took on a more casual demeaner.

"Looks that way. Do you plan to file charges against her?"

"Darn right I do! Give me the form and I'll do it right away."

"Follow me, Mr. James. Come to the back and we'll take care of the paper work. I need to make some phone calls while you fill them out."

The chief led Wilson to a small room where he sat at a table. In a few minutes, a clerk came in and handed Wilson some papers, which he studied intently. He was in the bowels of the building when they arrived with Cari at the station. She was led in with her head down and a look of utter defeat on her face. It was over.

She sat stoically as the detective questioned her but refused to say anything. *I wonder where Wilson is? Not that I care! But I hope they're not too rough on him. He'll never survive prison. Not that I care what happens to him! But it is a shame it had to end. Who knows what might have happened if we... stop it! He was only a mark, I don't care what happens to him.*

After a while the chief came in and sat down. "It appears your reign of terror is over, Ms. Stone. You'll be sent back to Las Vegas to face murder and kidnaping charges."

"Kidnaping?" Cari asked in astonishment.

"Oh, yes! He has filed kidnaping charges against you. Here, take a look." He slid a piece of paper across the table to her.

As she read, her anger grew. *That son of a bitch threw me under the bus to save his own pathetic skin! I should tell them this was all his doing!* "Is he under arrest too?"

"Not likely. It would appear he is another of your victims," the chief replied. That's all she would say.

About 1:00 p.m. Wilson returned to the police station and asked to see Cari. He was given two minutes and told they wouldn't be alone at any time. Cari had been brought to a small interrogation room and a female officer was standing opposite her. When Wilson came in she jumped up and had to be restrained by the officer.

"You son of a bitch! You're letting me take this alone! I hate you! Get out!" Cari screamed at him.

"I'm sensing some hostility. You need to breathe deeply and relax. These things have a way of working themselves out," Hhe said, placating her.

"Get out and leave me alone. I never want to see you again. Take me back to my cell," Cari told the officer.

As she brushed past Wilson he leaned in and whispered in her ear, "Don't fight extradition. Ask to be sent back to Vegas immediately, Blondie."

She looked back at him smiling as the guard pulled her out of the room.

"Mr. James, might we have a word before you leave?" the chief asked.

"I would love to chat, Chief, but I am exhausted from my ordeal. Today has been extremely stressful. Could we meet at, say, 8:00 tomorrow morning?" Wilson's shoulders drooped and he moved slow.

"That would be fine, Mr. James. You won't leave town, will you?"

"Of course not, Chief. I have no reason to." He immediately perked up.

After Wilson left the chief spoke to one of his officers. "Sergeant, put a tail on Mr. James. He is not to be let out of our sight at any time, understand?"

"Chief, that Stone woman wants to talk to you," another officer told him.

The chief went into the back where Cari was being held.

"I won't fight extradition. I want to go back to Vegas as soon as possible to prove my innocence," Cari told him.

"I'll make some calls. As soon as they send someone, you'll be on your way." *The sooner you're out of my hair, lady, the better.*

She sat down and watched him leave. *Should I trust Wilson? He's a fucking lunatic, but what choice do I have? No idea how to contact Baroque.*

"Captain? It's Harrison, I'm in Las Vegas, New Mexico... That's right, New Mexico. I picked up their trail... What?... When?... Where?... I'll leave first thing in the morning... Waived extradition? Fax me the papers here... Great news, Cap... We always get them in the end. Bye."

Harrison glanced in the mirror and saw a look of satisfaction on his face. He would have liked to have been the one to catch her, but at least he would have the privilege of bringing her back and parading her through the precinct.

It was a little before 7:00 a.m. when a car pulled up in front of the police station. A tall man in a suit emerged from the driver's side and a woman from the passenger side. She held some papers in her hand. They entered the building and went up to the desk sergeant.

"Good morning," he addressed the desk sergeant. "I'm Detective Harrison from the Las Vegas police and this is my partner Detective Abrams. We're here to pick up our prisoner, one Jessica Stone. I think you'll find the paperwork in order."

"The chief isn't in yet but the deputy chief will handle the transfer. I'll call him."

The two detectives stood casually looking around the room while the officer disappeared in the back with the papers they had given him.

"Detective Harrison, Deputy Chief Anderson," he introduced himself. "Your papers look fine. I'll just need a few signatures and initials. She's being brought out as we speak. Do you want her in cuffs?"

"No, we have our own, thanks," Detective Abrams replied.

Cari looked glum as they led her out. Suddenly she noticed the detective. *What the...?* An officer removed her handcuffs and Detective Abrams approached.

"Hands behind your back!" she told Cari gruffly.

"I didn't do it," Cari said as she turned around.

"Everybody is innocent."

"I really am!" Cari held her hands behind her while the handcuffs were fastened on. She couldn't shake the feeling something wasn't right.

"Tell it to a judge. Come on, let's go," Abrams instructed her.

"You two got here fast enough," Anderson observed.

"Took a redeye to Oklahoma City. Got a flight back this afternoon," the detective said.

"Long day."

"Thank you, Deputy Chief Anderson." Both detectives shook his hand.

"Thank you for taking her off our hands. Have a good one."

"And you too."

They led Cari to the car and placed her in the back seat, then slammed the door shut and were soon leaving the town limits. After a few miles, the car slowed and turned onto a small side road.

"I saw a sign back there. This isn't the way to Oklahoma City! And you're not Harrison! Let me see your badges!" Cari yelled at them.

The woman turned around to face Cari. "We don't need no stinkin' badges," she growled.

"That was good," her partner said. "From a Bogart film, right?"

"You can't beat Bogart," the woman responded.

"Excuse me!" Cari yelled nervously. "What is going on here?"

The woman stared at her. "Never you mind. Sit back and shut up, Blondie."

Blondie. *How did you ever pull this off?* she thought. Cari leaned back in the seat with a great deal more respect for Wilson, which still wasn't much.

They had driven a few miles north when the car slowed, turned into a narrow dirt driveway, and passed a gate with signs that read "no trespassing" and "trespassers will be shot." In the distance, Cari could see an abandoned farmhouse. The car pulled around behind it and stopped. A white car sat nearby. The woman got out and walked over to it. The door opened and Wilson stepped out. He handed her an envelope, they spoke briefly, and the woman returned. She opened the back door.

"Get out!" she ordered Cari, then took off the handcuffs. The woman got back in the car and it sped away. Cari walked toward Wilson and stopped in front of him.

"Heck of a day, Blondie!"

She threw her arms around Wilson and hugged him. He stood awkwardly for a moment before placing his arms around her. She was squeezing him and he could hardly breathe.

111

This is weird, Wilson thought. "We should go."

"Right. Go." Cari pulled back.

They got in the car and fastened their seatbelts.

"White for a change," she said in reference to the car.

"A new beginning," he replied.

"What took you so long to break me out of jail?" Cari asked.

"What took so long? You were in there for one night!"

"And a day. In fact, I was held 25 hours. Baroque would have had me out in 12."

"Can we not talk about that hack," Wilson grumbled.

"I must admit though, you did come through for me. I'm more surprised than anything that you could pull this off."

"That almost sounded like a compliment." Wilson smiled and tapped his fingers on the steering wheel.

"It wasn't. Don't get too full of yourself," Cari told him.

"No danger of that with you around."

"What's the plan now?" Cari asked.

"Breadcrumbs," Wilson replied.

"One word into the conversation and I have no idea what you're talking about." She stared at him with a puzzled look. And then caught herself lingering on his profile and turned forward again.

"We're going to leave a trail of breadcrumbs for the police to follow leading toward New York. When they think they got us figured out, we vanish. It's what magicians do. Distract the audience."

"We vanish? How?"

"It's a work in progress. I haven't figured it out yet."

"Why doesn't that surprise me? And how are we leaving the breadcrumbs? And what kind of bread? Whole-wheat, pumpernickel, or just plain white?"

"You're nowhere near as funny as you think. If you must know, we let ourselves be seen on some security cameras. We have to move on fast to keep ahead of the police."

"Do you think about your plans at all, or just make up stuff and hope it somehow works out in the end?" There was a cheerfulness in Cari's voice that made her uncomfortable.

"Do you have a third option?"

"I'm really curious, given your other plans to this point, how you managed to break me out?"

"Two words; Baby-Boy!"

"No! He has the connections for something like that?"

"I've been planning this book for years and covered all kinds of scenarios. That's how I found him. He was always glad to help because he thinks I'm going to immortalize him in the book."

"And if you don't?"

"You really want to know what he'd do to me?" Wilson glanced at her and shifted on the seat.

"Yes! I'll bet it would be something good, right?" A broad smile crossed her face.

"Shut up. And he didn't do everything. I found this car!"

"That must have been the toughest part!"

"I beginning to question my decision to get you out."

"Ahh, you would have missed my company and scintillating conversation. How did you find it? Walked into a used car dealership? That must have been rough."

"And easy to trace. No, I came up with a brilliant plan. Again."

Cari rolled her eyes.

"There was this free paper in town and I saw a 'for sale' ad by the owner. I called him after I escaped–" Wilson began.

"Wait a minute, what do you mean escaped? I didn't think they arrested you?"

"Didn't, but they had a cop following me and they were watching my motel room."

"How did you do it?" Cari asked.

"I called the front desk and said I couldn't sleep because the light outside my door was keeping me awake and would they please turn it off." Wilson was proud of his little ruse.

"And they did?"

"Not a minute later it went out. I opened the door enough to crawl through and went on the ground to the back of the motel and took off."

"And the car?"

"The owner was near the motel. I walked there, negotiated with him, and bought it."

"Where did you stay the rest of the night?"

"In the car behind that abandoned farmhouse where we met. And I got to tell you, it was freaky out there all alone." He shuddered.

"Still better than a cell."

Detective Harrison was bone tired and hungry when he pulled into town. He soon spotted the sign for the police station, stopped the car in front, grabbed some papers off the passenger's seat, and pushed his long legs out the door. He stretched and went into the building.

"I'm Detective Harrison from the Las Vegas police department," he told the desk sergeant and held out his badge. "Here to pick up a prisoner, Jessica Stone."

"Ahhh," the sergeant mumbled.

"Is there a problem? I have the papers here."

"Ahhh, could you wait a minute?"

Harrison looked around. "This is the right place, isn't it?"

"Yes sir."

"And you have my prisoner, Jessica Stone?"

The sergeant avoided Harrison's eyes and moved some papers around on the desk. "Kind of."

"What do you mean, kind of?"

"Excuse me a minute while I get the chief." He hurried into the back corridor.

Strange fellow, Harrison thought. *Must be new.*

"Detective Harrison, I'm Chief Cirka," the chief introduced himself after emerging from the back.

"Chief Cirka, nice to meet you. I'm here to pick up Jessica Stone."

"Could I see your papers?" the chief asked.

Harrison handed them to him.

"And could I have your badge for a moment?"

"Certainly. Is there a problem?" Harrison handed it to him.

"Back in a minute." Chief Cirka hurried into the back. "Sarah!" he yelled, "get me that captain from Las Vegas on the phone immediately!"

He sat at his desk studying the papers when his phone rang. "Thank you, Sarah. Captain Hodge, Police Chief Cirka again. Sorry to bother you, but could you describe Detective Harrison to me?... Okay... white hair... yes... No, there's no problem. He's here now. Can't be too careful... Oh, one other thing. Do you have a female detective named Abrams?... No?... Thank you, goodbye." He hung up. "Goddamn it!"

When he returned to the front the color was gone from his face. He carried a paper that he handed to Harrison. "This look familiar to you?"

Harrison scanned the sheet and replied, "Looks like the one I just gave you, except that signature isn't Captain Hodge's. I've known Hodge for twenty five years and that's not his signature. What is this?" Worry lines creased Harrison's forehead.

"This morning around 7:00 two detectives from Las Vegas, a man and woman calling themselves Harrison and Abrams, gave my deputy this paper, signed the release forms, and took your prisoner."

"Stone? You gave them Stone?" he asked incredulously.

"That's right. But their papers were good and we were expecting them, I mean you, so they weren't questioned."

"What about their badges?" Harrison leaned ominously on the desk.

"Well, that's the thing. They were never asked for. That's why my sergeant was suspicious when you showed up. That's why I called your captain and asked for a description of you."

"And you couldn't have done that before?" Harrison yelled, his voice rising in anger.

"I'm sorry and take full responsibility but shouting will get us nowhere," the chief responded.

"You're right. I apologize, Chief Cirka. What time did they take her?" Harrison took a deep breath and regained his composure.

"About 7:00 this morning."

Harrison looked at the clock behind the desk. It was nearly 4:00 p.m.

"They have a nine hour lead on me, but that's closer than I was. This had to be the work of James."

The chief perked up. "James? He was here also."

Harrison's eyes widened and he took a step toward the chief. "Wilson James? You have him?"

"Not exactly. You see, he came in here yesterday before we brought in Stone and filed a complaint against her for kidnaping him."

"Kidnaping? That's the same bullshit he tried on me. He's involved with her. I just can't figure out how. Where is he now?"

"He was supposed to come in at 8:00 this morning to be interviewed but–"

The detective rolled his eyes. "Let me guess, he never showed."

"I had a man on him all night, but when he didn't show by 9:00 we entered his motel room. Everything was there, including his car, but he hasn't been seen since," the chief said.

"I feel I have greatly underestimated Mr. Wilson James." He shook his head and looked to the floor.

"What do you mean?"

"He comes across as a dullard, but it seems he is disguising his true abilities as a mastermind. Never trust a writer, Chief. They're trouble in spades."

"Any way we can be of assistance, Detective, my department is yours. Whatever you need."

"How did you find them in the first place?" Harrison asked.

"They stopped at the drive-through at the local McDonald's and the woman went in to use the bathroom. Someone inside recognized her from the media reports and called police. We found them at a local motel and raided it at 6:00 yesterday morning."

Harrison looked perplexed. "But James wasn't there?"

"No. The car was gone and he said he had escaped before we arrived and had been driving around town looking for the police station."

"He's one clever son of a bitch, I'll give him that. This is going to be harder than I thought. You said his car is at the motel?"

"We had it towed. It's a rental from Las Vegas, New Mexico," the chief said.

"I know, I came from there. I was one day behind them. But if he left his car then he needed transport. He must have bought another one locally. I could use a list of the used car dealers in town, especially the shady ones who sell for cash without any questions." The thought revived Harrison.

The chief smiled and adjusted his utility belt. "I'll do you one better, Detective, I'll accompany you. I know everyone in this town and whoever sold him a car, we'll find him."

Detective Harrison, accompanied by Chief Cirka, spent a long evening searching car lots without any luck. Exhausted, Harrison gave up for the night and rented a motel room. Wilson James was making a fool of him. This had become personal. Early the next morning Harrison was sitting in a diner having breakfast when his phone rang.

"Hello... Chief Cirka how are... You found it?... Oh, where he bought it... Be right there." He left some money on the table and quickly drove to the station where the chief was waiting outside and jumped into his car.

"James bought the car from a young fellow not too far from the motel where he was staying," the chief began while Harrison settled in. "I figure he snuck out of the room and walked to the guy's place. But we'll get the details including the plate. Should have him in no time."

"I'm done underestimating Wilson James. He seems to have a brilliance I can't understand. It's as if he works on a higher plain of some kind," Harrison said as the two drove to the seller's house.

"Not many criminals out there like that."

"That's the thing, Chief. Technically he's not a criminal. If he sticks to his story of being kidnaped it will be hard to prove aiding and abetting Stone." Harrison's mouth flattened into a straight line, frustration coming off him in waves.

"But if he was kidnaped, and escaped, why would he go back to her? That proves he's in it with her," the chief attempted to put a positive spin on the situation.

"The Stockholm syndrome."

"You think that would hold up in court?"

Harrison shrugged. "With a good lawyer, and I'm sure he has the money for the best, it could be enough for reasonable doubt. But what I can't figure is the money angle."

"The money angle?"

"If you were on the run, how would you get money, Chief?"

"Bank card or credit card," he said.

"His bank card, credit card, and passport were stolen. And besides, they were never used after he left Vegas."

"He could have had a fake one made." The chief rubbed his chin, as was a habit of his when thinking.

"True, but you're talking a professional job if the card is going to work for longer than a day or two. And that would cost a lot of money and we believe he only had 500 dollars on him when they left."

"If that's the case, another way would be stealing."

"I've followed their trail and there hasn't been one robbery anywhere. Not one!"

The chief shrugged. "Then someone is supplying him."

"We checked his family, which includes two ex-wives, one brother, his parents in upstate New York, his lawyer in New York and his publisher. None of them has heard from him since they left Vegas. We've searched all his contacts we could find and no one has been in touch with him. Where's the money coming from?" The chagrin was obvious in his voice.

"Wish I could help more, Detective. There's the house on the right." He pointed to a shabby blue house with peeling paint. They pulled in, got out, and went to the door.

"Are they expecting us?" Harrison asked.

"No. Thought it better to arrive unannounced." The chief rang the doorbell.

"Yes? Can I help you?" an elderly woman asked as she held open the door.

"Police Chief Cirka and this is Detective Harrison. May we come in?"

The woman's eyes widened with fear. "Has something happened to my boy?"

"No, nothing like that, ma'am. It's about a white Chevy you advertised for sale?"

"I'm sorry but you're too late, Chief. My son sold it last night. An awful nice gentleman." She smiled at the thought.

"Is this the man?" Detective Harrison asked as he pulled out the photo of Wilson.

"Yes, that's the fellow. Sweetest man. Said I reminded him of his sister."

"He doesn't have a sister, ma'am," Harrison said.

She frowned. "Oh? He seemed so nice."

"They always do, ma'am. Could you provide us with the details of the car including the plate number?" the chief asked.

"I wouldn't have a clue, Chief. You'll have to go see my son. He works at the scrapyard on the west end of town."

He nodded. "Thank you for your time."

They headed for the scrapyard and found the young man, who provided them with the information they requested. Harrison was optimistic again.

When they reached Kansas, Wilson decided it would be best to get off the main highway and follow the many small side roads that crisscrossed the state.

"I think we passed that farm a while back. Are we driving in circles?" Cari asked him.

"We're not driving in circles."

"I'll bet Baroque wouldn't get lost."

"You got a thing for him?" Wilson asked angrily.

"Jealous?"

Wilson scowled. "No, but I know where he's going to be tomorrow night. Why don't I drop you off, then you'll be his problem."

"Problem? Is that the way you see me? Real nice!" She snapped.

"I think we're lost."

"I hope we have plenty of gas. We haven't seen any towns for a while."

"That's the point. Stay off the main drag and away from civilization."

"In other words, your plan is working perfectly!" Cari stated sarcastically. *Better ease up the Baroque thing. Don't want to push him too far. And besides, he did come back for me. He could have taken off. He's not a bad guy.*

"From the side, you look like that actress," Wilson observed.

"What actress?"

"The one from Tiffany's."

"Tiffany's?" Cari asked, confused.

"Yes. What was the name of it?" Wilson snapped his fingers. "Breakfast at Tiffany's?"

"You mean Audrey Hepburn?"

"That's her!"

"You think I look like Audrey Hepburn?" she asked incredulously.

He nodded. "Especially in profile."

"She was considered a beautiful woman." Cari could feel herself getting red. "Are you trying to seduce me?"

"What? No! I didn't mean it like that. Did you think–"

"Relax," she laughed. "I'm just kidding."

"Oh, yes. I knew that. I was playing along," he said, chewing his thumb nail.

"Sure, you were." *He's not that bad looking, either.*

They had driven for most of the day before finally returning to a major highway. Wilson followed it through a small town and pulled into a diner on the east side.

"Where are we?" Cari asked as they walked toward the diner entrance.

"Somewhere in Kansas. I need to find another atlas."

"Evening folks. Sit anywhere, hon," the waitress called to them as they entered.

They went to the far end and slid into a booth. The waitress took their order and soon they were eating their first meal of the day.

"Some food and water would have been good to bring along," Cari suggested.

Wilson sneered at her. "Twenty-twenty hindsight!"

"How long to Atlanta?"

"Don't say that," Wilson whispered. "Walls have ears. And I don't know for sure. Maybe three days. Do you think–"

"No, no, no! You have to pay first!" Wilson was interrupted by the shouts of the waitress. They turned around to see her blocking the entrance to a group of people in brightly colored clothes attempting to enter.

"The Lord is providing and keeping, good serving lady."

"Unless the good Lord is handing me cash up front you ain't getting served in here! Donny?" she called to the owner. "These freaks ain't got no money but want to preach for their supper!"

"Out, you bums! No freeloading in here! Out or I'm calling the cops!" Donny yelled from behind the counter. He had emerged from the kitchen and was arguing with the group.

"Excuse me, Miss?" Wilson called to the waitress.

"I'm sorry for the disturbance, hon. They'll be gone in a minute."

"I want to pay for their dinner."

She raised her penciled on eyebrows. "Pay for them? Do you know that tribe?"

"Never laid eyes on them before. How many are there?"

"Five, I think."

Wilson dug out some money and handed her 150 dollars. "This should do it. You keep the change."

"Oh my! This will cover it okay. And thank you, hon. Hey Donny, hold up." She went over to the group and talked to one of the women, then pointed at Wilson.

"I thought we were supposed to keep a low profile?" Cari whispered to him.

"Breadcrumbs. And it feels good to help someone, don't you think? Karma." Wilson spread his arms and grinned.

"Oh please! Don't give me that karma bullshit. I always did good things and look what happened to me!"

"You met me." Wilson started to smile when someone touched his shoulder.

"The good Lord seeks and He provides to the man standing tall in the field of wheat."

"What the hell does that mean?" Cari whispered to Wilson, who shrugged.

"I think he's trying to thank us," he said.

"You'll have to excuse the Man of God. He gets his passages mixed up sometimes." A woman in a bright dress walked up. "I'm July. He is trying to thank you for your kindness."

"No thanks are necessary. Doesn't the bible say something about sharing the wealth?" Wilson joked.

"It does." She was tall with long blond hair, a slim body and beautiful youthful face. She smiled at Wilson. "I better join them," she said after a moment's hesitation.

"She seems nice," Wilson observed after she left.

"You've got some drool on your chin," Cari indicated.

"What?" He wiped his chin. "There's nothing on my, oh. I see what you're saying and no, I have no interest in her."

"She does look like your type."

"I don't have a type."

Cari froze, her face white. "We've got company."

"Company? What are you–"

Cari pointed out the window at a Kansas State Police car behind their white Chevy.

"Son of a... We got to go!" Wilson told her, sliding out of the booth and knocking his drink over.

He stood and searched for the waitress. When he caught her eye, she hurried over. "Would you like something else, hon? Piece of pie?"

He handed her a fifty. "This should cover it. Keep the change."

"Thank you, hon, that's–"

"Is there a back door?" He interrupted her, looking around wildly.

"Around the end of the counter and through the kitchen. Can't miss it. Good luck!" she called out as they hurried toward the exit.

Wilson pushed open the door and surveyed their surroundings. Behind the diner was a gully with trees and brush growing along it. He grabbed Cari by the hand and they ran for cover. There was about a hundred feet of clearing before they reached the tree line and neither looked back until they were deep in the tangle of the vegetation.

"Think we're clear?" Cari whispered.

"We need to keep going. We'll follow this wash and get as far as we can from here then hold up until morning."

Cari knew there was no longer a plan. It was difficult maneuvering through the underbrush, a task made worse by the failing daylight. Cari slipped several times. Wilson hung onto her hand and helped her back up but knew they couldn't continue much farther. When he found what seemed like a dry spot beside a large cottonwood tree, he stopped.

"We'll stay here for the night."

Cari looked around. "Here? On the ground?"

"I thought you were tough. Prison and all."

"Even in prison we had beds to sleep on," she muttered.

"This is natural. Getting back to nature."

"Want to know where you can shove your nature?"

"It'll be fine. We'll snuggle up to this tree, catch a few hours of sleep, and move on as soon as it's light." Wilson tried to reassure her. Or maybe it was more for himself.

She sat down carefully and leaned back against the tree. He sat beside her.

Isn't this great! Cari thought. *In the middle of the fucking woods! I'm worse off than when I started. I picked the wrong mark. Wonder if he was kidding about knowing where Baroque is?*

Isn't this great! Wilson thought. *All that trouble to break her out, and look at us! In the middle of the woods surrounded by snakes! Why did I mention the darn snakes? Wonder what Baroque would do?*

Chapter 6: Pinky

Wilson had drifted in and out of restless sleep when the snap of a twig jolted him fully awake. The first rays of sun were shining above the horizon. He strained to hear any sounds. Cari woke and looked up at him standing above her.

"What is it?" she whispered.

"I thought I heard a car passing close by. We must be near a highway."

"How far did we go last night?"

"I don't know. Come on, maybe we can flag down a ride."

Wilson helped her up and they headed toward the sound. The creek they had followed crossed the road and they stayed on the edge of the trees until reaching the highway. He climbed up the bank and stood on the side of the road; not a single vehicle could be seen.

"We should start walking," he told Cari.

"Which way?"

Wilson looked at the long shadows and said, "east, facing the sun."

They crossed the road and started along the highway. After walking for nearly thirty minutes they heard an approaching vehicle.

"What if it's a cop car?" Cari asked.

"I don't see any lights on top. Wait, it's a van."

"Oh great! Another van," Cari sighed.

"But this one has something painted on it. Can't tell exactly but, yes, it's the Jesus freaks!"

"I am not riding with them!" Cari folded her arms.

"They're nice people."

"Based on what? The fact they haven't butchered us and dumped our bodies in the ditch? Yet!" She stepped back toward the ditch.

"Karma. The universe goes round and round." Wilson was waving his arms as the van slowed to a stop beside him.

"The brother has returned to the family as Lazarus rose and walked on the waters of the Jordan."

"Hello again," Wilson called to the Man of God.

There was a large Jesus face painted on the side of the van that slowly began to move. A woman stuck her head out. "Hello, the one who spreads the wealth. Remember me? July."

"That's my favorite month." Wilson smiled drunkenly at her.

Cari poked him in the ribs. "I'm not getting in there," she whispered in his ear.

"Need a lift?" July asked.

"Sure do," Wilson replied.

"We're fine. Really," Cari quickly added. "Just out for a walk enjoying nature."

"Isn't nature the best?" July responded.

"We do need a ride. If it's not an inconvenience?" Wilson asked.

"Spread the deeds of the Lord throughout the deserts of the seas," The Man of God intervened.

"Pay no mind to him. Get in. You two can sit in the back next to Cat."

Wilson turned to Cari. "We can sit next to Cat."

"No! I refuse!" Cari stood defiantly on the edge of the road.

Wilson climbed up and sat down.

"We don't bite," July assured her.

"Unless you want us to," a voice came from beside Wilson.

Wilson smiled at her and motioned with his head. Cari grimaced then climbed up and sat next to him.

"If I end up dead in a ditch somewhere, I'm never going to forgive you," she whispered in his ear.

July pulled the door closed. "Good to go, Ziggy. Our driver is Ziggy." Ziggy had long dirty blond hair and wore thick glasses on a face covered with a scraggly beard.

"Praise be to the elephants!" The Man of God shouted.

"And you remember The Man of God," July said.

"Is he high?" Wilson asked.

"He was a druggy once upon a time, but since joining our church he's been clean for more than two years. And this lovely creature beside me is Moonstone."

The Man of God had short brown hair streaked with grey and a small goatee. His face was deeply wrinkled. Wilson guessed he was in his sixties, but figured the drugs might have prematurely aged him. Moonstone had shoulder-length pink hair and metal studs in her lips, nose, ears, eyebrows, cheeks, chin, and anywhere else she could squeeze one in.

"And this ravishing vixen next to you is Cat, namesake of our church."

"It's a pleasure," Cat cooed as she rubbed herself against Wilson's arm.

"I'm Allen and this is Rose. What is your church, July?"

"We're the sacred church of the People Undertaking to Save the Souls of Youth."

"Sounds like a noble cause," Wilson said.

"You've got to be kidding!" Cari spoke up.

"Saving youth's souls is important," Wilson said.

"The acronym, dumbnuts," Cari told him.

"The acronym? What do you mean?" Wilson asked.

"P.U.S.S.Y! That's what I mean!"

"You mean you're the church of the sacred pussy?" Wilson laughed.

"Cat and I are founding members," July told them. "We're always looking for new members." She shot a hopeful glance at Cari.

"Thanks, but I'll pass. What are you smiling about?" she asked Wilson.

"This is too much! You see, July, I'm a writer working on this novel and you people would make great characters."

"Are there any sex scenes in the book?" Cat asked, again leaning on Wilson.

"No. It's not that type of book," Wilson replied, his face getting red.

"We could make it that type," she lifted a leg and draped it over his lap.

He scooted closer to Cari. "Perhaps for my next one."

"Any time," she purred.

"Where are you two going?" July asked.

"New York. And you guys?"

"A music festival in southern Texas."

"Lots of souls to save there," Cat added enthusiastically.

"I think I know how they support themselves," Cari whispered in Wilson's ear.

"You're welcome to come with us," July said.

"Thanks, but we need to keep going east," Wilson said.

"We'll be glad to give you a ride as far as Winfield, Kansas, then we turn south. We thought we would stop for breakfast soon. Next town we're going to give a sermon to raise some funds," July informed them.

"So, 'give a sermon' is what they call it these days," Cari whispered in Wilson's ear.

"July, I would be more than happy to give a donation to the church of the, ah, your church. There is no need for sermonizing for breakfast."

"Is that even a word, sermonizing?" Cari asked.

July beamed. "That is extremely generous of you, Allen."

"Would you like a receipt?" Cat rubbed against him again. Wilson hoped his face wasn't as red as it felt.

When Ziggy pulled into a café Wilson told July, "We'll wait here, if that's okay."

"Don't worry about it. We'll bring you back something," she replied, taking the money from him.

All five jumped out of the van. Cat dragged herself over Wilson's lap and smiled at Cari.

"I like girls, too," she said to her on the way by. They closed the door and disappeared into the café.

"Well this is just great!" Cari shouted.

"I told you they were nice people," Wilson said.

"Church of the PUSSY my ass! This is no church, it's a rolling brothel!"

He shrugged. "Maybe so, but they are still a nice group of people."

"A lunatic, a pimp, and his three working girls!"

"Like I said, a nice bunch of people. It's too bad we can't convince them to go all the way to Atlanta." He frowned.

Cari scoffed. "Maybe we could tell them there's a convention in town! And I don't think you would have any trouble convincing Cat to 'go all the way'!"

"Don't be rude to our hosts."

"You really want to go the rest of the way to Atlanta with them? Oh God, what did I just say? Of course, you do!"

Wilson smirked. "Cat seems nice."

"Oh pleeease!"

"Got you some donuts and coffee. That okay?" July asked as the door slid open.

"Fine," Wilson replied, smiling.

"Hope you guys aren't in a big hurry. We have to make a few stops in Wellington to visit some parishioners. Need to collect some donations for gas and such," she said.

"Nothing like a good ole sermonizer!" Wilson blurted out. Cari nearly choked on her doughnut.

After spending the afternoon patronizing members of their flock, the group picked up some supplies at a local store and headed out of town for the night.

"We prefer camping under the stars rather than staying in motels, if we can find a place."

"They probably spend enough time in motels sermonizing," Cari whispered to Wilson.

They finally found a secluded spot near a brook and some trees where they could have privacy. They pulled out a camp stove and lanterns and dinner was soon cooking. Ziggy was the chef. After dinner, everyone sat around on camp stools listening to The Man of God massacre verses of the bible.

"To the good man the flock shall be shorn." He finished, lay down by a tree, and was snoring within seconds.

"Guess that's our cue," Wilson observed. "Time to turn in."

"Sleeping under the stars again, I see," Cari said unenthusiastically.

"Here's a blanket for you two. And if you need a third," Cat offered.

"We're fine!" Cari replied.

"Oh, July. Could I speak to you a moment before we turn in?" Wilson asked.

"What is it, Allen?"

"Before you leave us could one of you buy a vehicle in the next town? I will give you the money. Something cheap and economical."

"Sure. It'll have to be me because I'm the only one with a driver's license."

Wilson sighed with relief. "I can't thank you enough for everything you've done. And for not asking any questions."

"We all have secrets, Allen. Goodnight."

"Goodnight, July."

When he got over to Cari, she asked, "Is she going to do it?"

"Of course. Heart of gold." Wilson winked.

"Great. By the way, they only gave us one blanket. Looks like you're out of luck. Goodnight." She snatched the blanket and started to roll over.

"After I rescued you from the jaws of the law?"

"The jaws of the law? I thought the only reason Baroque had a book instead of you was because of the way he looks without a shirt, not your lackluster wordsmith skills."

"What makes you think I don't look good shirtless?" Wilson asked in mock offense.

Cari smiled. "I like you too much to answer that. Goodnight."

What does that mean? Is she kidding? She is an unusual woman. No doubt about that. Certainly different from my ex-wives. Could she be...? Got to put that out of my head. I should have left when they arrested her. I'm in it deep now.

Wilson rolled onto his back and stared up at a million stars in the clear sky.

He felt her moving closer to him. He smiled and lay there looking at the heavens.

"Do you plan to continue with me or join the church?" Wilson asked her.

"I would think you're the one who's hot for the church!"

He laughed. "I'm considering it."

Detective Harrison was back on the road heading into Kansas. A report had come in that the car Wilson bought in Woodward had been found. It wasn't much, but it was all he had. He was back on their trail. Throughout his years on the force he had many difficult cases, but this one was different. Never had he run into such a perplexing set of circumstances. The case should be straight forward; Brentwood let Stone take the fall for the firm. She kills him in revenge. The problem was, there were so many holes in the story, nothing made sense. And even though his partner and several others back in Vegas were searching through everything, no connection could be found between James and Stone.

Harrison knew from experience that little in this world was random when it came to murder. But perhaps this was the one in a million case where two strangers accidentally meet and the rest, as the saying goes, is history. If he could only make sense of something in this case. He pulled into the diner and stepped out of the car.

"Sit anywhere, hon," the waitress called to Harrison as he entered the diner.

"Excuse me, I'm Detective Harrison," he flashed his badge at her. "Could I speak to you for a moment?"

"About what, hon?"

"Yesterday, a white Chevy was found abandoned in your yard. I'm looking for the couple who were in it, and would appreciate any help you could give me."

"I don't think I remember them." Her demeanor became cold.

"I have their pictures," he said, holding them out.

"Could be them. Maybe not. People come and they go. I don't stick my nose in their business." The woman turned away from him and began wiping down a table.

"Please look at the photos. Anything you remember would be helpful."

She took the pictures and glanced at them. "Maybe I remember them. Sat on the end, I think. Not sure. You see, officer, we had this group of hippies or Jesus freaks or something in here yesterday and we was involved with them. I didn't see these people leave."

Big tips equals bad memories, Harrison thought. "Is there another way out of here?"

"Back door. But it has an alarm if you open it."

"Can I see where it is?"

"You have to go through the kitchen and that ain't allowed. Don't blame me. It's the health inspectors!" She resumed her work.

"Could you at least tell me where the door exits?"

"In the back."

"Mind if I look around out there?" Harrison asked.

"Donny," she yelled to the owner. "Mind if this cop pokes around out back?"

"As long as he doesn't damage anything!" the reply came from the kitchen.

"It's okay as long as you don't–"

"Yes, I heard him. Thank you for your time." Harrison turned and walked out.

Harrison went behind the building and noticed two pairs of footprints heading toward the trees; one large and the other smaller. He followed the tracks to the brush line but then lost sight of them. He searched around in the woods for a while, but it was useless. If he could get a dog he might be able to track them. Most likely, they were long gone. He followed the line of trees for a long way before he could see the highway again.

If they came this way and made it back to the road, they probably hitched a ride, Harrison thought. He had an idea.

Harrison hurried back into the diner and went over to the waitress again. "Excuse me. You said there was a group in here about the time the couple left?"

She nodded once. "Jesus freaks."

"Why do you call them that?"

"Had a big face of Jesus painted on the side of their van and crosses and trees and I don't know what all. And one of them was preaching the bible, but it wont no bible I know."

"Which way did the van go when they left?"

She shrugged. "Didn't see them."

"Heard they stayed across the road out in a field," one of the customers piped up.

"What's that, Sir?" Harrison asked.

"They camped in the field across the road. Got thrown out this morning and headed toward Wichita. Least that's what I heard."

"Thank you." Harrison returned to his car. "A group of Jesus freaks might be inclined to pick up a pair of strangers."

Harrison was on his phone to the captain with a request to put out an APB for the van. It was a long shot but, if they were with the group, there would be no way out if they were stopped.

"Wake up!" Cat was shaking their legs.

"What's the matter?" Wilson asked groggily.

"Shhh. Cops. Up by the van." She pulled off the blanket. "Head down by the brook in the trees and wait till we come for you."

Wilson grabbed Cari by the arm and they ran for cover behind some bushes. They were breathing hard as they strained to hear the conversation. The Man of God was preaching up a storm and Wilson could see two state troopers. One was attempting to speak to The Man of God, but couldn't get in a word, and the other was talking to July. Wilson was nervous. Soon the cops were walking around their camp. It seemed to last forever. After about twenty minutes they left and July came over to where they were hiding.

"Allen? Rose?" she called out.

They stood and walked toward her. "Are they gone?" Wilson asked.

"Yes. They searched the van but found nothing."

"Were they looking for us?" Cari asked.

134

"No. They told us we were trespassing and thought we had drugs, but everybody in the group is clean. They were pissed when they couldn't find anything to charge us with. Threatened to give us a ticket for illegal camping, but decided to give us a warning. They didn't suspect you two were with us."

"July, I think we owe you an explanation," Wilson said.

"It's not necessary."

"I know, but you guys could get in a lot of trouble if they had found us. You see, Rose here, that's not her real name, is being framed by a rich guy for murder and I'm trying to get her out of the country."

July glanced at Cari, who grinned sheepishly. "That's admirable of you. It doesn't matter to us. We accept all into the church, and you're welcome to travel with us. We'll deal with the authorities if, and when, that happens."

"Thank you, July, but we have another destination to go to. You and everyone in your church are good people," Wilson told her.

"We'd best be going. We'll stop in Winfield and pick up a car for you. I have a parishioner who owns a dealership. We got our van from him."

"Go ahead up to the van," he told Cari. "I want to talk to July."

He counted out some money and handed it to July. "If you could, would you buy some clothes for Rose? We keep losing everything."

July took the money and smiled. "I hope she appreciates you. But if she doesn't, I'm unattached."

Wilson smiled back. "Thanks again for everything."

"Come on. We should be going. Don't want the others to talk." July entwined her arm with Wilsons.

In Winfield, Ziggy dropped off July, Cat, and Moonstone, about a block from the car dealer then drove to a parking lot to wait. Wilson was getting nervous as they were gone for over two hours. Finally, a car pulled in next to the van and the women got out. Wilson pulled open the door, stepped out of the van beside the car, and thought he was seeing things.

"Oh my God!" Cari yelled. "It's bright pink!"

"Don't you just love it?" Cat asked.

135

"It's too much, don't you think?" Moonstone asked.

July held out the keys to Wilson who was staring at the shiny pink car. "I thought we should get something a bit more conservative, but I was out-voted." She didn't look too disappointed.

"It's fine," Wilson responded after a few moments. "A bit much to take in all at once."

"Oh fuck! Come see the interior!" Cari called to him. "It's covered in hot pink fur! This is awesome!"

"There's a couple of bags on the back seat for her and some stuff for you. We guessed at sizes," July said.

Cari was already going through the bags with Moonstone.

"She's a keeper, don't you know," July whispered in his ear. Wilson grinned.

"We better be going."

"It's been a pleasure," July said and kissed Wilson on the cheek.

"Thanks again for everything, July. Great driving, Ziggy," Wilson told him while shaking his hand. "And Man of God..."

"The brilliance of the sun walks from the grave." As Wilson grasped his hand he leaned in close and spoke softly in his ear. "Godspeed, Brother Allen. I wish you success in your flight from the Man." He let go of Wilson's hand and winked at him.

Wilson looked at him and added, "Your secret is safe with me."

"Praise be the man with a cloak for his goat!"

"Hallelujah brother!" Wilson yelled out.

"Good luck, Allen. Too bad you two can't join us," Moonstone told him.

"Thanks. Be careful you don't rust." As he turned, Cat grabbed him and planted a kiss directly on his lips. He struggled to pull back, though not too hard.

Cat loosened her grip and stepped back. "Hope you like the car. I picked it out."

"I love it," Wilson told her.

Cari said her goodbyes and kissed everyone's cheek. They waved to the small group and entered the car. Wilson stared around him in disbelief as he fastened his seatbelt. The entire interior was covered with fake pink fur including the steering wheel and radio knobs.

"Look at the roof," Cari was pointing up. "It's a Hello Kitty poster."

"There is no way this is going into the book!" Wilson said as he grasped the steering wheel.

She giggled. "Are you kidding? This is great."

"Jason Bourne would never be caught in a hot pink car!"

"This is a stick! Could I drive Pinky?" Cari asked as they sat in the idling car.

"Pinky?"

"All cars with personality should have a name, and this one has loads of personality."

"You're good with a standard shift?" he asked.

"Love 'em. I grew up driving sticks."

He shrugged. "Okay by me. I don't really want to be seen driving a pink car anyway."

"Don't say that! You'll hurt her feelings!"

"Her? How do you know this car isn't a him?"

"Oh, come on. We're sitting in a giant vagina!"

"What? No! This is not–"

"No sense of humor at all." Cari laughed.

"I have a sense of humor. The problem is you're not funny."

"And you don't think trying to flee from the law in a bright shiny pink car is funny?"

"No! Okay, maybe it is a little funny." He peered around the interior.

"Let's switch and I can show you how this is done."

"No speeding. The last thing we need is to be stopped and I don't think we're going to blend in with the crowd," Wilson said as he got out.

He moved to the passenger's seat and fastened his seatbelt while Cari climbed over the shifting lever. *She certainly is different,* he thought.

"Where to?" Cari asked.

"Continue east. We need to stop at a gas station where I can get some maps or another atlas."

"Missouri is east of Kansas, right?"

"Yes, that's correct. Wait a minute. Missouri."

"What about it?"

"Every summer when I was a kid we went to a campground one of my uncles owned in Missouri. Where was that place? Let me think. It was near a lake. If I see a map I will remember. We could go there and hold up a couple days. Maybe things would cool down because people's attention spans are short. If something happens this week we will be old news." Wilson was enthusiastic about the new plan.

"Am I going to have to sleep on the ground with the rattlesnakes again?"

"Man, you're a baby!" Wilson laughed at her.

"Shut up! I'm a city girl."

Looking around the interior of the car he added, "There's no way this car is going to be in the book."

Cari shifted Pinky into gear and sped out of the parking lot. "We're like Thelma and Louise."

After a couple of stops Wilson was able to secure some maps and was busy plotting out their route.

"This uncle, does he like you?" Cari asked.

"Used to, but he's dead. I think my cousin runs the place now," Wilson said, without looking up from his map.

"Does he like you?"

"Used to hate me. I haven't seen him in about twenty five years. Maybe he's gotten over it."

"Over what? Why does he hate you?" Cari asked.

"If you must know, we fought a lot. I beat him up most of the time."

Cari laughed. "Was he born without arms?"

"You have a warped sense of humor," he stated as he shook his head.

"At least I *have* a sense of humor! Why did you lose touch?"

"After my parents split, he was my mother's brother, we stopped going."

"How old were you when they split?"

"Eighteen."

"That explains a few things." Cari's was nodding while staring straight ahead.

He groaned. "Oh no, not Freud again."

"Do you want to lay down for this?"

"I better not be getting charged."

"This is the best psychological evaluation you can get as produced by the federal penal system. Besides, you get what you pay for. I think this is the root of your commitment problems."

"My commitment problems?" He scoffed, scratching his neck.

"Two ex-wives. Do you have a girlfriend?"

"Coincidentally, she broke up with me by text while you were mugging me. She even took my dog!"

"Harsh! I'll bet Bar..." Cari caught herself. *Whoops! Better not push him on this.* "I mean, that's terrible."

"You, sympathetic?" Wilson asked in mock disbelief.

"There are some things even I wouldn't do, like take a man's dog!"

"What type of psychological problems do you have?" Wilson asked.

"How long you got?"

"As long as you need."

"Oh, right."

"How many times you been married?"

"I haven't."

"Long term relationships?"

"Do you consider three months long term?" Cari was visibly uncomfortable.

"No."

"Then now would be time to change the subject! Nice scenery. Ever been in this part of the country? I haven't." She spoke quickly, her sentences clipped.

"I've been through here before. And you don't have to worry about my cousin. If he still owns the campground he'll take care of us. He's kin."

"Kin? Where are you from, Alabama? Kin?"

"Yes, kinfolk. You know, relatives, family. He's blood and blood always sticks together."

"That's why you hear about some guy's mother turning him in to police after she recognizes his face on the surveillance camera," Cari deadpanned.

"Well, not mothers, of course. But I'm talking about a cousin."

"Ohhh, I feel so much better now."

Detective Harrison was sitting in his motel room studying documents on the computer when his phone rang.

"Harrison here... Yes, that's correct. A giant face of Jesus on the side door... Okay... Where?" He grabbed a pen and was scribbling frantically. "Got it... Yes, I'd like that... Tomorrow morning is good. I'm north of there... Okay, bye."

It was a call from his captain informing him the group in the van had been stopped and was being held by authorities. Maybe he could get something from them. He left early the next morning and was at the police station by 11:00 a.m.

"Detective Harrison from the Las Vegas police department," he told the desk sergeant upon entering the precinct.

"Detective Harrison, welcome. We've been expecting you. I'll call the detective in charge of the group."

Soon a woman approached him. "Detective Harrison, I'm Detective Pierce. Nice to meet you," she said, extending her hand.

"Detective Pierce, likewise. I understand you have some persons of interest concerning my murder investigation?"

"Come this way." Harrison followed her into an office. "Please, sit. I'm having the prisoners brought out if you would like to talk to them."

He nodded once. "That would be much appreciated."

"But I must tell you, I don't think they will be much use to you. I've talked to each of the five and their stories all agree." She sat with hands clasped across a desk from Harrison.

"I would like a shot at them anyway. Perhaps with the background I have on this case I can get something of benefit."

"This Stone woman killed some fellow in Vegas?"

"Looks that way. What did you pick them up on?" Harrison asked.

"Suspicion of harboring fugitives. We had figured to find drugs and arrest them on that, but there was nothing. We can't hold them much longer. That Dankforth seems to have some connections somewhere. There is a lawyer on his way. You got here just in time."

The phone rang. "Hello?... Thanks. The prisoners are ready," Detective Pierce told Harrison as she hung up the phone. "Let me fill you in on them. There are five; two men and three women. Only one woman, calls herself July, had any identification which is a Kansas driver's license. Her real name is Susan Dankforth from Kansas City. No record that we could find. One of the men has a record of drug possession but nothing in the last three years. Calls himself The Man of God and spews out nonsense. Guess his brain is fried from the drugs. His real name is Jeffrey Douglas, last address unknown. The other three are Ziggy, Moonstone, and Cat. No identification and those are the only names they will give. Fingerprints aren't on file anywhere."

"There was no one else in the van when it was stopped?" Harrison asked, his disappointment obvious.

"No one." Detective Pierce stood and exited the office, followed by Harrison. "And we printed the vehicle but found only the five occupants' fingerprints. If your guys were in that van, they wiped it down clean after. The first one is in there," she pointed to a door adjacent her office.

Harrison walked into the small interrogation room where July sat on the opposite side of the table.

"Susan Dankforth, I presume?" he asked as he sat down. "I'm Detective Harrison."

"July, if you don't mind. And why are we being held? We haven't done anything wrong. Why are we still here?"

"Only have a few questions then you'll be free to go."

"And why were we stopped?" July asked.

"Have you ever seen this man?" Harrison asked as he placed a photo of Wilson in front of her.

"Yes. Nice man. He bought us dinner two nights ago at a diner in Kansas somewhere."

"Know his name?"

"Didn't introduce ourselves. After the waitress told us he was paying I went over and thanked him."

"Ever see him anywhere else?"

"Never saw him again after that night."

"And what about her?" Harrison held up Cari's photo.

"Not sure. There was a woman with him but I didn't pay any attention. Could be her." She tilted head as she examined the image.

"And you never saw them again after that night in the diner?"

"That's right."

"Do you know what aiding and abetting a fugitive from the law means, Ms. Dankforth?"

"Do you know what 'talk to my lawyer' means?" July asked in a cold voice.

"How do you make a living, Ms. Dankforth?"

"I rely on the kindness of strangers."

"And that is working out for you?"

She smiled. "The good Lord provides."

"Thank you, Ms. Dankforth." Harrison stood and went to the door.

"Any time, Detective Harrison."

"Oh, one last question. Will the other four repeat your story?" He held the doorknob, his back to July.

"It's a free country, Detective. They can say whatever they want."

"Again, thank you."

When he stepped out of the room, Detective Pierce was waiting. "Number two, the loony, is in that room." She pointed to another door.

He went in without a word and sat down. "I'm Detective Harr–"

"The Lord guides and fires us." The Man of God was standing beside the table.

"Harrison. I wanted to ask–"

"Blackbeard is the angel of sequins."

Harrison sighed. "Recognize this man?" he placed the photo in front of The Man of God.

"Jesus Christ has risen! A miracle of the birds!" He flung his hands in the air.

"And this woman?" showing him Stone's picture.

"Grandma?" he asked, staring at the image and smiling.

"Thank you for your time."

"May the Lord bless your parakeet." The Man of God bowed low as Harrison departed.

"And yours also." Harrison sighed again.

"Anything?" Pierce asked when he came out. "Guess not by your look. Next is across the hall. Cat."

Wonderful, Harrison thought. "Hello, I'm–"

"One hell of a hunk!" Cat blurted out when he came in. "Married? Or does it matter?"

"I'm Detective Harrison and would like to ask you a few questions."

"Yes. To all of them," she purred.

"Have you seen this man before?" showing her the picture of Wilson.

"Not bad, but you're cuter. Who is he? Is he available?"

"Have you ever seen him before?"

"If I had I wouldn't need you!" Cat reached across the table toward Harrison's hand.

"Is that a no?"

"Yes." She raised and lowered her eyebrows as she stared at him.

"Lying to a police officer is a crime."

"Want to cuff me," she cooed and held out her hands.

"He bought you dinner two nights ago."

"He did? And I didn't properly thank him. Now I feel terrible." The corner of her lips drooped.

"He bought your group dinner but you never saw him?" Harrison asked.

"July and The Man of God went over to thank them while the rest of us found a table. Never saw him."

"And this woman?" He held Cari's picture.

"Not bad. I like girls, too."

"I suppose you've never seen her either?"

"Afraid not."

"Thank you for your time."

"Why don't you take the time to 'properly' thank me?" Cat rose slowly and moved toward Harrison.

He hurried out and slammed the door.

"Any progress?" Pierce asked. Not waiting for a reply, she pointed back to the first room again.

He walked in, saw Moonstone's piercings, and sat heavily in the chair.

"Ever see this man?" he asked.

"No," she replied.

"This woman?"

"No."

"Thank you." He got up and left.

"That didn't take long," Pierce observed as Harrison came out.

"I'm glad I didn't have to drive too far for this." He shook his head in disgust.

"Last one. Ziggy." Detective Pierce smiled half-heartedly.

He sat down opposite Ziggy who had a huge smile on his face and stared at Harrison.

"I'm Detective Harrison."

"Ziggy. You can call me Ziggy."

"Do you know why you were arrested?"

"Bad karma."

"No. Aiding and abetting a known fugitive from the law."

"Cool."

"A suspect in a brutal murder." Harrison leaned in close to him.

"Aren't all murders brutal?" Ziggy asked as he also leaned across the table.

"What?"

"Are there ever any non-brutal murders?" Ziggy was mere inches from Harrison.

"This is serious, son," Harrison said angrily as he pulled back.

"Murder always is, father."

Harrison glared at him and thought how much he would like to wipe that smile off his face.

"I'm looking for a murder suspect and–"

"A suspect?" Ziggy cut him off.

"What about it?"

"The person you're looking for is a suspect, not a criminal?"

"She fled the law and is guilty of that."

"Why do you want to catch her?" Ziggy asked. "Will it get you a promotion?"

"What? Never mind that. Have you ever seen this man?" he asked, his frustration growing as he held Wilson's photo.

"Looks like Sylvester Stallone."

"Stallone? He doesn't look anything like Stallone!" Harrison shouted.

"Can't see anything without my glasses."

"Where are your glasses?" Harrison asked.

"Don't have any."

"Ever seen this woman?" he growled, showing him the other picture.

"Looks like Audrey Hepburn."

Harrison got up and stormed out of the room.

"Sorry to have wasted your time, Detective Harrison," Pierce said after he slammed the door shut.

"I would bet my pension they know something!" He crumpled the edges of the pictures he was holding in frustration.

"I got that feeling also, but we can't charge them on that." Pierce shook her head.

"Have you got anything to hold them on?" Harrison asked in desperation.

"Nothing. In fact, if you hadn't arrived when you did they would already be out. They're doing the paperwork as we speak."

Harrison's shoulders slumped. "Thanks anyway."

Pierce looked at him, her eyes tinged with pity. "What next for your case?"

"Any idea where they were coming from?" Harrison asked.

"They said that diner was to the west. They must have been going east and probably turned south on US 177. That's US 77 in Kansas. It changes at the border."

"Any towns in that area?"

"Winfield, Kansas."

"Guess I'm going to Winfield. Thanks again, Detective."

"If there's anything we can do, don't hesitate."

"If you're ever out Vegas way stop in. I'll give you a tour of the town." He waved as he walked toward the door.

"I'll hold you to that," Pierce called after him.

Harrison slumped into the driver's seat of his rental and sighed. "Another dead-end! Where are you, Wilson?"

Chapter 7: Wee Willy

Detective Harrison was going through his email when he saw a message from the Kansas State police. It seemed that Susan Dankforth, better known as July, had purchased a car in Winfield from a dealer known to police. As Harrison was presently in Winfield, he decided to check it out personally and drove to the dealership.

"Good evening, Sir, and welcome to McShane's honest used car dealership. I'm Shane McShane owner and proprietor extraordinaire! I can put you in the finest of vehicles whether you want something economical, extravagant or, how about sporty to catch the eye of the ladies?"

"I'm Detective Harrison." He flashed his badge. "I would like to ask you a few questions."

"I run a legit business, Detective. You can check VIN numbers if you like."

"Not interested in how you conduct business. I want to know what kind of a car Susan Dankforth bought from you."

"Not familiar with the name. If you'll excuse me I think that's my phone ringing. Got to take it." He began to walk away.

"This won't take long. Maybe you know her better by the name July?"

"July?" His face lite up at the name. "Why didn't you say so? Lovely girl. I'm one of her parishioners. But haven't seen her in a long while."

"Then you wouldn't mind if I looked through your receipts for the last few days?" Harrison asked.

"Not at all. Always willing to co-operate with the law. As soon as you show me a warrant."

"That's not very co-operative of you, Mr. McShane. But if you insist I will return."

"You do that. In the meantime, I could put you in a fine automobile." He smiled and raised his eyebrows, gesturing to the lot around them full of battered vehicles.

"Perhaps next time. Oh, one other thing. Have you ever seen either one of these people?" Harrison held out the photos of Wilson and Jessica.

"Never laid eyes on either. Now, if there's nothing else?" He bowed slightly and walked away.

"Thank you for your time, Mr. McShane."

These people stick together, Harrison thought as he returned to his car.

"You know where we are?" Cari asked.

"Do I look like I know where we are?" Wilson glanced between his map and the surroundings searching for a recognizable landmark,

"No! It looks like you don't have a clue! That's why I asked."

"It's been twenty five years since I've been here and it's changed quite a bit from what I remember. Oh, wait, that fix-it shop on the left. I remember that! Turn there!" He was pointing across Cari's field of vision. "It should be about two miles down this road on the right. My aunt and uncle's house sits back from the road and the campground is behind it."

After a few moments he yelled out, "That's it! See, I remembered."

"I never doubted—oh God! Is that the place?" Cari grimaced at the sight.

The house was dirty brown with many patches on the roof, clapboards were hanging off the sides, the front porch sagged and the screen door had fallen off and was propping up one corner of the veranda roof.

"Looks like they fixed up the place since I was here last," Wilson said.

"Seriously? Is that the place?" *Now what has he got me into.*

"There he is. Turn in. And his name is Chris. Whatever you do, don't call him Christopher. He hates that." Wilson was excited at seeing his relative.

A large man wearing dirty blue jeans and a stained t-shirt was standing next

149

to the drive talking with a group of men. He held a can of beer. Cari pulled up beside and stopped. He leaned in the window much closer to Cari's face than she liked.

"Sorry folks, we're full up. There's a RV park a mile farther on," he said in a Midwestern drawl.

"Working hard or hardly working?" Wilson asked him.

The man leaned in causing Cari to pull back as far as she could.

"Well son er a bitch! Is that you under them whiskers, Wee Willy?" Chris asked.

Cari looked at Wilson and mouthed the name Wee Willy.

Wilson ignored her. "In the flesh, cuz."

He reached in to shake Wilson's hand which caused Cari to grimace.

"How long's it been anyways?"

"Too long. We need a place to hold up a couple days," Wilson said.

"Got that old trailer out to the end of the house by the woods. It's yours for as long as you need it."

"Thing is, Chris, I got the law looking for me."

"Mother-fuckin' law dogs! Them son er bitches come here they'll know something hit 'em." He banged his hands on the door, causing Cari to jump. "Don't you worry, cuz, you'll be good here. Pull around the house and we'll get you settled. Had supper?"

"Yes, we're good," Wilson replied.

"Follow me," Chris told Cari.

Chris spoke briefly to the group of men, who broke out laughing, then went in back of the house. Cari pulled the car up and stopped.

"Looks like the front is the best side," she told Wilson as she gazed at the house. "What the hell have you got me into?" she asked as she got out of the car.

"Your car?" Chris asked.

"Yes. Beauty, isn't it?" Wilson responded.

"The boys and me said we never seen a guy drive up in a pussy before." Chris broke into laughter again.

"This is Rose," Wilson introduced her to Chris.

"You always did like them fancy types, didn't you, Wee Willy?"

"How's Milly?" Wilson asked.

"Ahh, she left me last year and took the girls. The oldest boy, he works for me here at the camp."

"Sorry to hear that."

"Yeah. Caught me screwing some nineteen year old guest and said it was bad for business. Didn't mean nothing to me but she took it personal and split. Women! But I got me another, Jenny. Looks like you got yourself a fine one here," he was looking Cari up and down.

"Could we get to the trailer before dark?" Wilson asked.

"Sure, follow me. Leave the keys in the car and we'll put it out of sight. Come on."

They grabbed their few possessions and followed Chris a hundred feet to the edge of some trees and a tiny camper trailer. As they were walking down Cari whispered in Wilson's ear, "Don't you leave me alone with him!" while squeezing his arm.

"Ain't been used for a while," Chris said as he pulled open the creaking door. "Could be a might dusty inside but there ain't too many mice. I'll turn on the valve for the gas and you'll have lights. You can use the toilet but it ain't hitched to nothing. Runs down in the woods. It's okay unless we get a north wind then you might want to keep the windows shut. I'll send Jenny down with some blankets."

"Thanks, cuz. I appreciate it."

"Stay as long as you need. Won't nobody bother you. If you feel like it, we have a campfire every night and you two are welcome. And tomorrow night we're having a barbeque for the whole camp. Everybody brings something and you folks is welcome, but don't feel you need to bring nothing. Night." Chris began walking back toward the house.

"Goodnight."

They went into the tiny space and looked around. There was a sink with a two-burner cooktop next to it and a fridge under the counter on the right. To the left was a bench that converted to a single bed and a closet of a bathroom at the far end. As they stood looking around they could hear Chris up near the house yelling, "Jenny, get your ass down to the trailer with some blankets and tell Nicky to take 'em down that cot from under the porch."

"Who gets the cot?" Cari asked.

"When we were kids, Chris and I used to arm wrestle for things."

"We could arm wrestle for the bed. In other words, I get the bed." Cari stared at him with a smirk.

"Oh, you're hilarious!"

"What's hilarious is you thinking you have any chance against me!"

"Knock knock! Hi y'all, I'm Jenny." Jenny was stocky with short blond hair. She was neither ugly nor pretty and had a pleasant demeanor.

Wilson waved. "Wilson, and this is Rose."

"Brought you some blankets and towels and Nicky's digging out the cot for one of you." Jenny extended her armful toward Wilson.

"He's sleeping on the cot. Lost to me at arm wrestling," Cari informed her.

"That's not true," Wilson added.

"If there's anything you need, just holler. We can hear you up at the house." She had a wide smile.

"Thank you."

As she was walking away Cari whispered in his ear, "Bet she's not a day over sixteen."

"Hey, Uncle Willy." Nicky was tall, thin, and slouched as he carried a beat-up cot under one arm.

"Nicky, haven't seen you since you were a baby. I think you had just been born last time we were here."

"It's too bad you don't come visit. Ma and the girls is up in Jefferson City. If you get the chance they'd be happy to see you."

"I'll try to stop in."

"Here's your cot. Might want to brush the spiders off it. Night."

"Night." Wilson handled the cot gingerly. It was black with dust and mold.

"Spiders? You're definitely sleeping on the cot!" Cari told Wilson. "And look at it! Ewww!"

"Probably more comfortable than the bed." *Oh man, this thing is terrible!*

"Keep telling yourself that, Wee Willy! How'd you get the name? Is it because," she glanced down at his crotch.

"Hey! No! That had nothing to do with it! I was a small child that's all." He pulled the cot in front of himself.

"If you say so."

"This is cozy," he remarked. "We could stay here for quite a while."

"If you–" as Cari turned around their faces were nearly touching. "Ah, it's okay if you really like the person you're sharing it with."

"Guess we better not stay too long."

"Um, think I'll make up the bed. Can you set up the cot?" Cari turned away. "Warm in here." She fanned her face with a hand.

"I'll open the windows."

The cot filled the space between the bed and wall with just enough room left to squeeze through to the bathroom. After they had both settled in Cari lay on her side facing Wilson.

"Why is it when a man cheats on his wife, and gets caught, he always says it didn't mean anything? If you know it's not going to mean anything, why cheat?"

"I've been married twice, and both times they cheated on me. Perhaps you're asking the wrong guy."

"What happened with your girlfriend?"

"I don't know. It seemed fine when I left for the book tour. Then, a few days in I got that text. She even took my dog!"

"And you're still not over her yet?" Cari asked, a hint of amusement in her voice.

"I'm going to miss that dog."

Cari busted out laughing. *He's so pathetic! So why do I—stop it! Focus!*

All that matters is freedom. Ralph got what he deserved, now it's my turn to get what I deserve!

"Glad you find my misery amusing." Wilson said, cutting her thoughts short.

"Misery? Over a dog? Wait till they lock you away, then you'll know what misery is."

"You're such a ray of sunshine. Besides, we're doing great." Wilson continued to roll around trying to get comfortable.

"My cell was bigger than this camper. And my roommate better company. She was an axe-murderer."

"When you get sent up this time, maybe you two could share again. You have something in common now."

"That's not funny!" Cari shouted.

"It's a joke! Thought you had a sense of humor?"

"I do when something is 'humorous.' Unlike your mindless attempts."

"I guess you're—ahhh!" Wilson yelled out amidst a crash. The middle legs on the cot had broken and Wilson lay there with his feet and head elevated while his butt (without an e) was on the floor.

Cari flicked on a light and stared down at him then broke out in hysterical laughter.

"You're not a very sympathetic person, are you?" Wilson suggested.

Finally getting herself under control she said, "See how sympathetic you are after a few years in prison."

"I can't sleep like this."

"Don't look at me. You're not getting in here!"

"I'll fold up the other legs and sleep on the mattress." Wilson struggled to his feet, gathered up the pieces of the cot, and threw them out the door.

"Man, this mattress is thin! Might as well sleep on the floor," he complained.

"Still not getting in with me," Cari muttered.

"You're loving my agony, aren't you?"

"You keep me amused."

"Glad I can be of service."

"Seeing you're awake, and probably will be for a while, I want to ask you something."

"Anything." Wilson replied.

"I have this aunt in northern Missouri I would like to visit. She's in her nineties and if I get to Crete I may never be able to come back. If I don't make it, I may never get out, and I would like to see her one last time."

"Sure. We'll stay here tomorrow and rest up a bit and figure out how to find her place, then leave the next day. If we can push through, we should be in Atlanta two days later."

"What about papers? You can travel as Jason Bourke but I need new ones."

"I know people in Atlanta."

"You know people. This sounds like some cheesy crime drama," Cari giggled.

"I think it would make a great episode for CSI. There's only one problem."

"Yes, no one in their right mind would ever believe it."

"No, CSI isn't on anymore. The show finished."

"I hope that doesn't mean you have run out of ideas. Oh wait, you never had any ideas to begin with!"

"You're not a nice person, are you?" Wilson asked in a monotone voice.

"It took you all this time to figure that out? You are slow, Wee Willy."

"I won't be traveling on Jason Bourke's passport."

"You're going to get another one also?"

"I'm not going with you to Crete."

"What? What do you mean you're not going to Crete?" Cari smiled in the dark.

"No one knows about my place on Crete, but I do travel to Greece often. It would be logical that they look for me there. I could very well lead them to you. If we separate, they will have a harder time to find you. And I'm working on a plan that should throw them off your trail."

That's exactly what I was hoping for! Then why do I feel so...? "Stop it!" she blurted out.

"Stop what?" Wilson asked.

"What?"

"I said I wasn't going to Crete and you yelled out stop it."

"No, I didn't!"

"Yes you–"

"I think there is something seriously wrong with you! You're always talking to yourself and now you're hearing voices! And I'm not even going to mention the porn!" Cari shouted.

"Porn? What are you–"

"Is there a doctor in this camp? I'm almost afraid to ride with you."

"Afraid to–"

"And you need to get that temper under control. Why do you have anger issues?"

"I don't, I mean. What?"

"And you're confused a lot. I don't think it would be a good idea to leave you on your own. What are you going to do after I'm gone?"

"After you're gone? I figure six months to a year before everything settles down and I can work things out." Wilson sounded bewildered.

"But what if they arrest you? You could very well go to jail if they sort this thing out. It's going to be impossible for you to convince them I kidnaped you after you helped me escape."

"Yes, that part is going to be tricky, but I'm working on a plan."

"Oh fuck! You haven't got a clue, have you?"

"I'm working on something."

She shook her head, her stomach in knots. "Not a clue."

When Cari woke the next morning, Wilson was gone. She went outside but he was nowhere to be seen. Suddenly, she heard his laughter in the distance and walked toward it.

"He dragged the stupid fish into the boat and stood up to show his buddy and fell right in! Lost the fish and all his tackle!"

Wilson burst out laughing again. Cari stood watching him as he listened to a large woman who was wearing a striped dress. Wilson spied her out of the corner of her eye and motioned for her to join them. "Rose, this is Hilda. Hilda, Rose."

"So, you're the one he keeps talking about. His Rose. You're just as pretty as he said."

"He tends to exaggerate things," Cari replied.

"He can't stop talking about you, at least when I let him get in a word." Her laughter was loud and raucous and her whole body shook. "Best be getting back to my man. Poor thing, can't cope without me. Why, night before last he couldn't even open a can of beans without me. Couldn't find the can opener!" She burst into laughter again. "They're useless without us, aren't they dearie?"

"You can say that again," Cari agreed.

"Look forward to seeing you all at the party tonight. Going to be a good one!" she waved as she departed.

"One of the locals. Her and her husband Daryl come here every summer for three weeks. Why are you smiling at me like that? It makes me nervous. Are you up to something?" Wilson asked.

"Hey there, Wee Willy," Chris called to him as he approached.

"Morning Chris," Wilson replied.

He punched Wilson on the shoulder.

"Forgot how much fun we used to have together," Wilson said as he rubbed his shoulder.

"Can't stop to chat. Toilet's plugged in 17." Chris held up a plunger. "Got to shove some shit!" With that he continued on.

"Can't wait to meet more of your family," Cari laughed.

"And I suppose your family is perfect," Wilson stated with indignation.

"Well, at least they're not hillbillies!"

"I'll have you know I'm proud to be a hillbilly. It's in my blood." He puffed out his chest and put his hands on his hips, staring off into the distance.

Cari rolled her eyes. "Can we get some breakfast? I'm starving."

157

"Hilda invited us for breakfast."

"Okay by me. Do you really say nice things about me to people?" she asked as they set off.

Wish I knew what Rattler meant, Wilson thought.

After breakfast, Wilson took Cari for a walk to show her his favorite place to play as a kid. They strolled through the trees down a narrow path to a small crystal clear pond.

"Chris and I weren't allowed to come down here alone, which meant this is where we spent most of our time. We used to love frog gigging in the pond." Suddenly, Wilson was five again.

"What in hell is frog gigging?" Cari asked.

"Catching frogs with your bare hands. Want to try? I don't know if there are any frogs in here now, but we could try." He peered in the water, almost oblivious to her presence.

She stood on the bank with her arms folded. "Do I look like I want to catch frogs with my bare hands?"

"Oh right, I forgot. You're a city girl. That's okay. I'll catch one for you." He waded ankle deep into the water and bent over, searching.

"Is this some hillbilly attempt to woo me?"

"Darn, doesn't seem to be any frogs."

"You know, now-a-days they use a diamond ring instead of frogs."

"I don't see any of those in this pond either."

"Shut up!"

After several minutes, Wilson came out of the pond, lay down on the grass, and stared up at the sky.

"I hope there aren't any rats around here," Cari said as she stood looking down at him.

"None. They're afraid of the rattlesnakes."

"I hate you a little more each day."

He looked up at her. The sun glanced off her hair and formed a halo around her head. Her smile lit up the summer morning. *She's the most beautiful woman*

I've ever seen, he thought. *Where did that come from? Focus Wilson! You need to find a way out of this. She bought the story about going to Crete alone, that's good. Now all I have to do is think of a way to get her on a plane in Atlanta.*

"Penny for your thoughts?" she asked.

"I was thinking how beautiful it is in Crete this time of year."

Cari lay down beside him. "I'm so excited! I can't wait to get there." *Of course, now that I'm going alone, I'll have to find another mark when I arrive. Too bad, I could have milked him for a lot more. But he is sweet, in a goofy sort of way.*

They spent most of the afternoon studying the atlas and planning the remainder of their journey. They were both excited and apprehensive about that evening's festivities; he more excited, she more apprehensive.

"Cat bought me a nice dress. Do you think I should wear it to the party tonight?" Cari asked.

"You're asking my fashion advice?" Wilson raised his eyebrows.

"They are your kin. I thought you would know best what I should wear."

"My kin?"

"You know, your relatives, your blood."

"You're a real smart-ass, aren't you?"

"So, dress or no dress?"

"Can I see it first?"

"Sure, I'll try it on. Turn around."

"All of a sudden you're shy?"

"Shut up and turn around." She sneered at him. After a few minutes, she told him to look at her.

"Wow! If you wear that tonight everyone is going to be staring at you."

She frowned and looked at herself, smoothing the dress of non-existent wrinkles. "A bit much?"

"It's perfect. Definitely wear it. Do you dance?"

"Not well, especially to hillbilly music."

"Hillbilly music? You want to be the one roasted tonight instead of the pig?"

159

"Is that insulting?" she asked.

Wilson burst out laughing.

"You bugger! That's not nice. I'm just trying to fit in."

"Be yourself and everyone will love you. Let's go. We need to get in line ahead of Hilda and Daryl or there won't be anything left."

A large crowd had gathered by the time they arrived and people immediately came up to them and introduced themselves. There was food and hospitality in abundance and they felt among friends.

An eclectic crowd gathered every summer at the campground; most were regulars with a few new-comers each year. Chris screened applicants to maintain a certain, shall we say, down-home charm.

But everyone minded their own business and had no concerns about Wilson and Cari. Most had secrets of their own, so questions of a certain nature were never asked. All found this a refuge from the outside world, if only for the briefest of time.

After all had their fill of the barbeque pork, and had made several turns around the buffet table, they separated. The men gathered together on one side of the yard and the women on the other. Cari wanted to stay with Wilson but was whisked away by Hilda. Everyone complimented her on the dress and made double entendre remarks about her and Wilson to bouts of uncontrolled laugher. Cari joined in the laughter, but was uncomfortable that these people thought of her and Wilson as a couple. Meanwhile, Chris was introducing Wilson to his buddies.

"Want a beer or something harder?" Christopher asked him. "Got some nice weed."

"I don't drink or smoke," Wilson said.

"Don't drink or smoke?! You sure you're my cousin?"

He chuckled and shrugged. "Stopped a while back. Wife number two didn't like it."

"He always was a pussy," Chris told the other men to laughter.

"Did he always drive one?" someone shouted to more laughter.

Country music blared from several large speakers and the men had to shout to be heard. Occasionally, a couple would move into the open space between the groups and dance. Wilson tuned out the noise as he looked at Cari, who was talking with her new friends. She glanced up and caught him staring at her.

Chris and the others began ribbing him about dancing with Cari. Suddenly, Wilson was fifteen again, tall and skinny, and being teased by the others about asking a girl to dance.

"Excuse me a minute, boys," Wilson told them. He smiled at Cari and moved to his left toward the DJ, Tiny George Little. He was from the Littles in southeastern Missouri and had been coming to the campground most of his life, like many of the others here. In fact, Tiny had met his future wife at a party just like this one.

What is he up to? Cari thought, watching him head toward Tiny with a smirk on his face.

Wilson leaned close to the DJ, then turned and walked right up to Cari.

"May I have the pleasure of the next dance?" he asked her loudly, and extended his hand to her.

She shook her head no, but it was too late. All the women around her were shouting and calling for her to go. Like the crescendo from a clap of thunder the noise grew louder as her face grew redder.

"Go on, honey," one of the women called out.

"If you don't I will," someone else said, "and you won't get him back!"

The men whistled and cajoled Wilson.

"There's no music," Cari stated in a final attempt, but it was useless. He stood, half bowed in front of her, with the biggest smile she had ever seen. She placed her hand in his, he squeezed it, and pulled her onto the makeshift dance floor.

This will show them! Wilson thought.

"I'm going to kill you for this!" Cari whispered.

He pulled her close and signaled to Tiny. From the first sounds of the steel guitar wailing a wave of emotion spread through her as they stood alone, surrounded by the cheering crowd. They were swaying in rhythm to the music.

Cari closed her eyes as her thoughts drifted to what ifs and maybes. Would it be so bad staying with him? Was it time to change her ways? The idea caused her fear. Fear of the unknown. But it felt so good in his arms. When the song ended applause broke out amongst the crowd but they continued to dance. The applause and cheers grew louder until someone shouted above it all, "Get a room!" at which point everyone broke into laughter.

That will teach them! Even Baroque couldn't have done that! Wilson thought. But then he looked at her staring at him and broke into a cold sweat. *Why does she do this to me? I don't have feelings for her. She's not my type at all. But it felt so nice holding her. I certainly don't trust her after what Rattler... but then, maybe she was jealous of Cari. I just got dumped. Now is not the time. That's it. I'm feeling sorry for myself. I don't have feelings for her. Man, that's a scary thought. But it is so nice being around her.*

Later, walking back to their trailer, Cari said, "I'm still mad at you for dragging me up to dance."

"That would be more convincing if you weren't smiling."

"Shut up!" She hit his arm playfully. "Want me to take the cot tonight?"

"Of course not. I would have to listen to you complaining and swearing about it all day tomorrow."

Detective Harrison sat in his room in Springfield, Missouri, studying documents on his laptop, unaware he was less than a two hour drive from his prey. Unfortunately, for his case, he was beginning to have serious doubts about the guilt of his primary target. He had spent hours going through the evidence from Stone's fraud trial and found glaring holes in it. It appeared to him there was the possibility someone had set her up. And Miles Jacoby was his leading candidate. Unless she was much more clever than he believed.

Harrison's partner in Vegas had been digging along with him, and what they found on Mr. Jacoby did not bode well. Not only would he gain a tremendous fortune and control of Brentwood's company, it seemed he had a considerable gambling problem. And it was his testimony that was most damning to Stone at her first trial.

It also seemed to him that Stone wouldn't have killed Brentwood in the manner he was murdered. It was stupid to shoot him in the middle of the morning when guests were moving throughout the hotel. Someone would have seen her leave. And something else bothered him about the crime scene; the room had been wiped clean of fingerprints. From the eyewitness accounts, everything happened in too short a time for her to have done that. It was obvious to him at this point that Wilson James was a genius, and if he thought she was innocent, perhaps it was time to look at the case from the same point of view. That had to be the reason James was helping her. It would explain everything. But where was he taking her?

Detective Harrison was scanning through his emails when a message from the Kansas State Police caught his attention. They had raided Shane McShane's used car lot after reports he had sold a stolen car and, from the ensuing search, had discovered the car purchased by Susan Dankforth.

"Bright pink? Holy hell! They're riding in a neon sign!" Harrison blurted out.

Despite knowing their car, he still had no idea where they were headed. At least it was something. He had planned to return to Vegas, but decided to stay in Missouri a few more days to see if anything developed. His phone rang.

"Harrison here... What?... Where?... I'm south of there. Got the name of the campground?... No... Okay, I'll head up that way and see what I can find out, bye."

Another break. The pink car had been spotted in the Osage Beach area which wasn't too far north of where he was staying. He was back on their trail!

Chapter 8: The lion tamer

Wilson was up early, as usual, wandering around the campground.

"Morning, cuz!" Christopher yelled at him. "You look lost."

"Looking for the car," Wilson said, walking up to him.

"Hid it. I'll send Nicky to fetch it. You folks heading out? You're welcome to stay."

"I appreciate that but we got to keep moving."

"You know you're safe in this country." Chris slapped him on the shoulder.

"I know, but we got other plans."

"Here," Chris handed Wilson a cell phone. "It's a burner. You might need it. I'm the only one got the number. If I hear anything I'll let you know."

"Thanks, Chris." Wilson turned the phone over then slid it into his pocket.

Wilson returned to the trailer where Cari was packing up what few things they had.

"Good morning. Sleep well?" Cari asked.

"As well as could be expected."

"I suppose I'm going to have to listen to you complain all day about sleeping on the floor," Cari said in a cheery voice.

"That's more your thing." Wilson leaned on the door frame watching her.

"Wait till you hit a prison mattress."

"Very funny."

"Mind if I drive? It helps keep my mind off things," Cari asked.

"That's fine, as soon as they find our car."

Cari looked up, alarmed. "Pinky's missing?"

"They hid her somewhere. She'll be out soon."

"Knock, knock," Jenny called out from the door. "I brought you some food for the trip. Nothing fancy, just leftovers from the party. Too bad you couldn't stay longer. We was just getting to know one another. You'll have to come back."

"We'll try," Cari assured her. "Thanks so much for the food and everything. You're all so nice here."

"Our pleasure. Maybe you can come back for the wedding."

"Who is getting married?" Cari asked.

"Me, silly. As soon as I can convince that hunky man of mine!" She handed Wilson a cardboard box.

"We'll be here for that," Wilson called from the door.

After she left, Cari turned to him and said, "Why did you tell her that?"

"Unfortunately for her, she's history as soon as Chris finds something he thinks is better."

"You men are a bunch of fucking pigs!"

"With the exception of present company. Right?"

"I guess," she mumbled.

It seemed the whole camp came out to wish them well and say their goodbyes. Wilson and Cari greeted each one before departing. Everyone stood by the entrance waving as the couple pulled out of the driveway.

"This was fun," Cari said.

"Yes, it was. Been a long time since I enjoyed myself that much." Wilson settled back in the seat like it was his favorite recliner.

"We needed a break. And every one of them is like family." She stared out at the road, thinking. "Shit!"

Wilson jumped and turned to look behind them for a cop car. "What's the matter now?"

"It's your name! I can't believe I just made the connection!"

"Not 'Wee Willy' again."

"Of course! We're in Missouri!"

"You just figured that out?"

"Not your first name, your last," Cari clarified.

"My last? I'm glad you finally got it because I have no idea what you're talking about."

"Wilson James from Missouri. You're related to Jesse James! You're not hillbillies, you're outlaws! Now it makes sense."

"He was a distant relative, but that doesn't make us outlaws."

"And here I thought you were a dork, when all along you're outlaw royalty. I feel much better."

"It's not something I brag about, but that's why so many people know the family here in Missouri."

"Are your parents in the state?"

"No. My father owns a small convenience store and gas station in upstate New York and my step-mother is a second grade teacher. I was born in Missouri, and left when I was fifteen. But many people still know the name and also knew my father."

Cari's eyes lit up in mock excitement. "Wow! I'm being rescued by a member of the infamous James gang. What's your father's name?"

"I'm glad you're amused by my family tree." Wilson stared out at the passing scenery.

"Amused? I'm honored!"

Wilson smirked. "From one outlaw to another?"

"Hey, watch it!" She glared at him, the car speeding up a bit.

"Tell me about this aunt of yours we're going to visit."

"She's my great aunt and in her nineties. She likes to drink beer, smoke, and gamble. Bingo is her favorite. And she hates men," Cari added.

Wilson groaned. "That's nice to know! Maybe I should have waited for you at the campground."

"She had her heart broken when she was young and never got over it. Still carries a torch for the guy."

"When did you see her last?" he asked.

"I think it was about six or seven years ago. She sent me a letter after the story broke about my fraud charges. Said she supported me."

"That was nice of her."

Cari scoffed. "She never said she believed me."

"I'm sorry."

"It's not your fault. None of my family believe me."

"What about your sister? The one who gave you her car?"

She shrugged, sadness in her eyes. "She once told me she thought I was innocent, but it wasn't very convincing."

They passed through a small town in north-central Missouri and Cari slowed the car, turning into a tree-lined driveway. The old farmhouse sat on the right and had a wide porch with a swing that had seen better days.

"Want me to wait here?" Wilson asked tentatively.

"No," she said, exiting the car.

"I'm right behind you. On an unrelated topic, does your aunt own a shotgun?"

They stepped onto the porch and Cari knocked. An elderly woman with shoulder length hair, wearing an apron opened it.

"Yes?" Her voice shook when she spoke.

"Hello Doris. It's Jessica."

The woman stood stone-faced. "I recognize you. I suppose you want something from your aunt?" she asked coldly.

"No. I was just passing by and wanted to visit. How is Aunty?"

"Better before you showed up. And don't go getting her all worked up!"

Cari turned to Wilson. "This is Doris, my aunt's housekeeper. Doris this is–"

"Don't care who your latest man tramp is. Come in and I'll get your aunt." She waved her hand at Wilson and shook her head in disgust.

Cari went in, followed by Wilson. When he passed by Doris she growled, "Don't steal anything, tramp!"

"Wait in the living room." Doris pointed them into a large bright room to the left. "Miss Viney!" she called. "You got guests. Your ungrateful niece Jessica and some piece of trash she's dragging around like a homeless puppy dog." Her voice faded into the back of the house.

"She likes you," Cari told Wilson, forcing a smile.

"Jessica dearie," her aunt exclaimed as she entered. "Give me a hug, child."

She embraced Cari, and Wilson noted how spry she seemed for her age. She stood straight with silky white hair and had a warm presence about her.

"Aunty, this is Allen," Cari said, pulling him forward.

Viney stepped back and looked him up and down. "Honestly, Dearie, this is the worst one yet! Where did you find him? Some back alley somewhere?"

"He's a nice man, Aunty. He's helping me."

"I've heard about your troubles on the news. Oh Jessica, how could you do it? Didn't you learn anything from your last brush with the law? I know he was only a man, but did you have to shoot him in front of witnesses?"

"I'm innocent, Aunty! I did not kill that man or have anything to do with it! And I didn't defraud anyone! I was falsely convicted!"

"This is America, Dearie! We don't send innocent people to prison!"

"Well, America sent this innocent person to jail!" Cari's face was red, her breath coming in heavy pants.

"Why don't we take a break and cool off a bit," Wilson interceded.

"No one asked you to butt in. This isn't your business," Viney warned him.

"It is very much my business and you have no right speaking to your niece like that. She is family."

"Family? I'll have you know my family isn't a bunch of criminals!"

"Then you believe she is innocent and was wrongfully convicted."

"What?"

"If there are no criminals in your family, and she is family, she was framed and is innocent," Wilson said.

Looking at Cari, Viney said, "Your tramp is some kind of lunatic."

Cari's eyes brimmed with tears. "Maybe we should go. I thought I would be welcome but can see I was mistaken."

"No, Dearie. He's right, you are still family despite what you have done. You're welcome to stay for dinner and for the night. But I want you out first thing in the morning. And you two aren't sleeping in the same bed! You can have the guest room and he will sleep down here on the couch."

"Works for me," Wilson piped up.

Cari's aunt glared at him. "Dinner will be in an hour."

"I need some air," Cari said, brushing past Wilson.

"You have some good air in these parts. I think I'll join her," Wilson said.

As he walked out of the room, Aunt Viney looked at Doris. "What a piece of trash."

"Pure hillbilly," Doris added.

Later, Doris ushered them into the dining room where the table was set for company. As Wilson sat down Doris leaned toward him, "I'm going to count the silver after dinner."

He stifled a laugh. "Strange hobby."

"Don't steal anything, smart-mouth trash," she snapped.

He looked at Cari, smirking. "I've moved up from tramp to smart-mouth trash."

"You're not helping."

Viney came in and Wilson immediately stood up. She half smiled and sat at the head of the table.

"We don't get as many guests as we used to. I hope you will find the meal adequate."

"I'm sure it will be fine, Aunty," Cari assured her.

"What exactly do you do for a living, young man? Or dare I ask?" She stared at him beadily.

Cari gave him a look of needles. He smiled and leaned back in his chair. "Lion tamer."

"Oh God," Cari sighed to herself.

"Lion tamer?" Viney asked, perplexed.

"Yes, that's correct. I'm a lion tamer up in Canada. On sabbatical at the moment, traveling across the US, visiting colleagues. Met Jessica at a tamers' conference and I happened to be going the same way so decided to let her tag along."

Cari sat with her face in her hands.

"Are you serious?" her aunt asked him.

"Lion taming is very serious. A friend of mine was distracted for two seconds and lost his right arm clean to the shoulder. Lefty McConnell. You might have heard of him?"

"No, I can't say I have." She shook her head.

"He was big in Europe. Performed before the Queen."

Oh fuck, just let him stop! Cari thought.

"I'm not familiar with the profession," Viney said through tight lips.

"Of course, it's not like the old days," Wilson continued.

He isn't stopping! Cari thought, shaking her head.

"Political correctness," Wilson said as he pushed the chair back on two legs and rocked slightly.

"What does political correctness have to do with lion taming?" Viney asked.

"A few years ago, they passed a bill of rights for lions. Darned Democrats. The Republicans tried to stop it, but they tacked on a rider about Obama-care, and there you have it. We couldn't use whips and pistols anymore. Overnight the business shut down. Ever tried reasoning with an angry lion while holding a plush toy? You wouldn't believe how many friends I lost. And, of course, the bleeding heart Brits followed suit. Long story short, Canada was the only place left. After all, any people who club seals have no problem whipping lions. That's why I work in Canada."

Cari's aunt sat dumbfounded, staring at Wilson who had a wide grin on his face.

"And this is your man?" Viney asked Cari.

"Oh God yes, he's all mine," Cari replied, shaking her head. *I definitely should have left him when I had the chance!*

Doris brought in the food and conversation died. Wilson felt rather proud of his lion tamer story. Perhaps he wasn't blocked after all. Maybe Cari was right. All he had to do was sit down and write. Hopefully, it wouldn't be from a prison cell.

After dinner, Cari and Wilson went out and sat on the porch swing. It creaked as he pushed it. She was very quiet and he wondered if she was angry at him.

"Jessica," Doris called from inside the door. "Telephone."

She shot up off the swing, panic radiating from her. "Phone call for me? No one knows I'm here. Who is it?"

"It's your father."

"My father?! I don't want to talk to him! And how does he know I'm here?" Cari was extremely agitated.

"Miss Viney called him."

"Tell him I don't want to talk to him!" She went to the far end of the porch.

Doris went inside. Cari stood with arms folded and a scowl on her face.

"Jessica Stone you get your butt (definitely no e) in here this instant and talk to your father!" her aunt ordered her.

"I'm not talking to him!" Cari responded.

Viney stepped out onto the porch. "You listen to me young lady. I don't care how you feel about him, he is your father and you will respect him! Now get in here before I come out there and drag you in!"

This ought to be good, Wilson thought.

Cari turned and went in with her aunt.

"You stay out here!" Doris told Wilson. "And I'm locking the door!" He heard a click.

Wilson could hear muffled voices in the living room but could not make out what was being said. After several minutes, Cari came back out, slammed the door behind herself, stomped across the porch, went to the car, and sat on the hood. Wilson got up, walked over, and sat beside her. She was silent for a long time, but Wilson knew she would talk when she was ready.

"He says he loves me despite everything I've done. Isn't that the sweetest thing? Well fuck him, fuck all of them! I have no family! No one believes me! Not one of them!" Anger lined every feature on her face, her cheeks red, hands shaking.

172

"I believe you," Wilson spoke softly.

Her gaze snapped to him. "You do?"

"I admit, at first I was only interested in the possibility of getting a book out of this, but as we've spent time together I have come to see what an intelligent, sweet, and nice person you really are. I feel you are not only innocent of the murder, but the fraud as well. I believe in and support you completely."

"Really?" Cari's features softened.

"Really."

"Thank you. That means a lot to me."

"You're welcome."

She stared at him in the moonlight. "That was the biggest pile of bullshit I've ever heard!"

"Thought I could pull it off, but I'm not much of an actor."

"You can say that again! Better stick to writing. Oh wait, you can't do that either because you`re BLOCKED!"

"You aren't a nice person, are you?"

"Took you this long to figure that out? Kind of slow, too."

Wilson looked at her and smiled.

"I'm going to bed. We should leave early tomorrow," Cari told him.

"Looking forward to sleeping on the couch. That thing is hard as a board!"

"You're such a baby! Wait till you get on a prison mattress! My aunt always has the most comfortable mattress in her guest room. Can't wait to sink into that."

"I hate you."

She slid off the hood. "Goodnight."

"Wait! Don't go without me." He hurried to catch up.

"Scared all alone in the dark?"

He chuckled. "Don't want to get locked out again."

Doris was waiting in the hall for them. "It's time for bed. You're upstairs, first door on the right." She stepped in front of Wilson. "In there." She pointed toward the living room. "This is yours." She shoved a pillow and blanket into his chest and knocked him backwards a bit.

"That's mighty kind of you," he replied.

"Humph! Lion tamer my ass!" Doris turned and walked toward kitchen. "And I best not hear you going up those stairs or there's gonna be a whole lot of pain on you!"

No one trusts the lion tamer. Wilson made up the couch and settled in. *The floor is probably softer,* he thought, but soon drifted off to sleep.

Detective Harrison had to ask several times for directions until he finally found the campground Wilson and Cari had recently left. It was late, almost 10:00 p.m., when he drove past the dilapidated house beside the entrance. As he pulled in, Chris saw him and told Nicky to spread the word. He could spot a cop a mile away!

"We're full up," Chris told Harrison as he drove in.

Harrison stopped the car and flashed his badge. "I'm Detective Harrison and would like to ask you a few questions."

"Bout what?"

Harrison stepped out of the car and held out the two photos. "Have you seen these two people around here?"

Chris looked at the pictures. "Never seen them before."

"The man is your cousin." Harrison tapped Wilson's photo.

"Got lots of cousins, mister. Don't know half of 'em." He spit on the ground.

"Reports suggest they are driving a bright pink car."

Chris laughed. "Wouldn't forget a thing like that."

"Witnesses say they saw the car headed this way."

"Guess I missed it when they went by."

"Mind if I look around? Maybe talk to some of your guests?" Harrison asked as he retrieved the photos.

"Knock yourself out."

"Can I leave my car here?"

"Suit yourself." Chris spit again. "I'll see nothing happens to it."

"Thank you."

Harrison walked up the road as Chris leaned on the hood of the car. He went up to the first camper and knocked.

"Yes, can I help you?" the woman asked in a pleasant manner.

"I'm Detective Harrison, ma'am."

"Hilda."

"Ever seen these two people around here?"

Hilda looked at the pictures. "Never seen either one. Daryl, come here! Daryl is my husband. This policeman wants to know if you ever seen these two?" She pointed to the photos as Daryl squeezed into the doorway.

After studying the pictures, he shook his head. "Never seen them."

"Thank you for your time."

"That's okay, we're on vacation. Got all kinds of time. Like some coffee, officer?"

"No thank you, ma'am." Harrison moved on to the next camper, and the next, and the next, all with the same results. Everyone was polite and studied the pictures but no one had ever seen the couple.

"Any luck?" Chris asked Harrison when he returned.

"Not a bit," he replied. *As if you didn't know that before I left.*

"I would offer you a place for the night but we're full." Chris stood, arms folded, a defiant look on his face.

"Yes, I remember you saying that when I arrived. I want to thank you for–" Harrison's phone rang. "Excuse me." He took out his phone, glanced at the screen, and walked a short distance away.

"Harrison here... What?... You found them?... Where?... Email me the location, I'm on my way." Turning back to Chris he asked, "Do you have wi-fi?"

"Do I have what?"

"Never mind. Thank you for your help." Harrison hurried into his car.

"Have a nice day." Chris waved as the car backed out of the drive. "Asshole!" he muttered, and took out his phone.

Wilson jumped up at the sound of his phone ringing. Fumbling with the buttons he held it up to his ear.

"Hello?... Chris... What?... Harrison?... They do?... Thanks, cuz." He flicked on a lamp and glanced at clock. It was 11:30 p.m. He slipped the phone in a pocket and hurried across the room.

Where is she? He tried to remember as he crept up the darkened stairs. At the top, he looked both ways, then approached the door on the right. He certainly hoped he was right as he pushed the door open. He could barely make out the features of the room in the low light from the moon in the window. He crept to the bed and turned on a light on the night-stand. A sigh of relief came over him when he saw Cari lying on her side.

"Wake up," he gently shook her.

"What? Who is it?" she asked groggily.

"Shhhh. It's me. We have to go," Wilson whispered.

"What time is it?"

"11:30."

"In the morning?"

"No, at night. Come on, hurry."

"We're not leaving this early. Come back in a few hours."

He grabbed her arm and rolled her toward him. "Get up and get dressed. Hurry, we've got to leave now. Where are the rest of your clothes?"

"I left them in the car."

"Good. Come on. And be quiet!"

She dressed and Wilson turned off the light. They made their way to the stairs on tip toe. There were several creaky ones and the sound seemed amplified in the silence of the house. At the bottom, he fumbled with the lock, heard the click, and reached for the doorknob as the lights came on.

"Thieves!" Doris screamed. "Just as I thought! Make one move and you'll get it!" She held a fireplace poker menacingly over her head.

Wilson pushed Cari behind him. "If you make another sound, Doris, I swear to God I'm going to take that thing from you and wrap it around your ears! Go!" he ordered Cari.

Holy hell! Who is this guy? Baroque? Cari thought as she ran out the door followed by Wilson.

They reached the car, Wilson fired it up, and tore off toward the road.

"You know any side roads near hear?" Wilson's adrenalin was flowing.

"Side roads? Why? What's happened?"

"Side roads!" he shouted.

"Ah, to the right a little ways. I think there's a dirt road on the right."

He spun up the gravel as he turned hard. The car swerved, then straightened. He spotted a country road on the right and turned hard again. When he was on the road he gunned the car and they sped off into the night.

"What is all this about?" Cari asked, gripping the edges of her seat tightly.

"Chris gave me a phone when we left and he called me a few minutes ago. Our friend Detective Harrison stopped by the campground looking for us."

Cari's face went white. "Shit! How did he know?"

"Must have traced the car. Chris overheard Harrison on his phone saying they knew where we were. Someone tipped them we were here and the cops are on their way any minute."

"Fucking family!" Cari started pounding her fists on the dash. "Fuck, fuck, fuck, fuck!"

"Stop it!" Wilson yelled as he grabbed her hand. The car swerved before he pulled it straight.

"My fucking family turned me in!" Tears fell down her angry face.

"And I pulled you from the teeth of the lion! Again!"

"Baroque couldn't have done any better." She reached over and squeezed his arm.

"You still swear too much. And look at the bright side," he added. "You got hillbillies and outlaws for family now."

"And how's that? Are you planning to marry me?"

"What? Ah, well it's–"

"Kidding!" She wiped her cheeks. "What now?"

"We have to ditch the car."

"Oh no! Not Pinky!"

"Afraid Pinky is history."

"Shhh! Don't say it in front of her. God you're insensitive sometimes."

Wilson smiled. "Find the atlas so we can plot a course south."

Cari dug around in the back and pulled it out. "How far south?"

"All the way, then east into Tennessee."

She searched the paper for a few minutes before looking up at him. "I can't find this road on the map."

"Scale is too big. These country roads never show up on an atlas. I'll have to rely on my navigational skills to get us there."

"You have skills?" Cari asked.

"Still not funny."

She paused. "Are you going to include my back-stabbing family in your book?"

"It might make an interesting plot twist."

"And Pinky?"

"Readers will never believe a pink car in an action thriller." Wilson shook his head.

"Is that what this will be? An action thriller?"

Wilson nodded. "Just like Jason Bourne."

"Describe the main character as you're planning to write it."

"Let's see, tall, dark and handsome," he started.

"Excuse me? I'm the main character! I thought we sorted this out."

"I said the main character should be male and you threatened me."

Cari smiled. "Exactly! It's all sorted out! The main character is female, me. So, describe me."

"Well," he hesitated. "I haven't thought this out yet. I'm concerned with plot and not the characters at this time."

"Oh great! You come up with that stupid lion tamer story but you can't describe your main character." She sat back and folded her arms.

"Okay, I'll give it a shot. First, she must be tall with dark hair."

178

"Why not blonde?"

"Too flashy. Remember, she's fleeing for her life and wants to remain inconspicuous. Blondes stick out more."

"I suppose that makes sense. Continue."

"Large dark penetrating eyes that instill fear in her enemies."

"I think you mean large 'green' eyes. My eyes are green," Cari corrected him.

"I know," he answered quietly.

She stared at him, mouth slightly ajar. "You know what color my eyes are? I was with Brentwood's firm for five years and we dated for one and he didn't know that."

"To continue," Wilson said, "she is very pretty, nice slender nose, and roundish face. Her hair is shoulder length, though she cuts it for the journey. Her build is athletic, as she is trained in the martial arts."

"You realize you're describing me?"

"It's based on you."

"You think I'm pretty, right?" she asked, not looking at him.

"What?" he glanced at her.

"You hesitated. You don't think I'm pretty?"

"No, I didn't—"

"You don't think I'm pretty?"

"Yes, I think you're pretty." Wilson was flustered.

"Are you coming on to me?"

"What? No, it's—"

Cari burst out laughing. "Kidding! I would think by now you would start to catch on, but noooo."

"I hate you!"

She smiled. "I'm going to try and sleep. Wake me if you want me to drive."

"I do think you're pretty."

"Too late."

Detective Harrison was close to Jefferson City when his phone rang.

"Harrison here, hello... Not again!... How long?... No idea which way they went?... Okay, I'm on my way there. I would like to interview those involved if I can... Good. I should be there by morning... Goodnight." He hung up. "Son of a bitch! This guy must have lady luck riding on his shoulder! He's always two steps ahead of me. Where in hell are you going James? Where are you going?" Harrison shook his head as he drove into the darkness.

It was early the next morning when Harrison found the farmhouse. A state patrol car was parked by the entrance to the driveway. He stopped, showed the officer his badge, and was waved in, then pulled up by the porch and got out.

"Are you Harrison?" A tall man with a massive grey mustache asked him.

"Yes."

"I'm Detective Monroe, state police. I just arrived myself. We'll go in and you can question them if you like. I'm not too familiar with the case."

Harrison sighed. "Sometimes I wish I wasn't familiar with it either."

"One of those, is it?"

"I've never come across a guy like this Wilson James. He's a genius! It's like he knows what I'm going to do before I know."

"I know the feeling," Monroe sympathized. "They told me the old woman here is Stone's great aunt and the younger old woman is her housekeeper."

"Who called it in?"

"The housekeeper, Doris Blanchard. Been with the woman for years."

"Is she related?" Harrison asked.

"No." Monroe knocked.

"Yes?" Doris opened the door.

"I'm Detective Monroe and this is Detective Harrison. May we come in?"

"You're too late! They left hours ago," Doris berated them.

"We know, ma'am. Are you the housekeeper?" Monroe asked.

"Yes. Come in."

"We'd like to talk to you first."

"Come and sit in the living room. He slept right there," she pointed to the couch.

"They are not sleeping together?" Harrison asked.

"Oh, they wanted to but I wouldn't allow it! Downright rude he was. Jessica is some naive and he has her under a spell of some kind. He just told her everything to do as if she had no mind of her own. That's why I called the police. He's a maniac and dangerous. Claims to be a lion tamer from Canada! Insane! And he threatened to kill me!"

"He threatened to kill you?" Harrison's eyebrows raised in surprise.

"I caught them trying to leave in the middle of the night, not long after I called police. I grabbed a poker from the fireplace and stood between them and the door. Well, he grabbed that poker from me, knocked me to the floor, and stood over me ready to strike! Said he knew I called the police and he was going to bash in my head!"

"Did he hit you? Do you require medical attention?" Monroe asked as he looked at her head.

"Jessica stopped him. Pleaded and begged him to spare my life. If she hadn't intervened I would surely be dead by his hand! Makes you wonder how many others he's killed along the way. He's a dangerous man leading poor Jessica down the evil path. You need to order a shoot to kill when he's found! Just be careful not to hit Jessica. I wouldn't be surprised he's the one who killed that fellow in Las Vegas!"

"You've been most helpful, ma'am. Could we talk to Stone's aunt now?" Harrison asked her.

"Of course, but I must warn you she is forgetful at times. You have to take what she says with a grain of salt."

In a few minutes, great aunt Viney entered the room.

"Morning, ma'am. I'm Detective Monroe and this is Detective Harrison. He'll be asking the questions."

"Thank you again," Harrison said to Doris. "We would like to talk alone."

Doris excused herself and left the room, but stayed within listening distance.

"Dreadful business, this. Poor Jessica. She's not a bad girl, but made some terrible decisions. First that fraud and now killing her former boss. Dreadful business."

"You believe she did it?" Harrison asked.

"Whole family believes she did it. And now she's hooked up with this Allen fellow."

"Allen? Any last name?"

"Never said. Made up this ridiculous story about being a lion tamer from Canada."

"Did he threaten violence to you or your housekeeper that you know of?" Harrison asked.

"Threaten violence? Oh no, officer, not that man. I doubt he has it in him to threaten so much as a mouse! Not much of a man if you ask me. Jessica always had such poor taste when it comes to men. Some things never change."

"Did they say anything at all about where they are headed?" Harrison was busy writing notes.

"When she talked to her father on the phone, I believe she mentioned something about New York. You'd have to ask him. I can give you his number. He lives in Philadelphia."

"That would be most helpful."

"Anything else, officers?"

"The car they were driving?" Harrison looked up from his notepad.

"A hideous pink thing. Dreadful!"

"Thank you. We'll show ourselves out." The two detectives went out to Harrison's car.

"What do you make of that?" Monroe inquired.

"I think the housekeeper is full of shit. I interviewed James in Vegas before he ran and believe you me he is not the threatening type. What the aunt said reflects his personality. I figured from the beginning it's Stone that is running the show. She must have him wrapped around her little finger if he's willing to face jail time to help her. But I can't figure what he's getting out of it? He was married to two models, he's not bad looking, and has substantial wealth. It doesn't make sense to me."

"This guy was married to two models? And he's some kind of a genius? Sounds like James Bond! You got your work cut out for you on this case." Monroe removed his hat and scratched his head.

Harrison scoffed. "Tell me about it."

"What's next?"

"Think I'll talk to the father. If she let it slip they're heading to New York that's the only lead I have to go on at the moment. And if they're planning to leave the country, they need fake passports and New York is the best place for them to get some. They already bought one set in Phoenix but got robbed and lost them."

"I wish you luck." Monroe reached out and shook his hand.

"I need it with this pair. Thanks for all your help."

"If anything turns up, I'll be in touch. Let me know when you get them."

"Will do." Detective Harrison slid into his car. He had hit another dead end.

Chapter 9: You have never seen a dog with so many teeth!

"What a story! Snatched from the jaws of justice! By me! And it's all true, unlike Baroque's book. I'll bet his is based on events that never happened. I can't believe how much better I am than him." He glanced over at Cari, who was still asleep. *She's not so bad. A little rough around the edges, but that's from prison. I wonder if she did it?*

Wilson drove all night along narrow, unmarked dirt roads, weaving south through Missouri. He was forced to turn around several times after driving to dead ends. Cari was still sleeping as the first rays of morning sun began to light the countryside. They were going through farmland as he wanted to avoid major towns and cities until he could find another vehicle.

"Good morning," Cari said, stretching. "What time is it?"

"Early. Sun is just coming up."

"Where are we?"

"Not sure."

"What's the new plan?"

"I'm working on it."

"Why do I ask?"

"I would think by now you would have learned." Wilson ginned slightly and cast a quick glance her way.

"It's too early for your lame attempt at humor. Are we going to stop somewhere soon?" Cari yawned and tried to clear her head.

Wilson nodded. "Need to find another vehicle. Want to drive?"

"Not unless you need me. Don't feel like it today."

He looked at her, concern in his eyes. "You okay?"

Cari shrugged and looked at her knees. "I'm kind of bummed about my family. It would be nice if they supported me, at least a little, instead of turning me in to the cops."

"Were you close before the trial?"

"Not so much. My sister could do no wrong and I was always trying to impress my parents, but it never amounted to anything. Then I sort of rebelled." Her tone became cold and detached.

"Sort of?" Wilson asked.

"Started dating bums my parents hated and sleeping around and drinking and drugs. Not proud of it. I straightened out and went to college. I always liked math and got into accounting and investment banking. Did a masters in finance and was considered a wunderkind. Had lots of offers but accepted with Ralph's firm. By my third year I was pulling down a quarter mil a year. That was before the collapse when we were flying high. Clients were lining up to be represented by me, but my family still had no respect for me." The disappointment in her voice was obvious. "My sister is a nurse and they faun over her. What I did was never good enough. And, of course, she lived down the block from them and I moved to New York. When everything got fucked up in the collapse, the FCC started nosing around.

"At the beginning, Ralph supported me. When I was charged, Miles came to see me and said it wouldn't look good for the firm if they helped me because they were trying to get a big handout from the government. Everything I had was seized. I asked my father for a loan. He's a surgeon. Said I had got myself into the mess, it was my responsibility to get out. Ended up with a court appointed asshole lawyer on his first trial case. Wanted me to settle, but I thought they would never convict me. Guilty; two to five years in federal prison. My parents never even came to visit me. My sister came once. I guess I shouldn't be surprised." *He doesn't need to know everything,* she thought.

I wonder if there's any truth to that? Wilson thought.

She looked at him and smiled.

"Did you see that?" Wilson called out, slamming on the breaks.

Cari jumped and looked around wildly. "No! What is it? What's the matter?"

"Next to the road. Back there a bit. A pickup for sale."

"A truck? I thought it was the cops or something. You're a fucking lunatic, you know?"

"Here, you take the car, drive up the road, and wait somewhere. I'll see if I can make a deal. If I'm not back in an hour, leave!"

He jumped out of the car and started walking back. Cari slid into the driver's seat, watching him in the mirror. "What did he mean 'if I'm not back in an hour'? He's such a fuc–, right, less swearing. Oh God, he's starting to get to me." She sped off.

Wilson arrived at the truck and walked around it. It was old, but looked to be in good shape and was exactly what they needed. It would be difficult for the police to trace them driving this and, by the time the cops figured it out, they would be in Atlanta. Happy with his find, he headed down the driveway to the house. A large dog was barking and he faltered a step. The barking increased when he knocked on the front door.

"Yes? What is it?" a woman's voice called from inside.

"I'm interested in your pickup," Wilson shouted through the door. "What are you asking?"

The inside door opened which left only a screen door between him and what had to be the biggest and ugliest sounding dog he had ever come across. He casually pressed his foot against the bottom of the door to hold it closed. The dog growled and snarled at him.

"Sit, Sweet 'ums!" the woman commanded the dog. He stepped back and sat.

Sweet 'ums? You've got to be kidding!

She was middle aged with dark, shoulder length hair, and wore wire-rimmed glasses.

"Seven hundred, cash. Firm." The woman casually looked him up and down.

"May I try it?"

"No!" she snapped. "Runs good."

"Starts okay?" Wilson asked, thinking of Ol' Bill.

"Yep. Seven. Take it or leave it. And if you plan to attack me, my dog will rip out your throat."

Wilson swallowed hard. "Only interested in buying the truck. Nothing else. I swear."

"Come in then." She pushed the door open and the dog immediately sprang up. "He won't bother you unless I say to."

Wilson eyed the dog nervously and walked in. *Baroque would never dare enter!*

"Come in the kitchen and sit. I'll get the papers."

He settled slowly into the chair she pointed to before she disappeared to another room. The dog stood about a foot from him growling, teeth bared.

"Sweet 'ums is it?" Wilson asked the dog. Sweet 'ums moved a bit closer.

"Here we go," the woman told him upon returning. "First the money, then I sign."

Wilson hesitated. "Ma'am, the money is in my pocket and I don't want to upset your dog when I reach for it."

"Sweet 'ums, sit!"

The dog sat. His head, and more importantly to Wilson, his bared teeth, were in line with Wilson's throat. Very slowly Wilson slid his hand into his front pocket and pulled out a roll of bills. He counted out seven hundred dollars and gingerly placed it on the table.

"There you go, ma'am. Seven hundred, cash."

She picked up the bills. "Twenty... forty... sixty... eighty... one hundred... one hundred and twenty. Would you like something to drink?" She smiled.

"No, I'm fine. Thank you." Wilson rolled his eyes at the dog and tried not to shake.

"Where was I? Twenty... forty... sixty... eighty..."

"Ma'am, if you could–"

As Wilson leaned forward Sweet 'ums jumped up. Wilson froze. Sweet 'ums was about six inches from his face.

"What's that?"

"Nothing. Continue." He hardly dared blink.

"Let's see. Twenty... forty... sixty..."

Sweet 'ums continued to creep closer and closer to Wilson. He had reached a point where he was drooling on Wilson's leg.

"Six hundred and eighty... seven hundred! Exactly correct! Now I'll sign it over to you." She signed the slip and handed it to Wilson.

"Thank you. The key?"

"Yes, of course. I have two. Now, where did I put them?" She got up and went to a cupboard. "Here they are. Oh wait, there's only one. I know, the other is upstairs. Be right back."

"One is fine," Wilson protested.

Sweet 'ums continued to growl and drool on him.

"She's gone to get the other key. No need for you to stay if you have to be somewhere. Maybe got a cat to chase. Neighbor to mutilate." Sweet 'ums growled louder.

Wilson could feel the sweat running down his temple. *So, this is how it ends. I wonder how it feels to be ripped to shreds by a dog.* "Could you make it quick? As a personal favor to me," he said to the dog.

It seemed like the woman was gone forever. Wilson wanted to look at his watch but did not dare move and was barely breathing. Finally, she returned to his great relief.

"Found it upstairs next to my bed."

He turned to look at her and noticed the change immediately. She had combed her hair and applied lipstick.

"You're kind of cute, you know?" she suggested. "Single?"

"Ahh, no, married. In fact, my wife is outside waiting," Wilson replied nervously.

She smiled coyly. "Ever do it on a kitchen table?"

"If I could have the key I really ought to be going," he pleaded.

"Don't worry about your wife. Invite her in. She can join us."

"I really need to go," he told her. As Wilson stood up the chair tipped over backwards, Sweet 'ums barked and lunged at him.

"Sweet 'ums, sit!" the woman yelled.

Wilson felt a breeze as Sweet 'ums' jaws snapped shut and brushed the hair on his arm. He backed cautiously toward the door.

"Don't forget your papers." She handed them to him along with the second key.

"Thank you. It's been a pleasure doing business with you."

"I could give you more pleasure." She winked at him.

"I'm sure you could."

He reached the door and slipped through.

"Would you mind keeping Sweet 'ums inside until I leave?" Wilson called over his shoulder as he bolted for the truck.

"I'll give you five minutes before I let him out."

"Fair enough."

Pulling open the door of the truck he jumped in, slammed it shut, and breathed a sigh of relief. He was shaking. He put the key in the ignition and turned it. Nothing. Wilson jumped out of the truck and ran to the hood. He propped it opened and scanned the engine and noticed one of the battery cables was unhooked. He forced it onto the post, slammed the hood down, and went back to the driver's seat.

"Please Lord, let it start." He turned the key and the engine groaned, clicked, then turned over twice and started. He noticed Sweet 'ums in his side mirror running toward him.

He put the truck in gear. It lunged ahead and stalled. He turned the key again, it sputtered, and started.

The truck moved ahead just as Sweet 'ums grabbed the back tire. But it was too late. Wilson made it to the road and gunned the engine. He looked back to see Sweet 'ums fruitlessly chasing him. It was a victory! Even if it was a victory over a dog, he would take what he could get. Speeding down the road, he almost drove past Cari who had parked the car behind some bushes and was standing near the road. He stopped and backed up to her.

"Another pickup. What is it with men and pickups? I better not have to crawl under the hood to start this one!" Cari told him.

"Don't complain about the truck. I darn near died getting it!" Wilson stated triumphantly.

"Oh yeah, I'm sure. What about the car?" She jabbed her thumb over her shoulder at it.

"Follow me for a ways then we'll ditch it. Don't want them to find it near where I bought this one."

Cari returned to the car and was soon behind Wilson. They drove for twenty minutes before Wilson spotted an abandoned farmhouse set back from the road and stopped. "Give me the stuff then park the car behind that house out of sight."

A few minutes later she was walking back to the truck.

"At least it's cleaner than the last one," she observed as she looked around the interior.

"Darned near died for this truck," he repeated.

Cari sighed. "Okay, tell me the story of your heroism."

"The owner was a woman and she had the biggest dog I have ever seen. He must have been four feet at the shoulder! Maybe more! Some kind of Rottweiler, Doberman, German Shepard killer cross. You have never seen a dog with so many teeth! And he had all of them pointed at me! He was standing right beside me growling the whole time I was sitting there. I was positive I would never make it out alive. Then, when I left, she let him out and he bit the back tire as I was driving away."

"A big dog shouldn't scare a lion tamer!"

"Oh, I see. No, okay, the lion tamer was just a story I made up to tick off your aunt, but the dog is not a story. This is true!" Wilson was shaking his finger at her.

"Oh, I believe you." Cari shook with silent laughter.

"Don't patronize me!"

"It was probably a Chihuahua." She held her hands out, six inches apart.

"Go ahead, laugh. But this is a true story. That dog, his name was Sweet 'ums, he–"

191

"Wait! His name is Sweet 'ums? This is too good."

"Yes, well, you wouldn't have thought it funny had you been the one facing all those teeth! And when I was ready to leave she propositioned me!" Wilson shuddered at the thought.

"Oh, this is too much. First the dog attacked you then his owner. Did she at least have big boobs?"

He scowled. "Just for that I'm going to have the dog attack the main character and leave her horribly disfigured."

"Her?" she asked, bringing herself back under control.

"What?"

"You said leave *her* disfigured. You've come to your senses and realized I'm the main character?" A big smile spread across Cari's face.

"Did I say... wait, I didn't—"

"Too late! No take backs. I'm the main character. Period."

"Okay, yes, I think the book would work better if the main character was a woman."

"Cool. Who do you think should play me?"

"Play you?" Wilson looked at her in confusion.

"In the film. Who do you think should play me?"

"How about Big Bird?" Wilson replied.

"You're still not funny. Maybe Angelina Jolie."

"Jolie?"

"Yes. She's beautiful and athletic. And I kind of look like her. She would be perfect, don't you think?"

"I think you're delusional." Wilson shook his head.

"You're just jealous. They'll have to find someone really nerdish to play you."

"Nerdish? Is that even a word? And I'm not a nerd. Would a nerd have faced down a man-eating dog for this truck? And don't forget the way I fought off Doris last night when she stood in our way!" he reminded her.

"You threatened a 75-year-old woman. My hero!"

"She was armed."

"Armed? She could barely lift it."

"I was protecting you."

"She never would have hit me. You saved yourself."

"Well if that–"

"Kidding! I actually thought it was brave of you to threaten her and get us out. And if you ever tell anyone I said you were brave, I'll kick your ass!" She poked him hard in the arm to make her point.

"You even make a compliment insulting."

"Well, that's all you're going to get." Cari shrugged.

"The dog story is true," he said in a low voice.

"Oh, shut up and find us something to eat." *He's such a kid!*

Wilson spotted a café with a large sign that read 'Eats' in faded red letters. It didn't look too prosperous, but they were in a small town somewhere in central Missouri, and their choices were limited.

"How long to our destination?" Cari asked Wilson after they had settled into a less than clean booth.

"I think we can make it in two days." Wilson brushed crumbs off the table. "We'll head into the mountains of Tennessee and stick to the back roads which means it might take a little longer. When we get closer I'll call my guy to get things moving for papers before we arrive."

Cari nodded. "I'm going to owe you when this is done."

"I told you, I need a new broker to manage my portfolio. You can pay me back a little at a time." *I'm not counting on it.*

"I imagine with the rate of pay you'll give me it's going to take a long time to pay back that twenty."

When he looked up, Cari was smiling.

"Best get back on the road," Wilson suggested when they had finished their greasy burghers.

"You want me to get this?" she asked, a twinkle in her eye.

"You can get the next one."

"That was almost funny." *I wonder what it would be like to manage his money. I could siphon off a little at a time... Maybe it's time to go legit.*

They had driven late into the afternoon when there was a loud noise and the truck swerved across the road. Wilson jumped the brakes and brought it to a halt.

"You okay?" he asked.

"Yes. What was that?" Cari looked back, shaken.

"From the way the truck is sitting I would say the left hind tire is flat. The one Sweet 'ums sunk his teeth into."

"Oh right! A dog caused a flat tire. Give me a break." She shook her head.

He stared at her.

"What?" Cari asked.

"Aren't you going to change the tire?" he asked.

"You bought this thing, you change it." She folded her arms.

"Equal rights for woman, and all."

"Not even close to being funny. Stop staring at me and fix the tire."

"Look under the seat for the jack and tire wrench," he told her.

"God, I have to do everything!" She bent over and rummaged around under the seat.

"Find it?" Wilson called from behind the truck.

"No."

"There's no spare either." He leaned on the tailgate.

"Now what?" Cari joined him.

Wilson noticed dust rising in the distance. "Looks like that," he pointed toward the dust cloud.

"Hope it's not the cops."

"Not likely in this part of the country."

"What do you mean?"

"I grew up not far from here." Wilson pointed off in the distance.

"Seriously?"

"Yes. Probably five miles."

"Can we go visit your old home?"

194

"We'll see."

The cause of the dust cloud was a pickup truck that slowed as it approached then stopped. Wilson walked over to the driver.

"You folks okay?" the driver asked.

"Yes. Flat, and haven't got a spare, jack or wrenches," Wilson told the gentleman.

The old man driving the truck sat in silence, staring at Wilson, who was beginning to get uncomfortable.

"If I didn't know better," the old man began, "I would swear you're Frank James' boy, Wilson."

Wilson looked at the man and a wave of recognition came over him. "Are you Mr. Perkins?"

"One and the same. How the hell are you, son? Ain't seen you round these parts in a donkey's age."

"It's been a long time," Wilson replied, shaking the old man's hand.

"How old were you when you worked for me?"

"Started at thirteen for three summers."

"You were one good worker, just like your pa. And quite the hell raiser if I remember right."

Wilson chuckled. "I did get into a few predicaments."

"Predicaments? Hell son, if it weren't for your pa you never would have stayed out of jail! That name of yours was worth something back then."

Cari had worked her way over and nudged Wilson.

"Mr. Perkins, this is my friend Cari."

"Nice to meet you, young lady." He reached out the window to shake her hand. "And the name's Ted. Hope you been able to tame this one here." He laughed, pointing at Wilson.

"A hell raiser?" she asked in disbelief.

"Never mind. It was a long time ago," Wilson said.

"I got some tools in the back. You pull that tire off and I'll run you up to the house. It's just down the road a piece. The missus is there, she'll take care of

195

you, and I'll drive into town to get your tire fixed. By boy Phil, remember Phil, my youngest? He runs a garage in town. Get it fixed up right quick and have you back on the road."

"That's much appreciated, Mr. Perkins."

"Ted."

Wilson climbed in the back and handed a tire wrench and jack to Cari. When he was taking off the tire, she squatted down beside him.

"I'm curious. Why did you introduce me as Cari and not Rose like everywhere else?"

"This is home. These people would never turn us in no matter what we did. You don't think Ted watches the news? He recognized the name on the first broadcast. If he wanted to turn us in the cops would be here by now."

"How can you be so sure?"

"He has a cell and his oldest son is the chief of police for the county."

Cari blanched. "Oh fuck! Are you kidding?"

Wilson pulled off the tire and threw it in the back of the truck. Ted turned around and they were soon at his house.

"Come on in. Wife's inside." Ted limped in ahead of them.

"Victoria!" he called when they entered the house. "You'll never guess who I run into down the road."

Victoria was short and stocky with gray hair and a wide smile. "Well if it ain't little Wilson James. I would recognize you anywhere, even with all them whiskers." She came up and hugged him. "And who is this beautiful young thing with you?"

"I like her!" Cari replied as Victoria grabbed her in a hug.

"Mrs. Perkins, this is Cari."

"Always a gentleman, this one. Call me Vicky, dear."

"It's nice to meet you," Cari said, smiling.

"Got a flat, Vic, and no tools. Tire's in the back of my truck. I'm taking it to Phil and leaving them here."

"You'll stay for supper," Vicky informed them.

196

"We don't want to impose," Cari said.

"She wasn't asking, young lady. Be back in an hour," Ted said as he left them.

Vicky turned to them. "You got a place to stay?"

"We're fine, Vicky, really," Cari tried to reassure her.

"Won't hear of it! We got a spare room all made up for company. Usually got some grandkids around but no one tonight. Sometimes I think we run a hotel out here!" Vicky laughed.

"That's very kind of you," Cari replied.

"Would you like something to drink? Tea? Coffee?"

"No thank you."

"I'm good, thanks," Wilson added.

"I'll put the kettle on in case you change your mind."

"We're staying here?" Cari whispered after Vicky had gone into the kitchen.

"Looks that way. Don't worry, we'll be safe."

"This one here, he was quite the hell raiser, let me tell you," Vicky said as she entered the parlor where Cari and Wilson were sitting.

"I don't think Cari wants to hear about those times," Wilson attempted to dissuade her from reminiscing.

"Yes, I do." She was looking at Wilson and smiling.

"There was this one time when he was working for us. Well, they were over at the Turner place about three miles away–"

"I don't think she needs to hear that story," Wilson interrupted.

"Yes, I do!" Cari sat bolt upright and stared at Vicky.

"See? She wants to hear it. You hush up! Anyway, they was working over there and old Turner had this beautiful daughter. Wilson here was, what? Fifteen at the time? And Turner's daughter was eighteen."

"This gets better and better," Cari said and nudged Wilson.

"What was her name, Wilson?"

"Maria."

"That's it."

"You remember her name?" Cari asked, staring at him.

"Anyway, they was working when Ted noticed Wilson here wasn't around. Then, this Maria had a boyfriend, the jealous type if I remember right, and all of a sudden there's a hollerin' and Wilson comes running out of the barn, naked as a jaybird, and her boyfriend is behind him with an axe. Then she comes out yelling at her boyfriend and she's carrying her clothes in her arms. Naked as a jaybird she was!"

Cari was laughing along with Vicky while Wilson sat stoically.

"Wilson was staying with us and he run all the way back here through the corn fields naked! I looked out back and he was pulling clothes down off the line and putting them on. When he came in I asked but he went right up to his room. But I got the story when Ted got back."

"That is too funny!" Cari said between gasps of laughter.

"It's not like anything happened," Wilson said.

"Nothing happened? You're fifteen and in a barn with an eighteen year old girl, and you're both naked, and nothing happened? Yeah right. Sell that to someone else buddy!" Cari chastised him.

"She was helping me with my studies," Wilson pleaded.

"Studies of anatomy!" Vicky added.

"Glad I could be a source of humor for you two," he stated, his face red.

"Come on, dear, help me get supper ready. We'll leave him here in his misery." Vicky rose and headed toward the kitchen, still laughing.

"I like her," Cari stated. Before she got up she leaned over and kissed Wilson on the cheek, then followed Vicky into the kitchen.

That was strange, he thought. *She lingered a bit too long to be friendly. It was more like a, no, can't be. She barely tolerates me. I'm reading too much into one kiss. She meant it as a friend. I'm positive.*

Soon bouts of laughter could be heard coming from the kitchen, at his expense, he believed. Just then he saw Ted turn into the drive.

"Ted's back with the tire. I'm going to get the truck," Wilson called as he walked out the door.

"Got her all fixed," Ted told Wilson as he approached the truck. "Phil said it was the funniest thing, two small holes. He thought it looked like a dog had bitten the tire! Strange."

Wilson smiled to himself but decided it was best not to tell Ted the story. When he came back with the truck he parked in front of the house and went triumphantly into the parlor where Cari was stretched out on the couch.

"Phil said the tire went flat because of a dog bite. So there!" Wilson proclaimed proudly.

"My hero!" Cari replied sarcastically.

"Supper's ready, you two. Come on in," Vicky called to them.

Cari stood and linked her arm into Wilson's as they went into the dining room.

After dinner, they sat in the parlor reminiscing but Wilson could barely keep his eyes open. Finally, Cari suggested they call it a night, not expecting they would be in the same room with one bed.

"This is cozy," Cari said as he closed the door.

"Which side you want?" Wilson asked between yawns.

"Doesn't matter. I'm going to the bathroom."

When she returned, Wilson was lying on his side on top of the quilts. She sat on the bed by his feet.

I could make a fortune once I got hold of his accounts. He wouldn't even notice. Wonder what it would be like to be married to a writer? Fuck! Where did that come from? Focus! He's only a mark. Another Ralph, but dumber. She could hear him breathing softly. *He does seem to be a nice guy. It's not as if any of my relationships have been good. Maybe…no! Stick to the plan. Besides, he doesn't seem interested in me. But then, he did just lose his dog.*

When she woke the next morning Wilson was gone. She got up and went to the window. There was a police car sitting in the driveway.

"So, this is how it ends." Cari got dressed and sat on the bed. She was shaking.

Detective Harrison had called Jessica's father. She had let it slip to him that they were heading to New York. They most likely would not follow interstates or main highways, which meant it would be next to impossible to intercept them on the road. He believed his best bet was to get ahead of them and see if he could find out who they might approach for passports, then set a trap. He would fly to New York and have plenty of time to make the arrangements. That was the plan. For the first time since this started, Harrison felt he was about to get ahead of them.

It won't be long before you're mine, Mr. James.

Harrison was sitting at the departure gate of the airport in St Louis when his phone rang.

"Harrison here... What? When?... Where?... Okay... Bye."

He went over to the counter.

"Yes sir, how may I help you?" the attendant asked.

"I'm Detective Harrison, Las Vegas police. I'm booked on this flight to New York but a police emergency has come up and I won't be able to go."

"That's not a problem, sir. May I see your boarding pass?" She held out her hand.

He handed it to her and waited while she typed on her computer keyboard.

"There you are, sir. It's all taken care of." She smiled in a 'I don't care one way or the other' manner.

"Thank you. Which way to the rental cars?" Harrison asked.

"Follow the exit signs and you'll find it."

Harrison left the departure area and hurried through the airport. After renting another car he was soon headed southwest. They had found the pink car. When he arrived at the abandoned house where the car was still parked, Detective Monroe was waiting.

"We meet again," he said as Harrison approached.

"This where you found it?" Harrison was studying the area.

"Yes."

"Positive it's the one they had?" His attention focused on the car.

"Plenty of their fingerprints. It's definitely the one."

"Any dealers near here?" He leaned in the driver's side door. It was as if he could sense Wilson's presence.

"None. I figure they saw something for sale beside the road and grabbed it. A lot of people sell their vehicles that way around here. I got men out in a five mile radius asking if anyone sold something."

"They manage to stay two steps ahead. No matter how close I get, two steps ahead." Harrison slammed the door in frustration.

"Don't worry, we'll get them. We always do," Munroe tried to reassure him.

"I thought they were heading east to New York. Now they're going south. Doesn't make sense." Harrison shook his head.

"Yes, it does."

"What?"

"Toward the south is where he's from. I started out as a patrolman down in that region. Know it well. James has still got family and lots of friends down there."

"I best be heading there. Where is it exactly?"

"I'll take you but I can tell you now it's a waste of time. You won't get anywhere with those folks. They're a tightknit bunch. They'll never give him up." Monroe shook his head and looked at the ground.

"I talked to a cousin of his who owns a campground near Osage Beach," Harrison told him.

"Chris. I know him well. No one to fool with. That bunch has been into everything, but we've never been able to prove anything. Same where James is from. And you know the ironic part? His father was sheriff there. I worked under him."

"Crooked?"

"As a dog's leg! Finally got busted by the FBI but they couldn't make any charges stick. They made a deal to let him resign and move out of state."

"Maybe that is why James is good at this. It runs in his family," Harrison said.

"You know who else he's related to?" Monroe asked.

"Who?"

"Jesse."

Harrison's eyebrows rose. "The outlaw?"

"One and the same. His kinfolk came from the northwest of the state but moved to the southeast a while back. Didn't take them long to establish themselves there. I can take you, but don't expect too much. Excuse me, that's my car radio." Monroe went to his car while Harrison examined Pinky.

"A pink car!" Harrison shook his head. "What were you thinking, James?"

"Like dogs?" Monroe asked when he returned.

"Not particularly. Why?" Harrison scowled.

"They found where James bought a pickup truck yesterday morning. It's not far. You can leave your car and I'll take you."

Soon they were at the woman's house where Wilson had purchased the truck. Monroe pulled into the driveway and could hear the dog barking before they got out of the car.

"You got your gun?" Monroe asked.

"Afraid not, you?"

"Yes. May unlatch the safety by the sound of that. The officer who interviewed her didn't dare go inside." Monroe placed his hand on his revolver as they made their way to the front door.

"I'll walk behind if you don't mind," Harrison said.

Monroe knocked on the door.

"Sweet 'ums, sit!" She ordered the dog from inside.

"Sweet 'ums?" The two detectives looked at one another and repeated simultaneously.

"Yes? Can I help you?" the woman asked as she opened the door. Monroe placed his foot against the screen door as Sweet 'ums growled and snarled at him.

"I'm Detective Monroe, state police, and this is Detective Harrison. You told another officer you sold a pickup truck yesterday?"

"That's right, officer. Nice man, but a bit henpecked by his wife," the woman replied.

"Is this the man?" Harrison asked, showing her the picture.

"Had more whiskers, but yes, that's the man." She pointed emphatically at the image.

"And did you see this woman?" He showed Stone's picture.

"Never laid eyes on her before. She the wife?"

"Did he say anything about where they were going?" Harrison asked.

"Not a word. He was a nervous fellow, though. Don't think he liked dogs. Would you gentlemen like to come in?" She attempted to open the screen door, but Monroe's foot still held it fast.

"Thank you, no, we have to be going," Harrison replied anxiously.

"What did he do?" she asked.

"We can't discuss the case, ma'am."

"Rob a bank? Is that it? Bet they robbed a bank. You ain't going to take the money he gave me, are you?" She became concerned.

"How much did he pay?" Harrison inquired.

"Seven hundred, cash."

"What size bills?"

"All twenties."

"Thank you for your time," Harrison said.

"Did he kill somebody?" she asked enthusiastically. "He looked the type. Real shifty like!"

"Goodbye, ma'am." Harrison cast a glance at Sweet 'ums, and hurried off the porch.

"What are you thinking?" Monroe asked him after they were back in the car.

"I'm thinking he has a lot of balls if he went in that house, but also the fact he paid all in twenties. Most likely means he's getting his funds from a bank machine. What is he using for a card? His bank card, license, and passport were stolen back in New Mexico, but he keeps getting money. We froze every account he has. I talked to his lawyer and broker and no one knows of any other account. Where is he getting the money?"

"That's a puzzle alright," Monroe conceded.

"If we could shut down the money he wouldn't get far. And where in hell is he going?" Harrison squeezed his hands into fists.

"You want to head south? I'll take you down in his country but, like I said, it's most likely a waste of time."

"Maybe so, but it's the only lead I have at the moment."

Chapter 10: Praise be the fishes in sandals!

Cari jumped at the knock on the bedroom door.

"How are you this fine morning?" Wilson asked as he came into the room.

"How am I? What the fuck?" She was pale and shaking.

"What's the matter? You look like you saw a ghost!" He stopped abruptly.

"I wish it were only a ghost! That I could handle. Didn't you look out in the driveway?"

"The driveway?" Wilson went to the window and drew back the curtain. "What am I supposed to be looking at?"

"The fucking cops, that's what!"

"There are no cops out there." He turned back toward her, a puzzled look on his face.

"What?" Cari sprang up and went to the window.

"Oh, I know what the problem is. Ted's oldest son, Collin, he's the sheriff around here. He stops in for coffee every morning and to check on his parents. I've been chatting with him. Catching up on old times."

"So, we are not surrounded by the police?"

"Surrounded? This isn't some old gangster movie." He waved at her dismissively.

"This guy knows you, this Collin?"

"Grew up together."

"And he knows you're on the run?"

"I expect everyone in the county knows. I'm getting famous." Wilson puffed out his chest.

"I thought you were already famous?"

"For writing children's books? In this county? You have got to be kidding. I'm finally getting some recognition in my old stomping grounds."

She jumped up and hugged Wilson, who stood uncomfortably, arms at his sides.

"Come down for some breakfast so we can get back on the road. Two more days and we'll be in Atlanta." Wilson gently pushed her back.

After breakfast, they said their goodbyes with hugs and then hit the road in the truck once more.

"Tell me, why is your family famous in this part of Missouri?" Cari asked.

"My father was sheriff here from way back before I was born."

"Sheriff? Now this makes more sense. You were a badass kid and had a cop for a father. That's why you're good at this escaping stuff. You had an inside track."

He looked at her. "You think I'm good at this?"

"Yes, I do. But don't go getting all full of yourself or I'll have to take you down a notch."

"I wouldn't want you to do that."

"And don't think you're going to be leading me into some barn any time soon!" Cari stated in mock anger.

"She led me in that barn, I'll have you know. I was an innocent victim," he protested.

"Oh pleeeease!" Cari stifled a laugh.

"It's true."

"Your father must have been good at his job. Why did he leave?"

"My father was an old fashioned cop. More frontier lawman. He didn't arrest a lot of people but would bust their heads. Most wouldn't do it again. He did a lot of favors for people and that's why so many still love him around here. Collin, for example."

"The sheriff?" Cari asked.

"Yes. He robbed a liquor store up in Jefferson City when he was sixteen. My father found out and caught up to him. Story is, he held Collin up by the throat with his feet dangling and told him he had three choices; go to jail, straighten out, or die right there."

"Oh fuck! He was something. I take it Collin went with choice number two?"

"Yes. Went back to school, then on to law enforcement. That's why I wasn't worried about him this morning."

"What happened? Why did your family leave here?" she asked.

"My father had a family to support and wasn't paid much. If he stopped you, and you handed him a twenty, he would forget about writing you a ticket. He also laid beatings on a few people. The FBI got after him but they didn't want to put him on trial, thought there would be trouble, and there would have been, so they cut a deal. He quit and moved out of state, they dropped the investigation."

"I was thinking, seeing you know everyone in this area, maybe we should stay here instead of going to Crete. We could get a place and get married."

"Married?" Wilson shot her a look. "You want to get married? Oh, wait, I see." He relaxed. "You almost had me again. I'm on to you. I say that's a good idea then you come out with 'just kidding.' I'm not falling for it this time."

"You're right, almost had you," she said half-heartedly. "Where to now?" she continued after a few minutes of sitting silent.

"Ah, I know this guy in Tennessee. We're friends. He has a cabin in the mountains and I know where the key is. It's usually stocked and he probably won't be around. We can stay there tonight and drive to Atlanta tomorrow." Wilson glanced at her.

"Sounds good." She was staring out the window.

Did I miss something? Wilson thought. *She must be kidding. It's a preposterous idea! Who ever heard of such a thing? I mean, she's not terrible. Sometimes not even half bad. And kinda funny. Not bad looking. And it's not like I've been too successful in my relationships up to now. She is different. Maybe she's just what I need.*

Detective Monroe pulled in next to the sheriff's office followed by Harrison in his car. They walked in and asked to see the sheriff.

"Collin Perkins, sheriff. What can I do for you gentlemen?" he asked, shaking their hands.

"Detective Monroe, state police, and this is Detective Harrison."

"Have you seen either one of these two around anywhere?" Harrison asked as he held out the pictures of James and Stone.

"Well I'll be!" Collin exclaimed. "That's little Willy James. We grew up together. But I don't know the woman."

"When was the last time you saw James?" Harrison asked.

"The last time? Oh, man, it must be thirty years if it's a day." He rubbed the back of his neck as if trying to recall a long lost memory.

"He isn't in the area as far as you know?" Monroe asked.

He shook his head, frowning. "He made some enemies when he was growing up and if he were to come back, someone would report it."

"You've seen the news?"

"Heard something about him being involved in a murder in Las Vegas. That true?"

"He's not a suspect in the murder, but is helping this woman to escape." Harrison touched her photo.

"Well, detectives, if I hear any reports of him in the county you'll be the first to know." Collin smiled.

"Thank you. We appreciate your assistance in this matter," Harrison said.

When they were back outside Monroe asked, "What do you think?"

"He's lying through his teeth." Harrison looked back toward the office.

"I hate to say it, but like I told you, you aren't going to get any help from people in this county. What now?" Detective Monroe asked Harrison.

"What's your best guess which way they headed?"

"Maybe south. If they need papers they might find someone in Memphis.

That's a specialized business to make fake passports that will get through security. I would think they have a better chance in Atlanta. At least there is a better flight hub there to get out of the country."

"How long to Atlanta from here?" Harrison asked.

"Two days, maybe less if you stick to the freeways."

"I believe they will stay on the back roads. Of course, if they don't think we know what they're driving, they could be careless and make a mistake," Harrison said, though he doubted James was likely to err.

"I already got the description and plates out on the wire." Monroe tried to reassure him.

"Maybe this is the break I've been waiting for. Thanks for all your help." Harrison shook his hand.

"Any time. Where you off to?" Monroe asked.

"Atlanta."

"Let me know how this all turns out."

"I will."

With that, Detective Harrison got in his car and headed to Atlanta.

"You've been uncharacteristically quiet this morning," Wilson observed.

"No more than usual." Her tone was downcast.

"Most of the time I can't get a word in." He smiled.

"Ha, ha. It's just that cop car spooked me this morning. I thought it was over and I would never see you a..." She trailed off, eyes wide.

"You were afraid you would never see me again?"

"No! I was going to say, I would never have to see you screw up again."

"No, you weren't."

"Shut up!" Cari folded her arms and stared out the window.

Wilson looked at her and smiled.

She threw him a glance. "Shut up!"

"Everything is going to work out," Wilson attempted to reassure her again.

Or maybe it was to reassure himself.

"Yeah, well, you're not the one facing prison."

"I am now."

"Oh right, and because of me! That makes me feel a whole lot better!"

"I still believe we're going to succeed. And look at the bright side, if I get you out successfully I have the material for an adventure thriller. If you get caught, I'll be there every day at the trial and can write a courtroom drama. And, if you're convicted, I'll visit you every day and write a prison story. You see, it's a win, win, win scenario!"

"You really are a lunatic! A win, win, win? With me on trial or in prison? How is that a win, win?"

He shrugged. "Well, I meant for me."

"I hate you! When do we get to Tennessee?"

"Entered the state when we crossed the Mississippi."

"Geography wasn't my thing."

"Any good stock tips for me?" Wilson attempted to chance the subject.

"Hire me to manage your portfolio. How much are you worth?"

"That's rather personal."

"Personal? We've been together nonstop for I forget how long. I think we're beyond personal. The point is, never mind. You're right, if you don't want to tell me it's okay. Forget I asked." Cari slumped down in the seat.

"I don't know exactly, but I bet my ex-wives do. At least their lawyers do. But I did sell the movie rights to the Willikers a few years ago for two and a half million."

"Holy hell! You sold the rights to the Willikers for two and a half mil?" *I could go a long ways on that. Wonder how much is left?* "I suppose I have to sign a pre-nup?" *Fuck! Why did I say that?*

"Man, you're sure interested in getting married, aren't you?" Wilson asked, still wondering if she was kidding.

"You're aware there is a law that prevents a man from testifying against his wife?"

"Now it makes sense!" Wilson slapped his leg.

"Though that may not apply to a lunatic."

It was slow going through the back roads but finally they reached the last stretch for the day as Wilson turned onto a narrow, paved road.

"Almost there," Wilson told her.

"What is this place?"

"A cabin a friend of mine built several years ago. I go there sometimes to write. He's a writer too." Wilson was busy watching for the turn.

"What's his name?" she asked.

"It's best you don't know."

"Why?"

"It's just best this way. There's the turn." Wilson pointed ahead on the right.

That's strange. Why won't he tell me the name? Maybe he's getting suspicious again. I'll have to bring up Baroque.

He pulled the truck into a narrow dirt driveway that was steep, uphill, and winding. At the end was a log cabin.

"Oh wow, this is nice. And no one is here?" Cari asked.

"No. I talked to him this morning and he said it's all ours."

They left the truck and Wilson hunted around in some flower pots on the front porch eventually finding the key. "Come on in."

The interior was decorated with deer skins and trophy heads on the walls and a bear skin on the floor in front of a fireplace.

"I hope you're not a member of PETA." Wilson laughed as she came in.

"Wow, this place is cool. Very romantic."

"Romantic? It's a hunting lodge."

Damn, why did I say romantic? she thought.

"There should be plenty of food and two bedrooms. You don't have to worry about your virtue," Wilson assured her.

"That was almost funny. I don't suppose there's a barn out back?" She touched his arm.

"I'm going out to see if I can get a signal on this phone. I got nothing in here. I want to call my guy in Atlanta and get him moving on this project."

"You going to fill me in on the plan?"

"When I come back. I'll know more after I talk to him."

"What kind of silly code name does he have?"

"His name is Lenny."

Cari scrunched up her face. "Not very imaginative."

"Be back shortly."

Cari began searching through the cupboards and soon found a bottle of wine and some candles. She put two glasses on the table and lit the candles.

"Maybe we can work on this virtue thing tonight," she said while admiring her work.

"Damn, damn, damn!" Wilson shouted as he slammed the door and threw the phone on the table.

"What's the matter? No reception? We can call tomorrow."

"He's dead!"

"Who's dead?" Cari asked.

"Lenny! My guy in Atlanta. The one who made the Jason Bourke papers." Wilson paced around the room, extremely agitated.

"What happened?"

"I called the number and his brother answered. Said Lenny got popped two weeks ago by another gang." He threw his arms up in exasperation.

"We'll find someone else."

"No, you don't understand. It took me almost a year to gain the trust of Lenny before he would deal with me. His brother isn't into that stuff and knows no one who is. This is it. I failed. End of the line." Wilson sat down and rested his head in his hands. He swayed slightly and was moaning.

"No, it isn't. And you haven't failed unless you quit. Look at what you've done so far! This has been impressive and I know you will figure out something. Everything will work out, you'll see. We'll find someone to make the passport. We can hold up in the city somewhere for as long as we have to. I'll make it to Crete."

He looked at her. "You sound like me."

"There's no need to be insulting!" she blurted out.

"Shut up." He put his head down again.

"You going to let Baroque get the best of you? He wouldn't quit. He would figure out something."

"Man, you in love with this guy?"

"You turned down my proposal. You had your chance. On to Atlanta?" she asked tentatively.

"On to Atlanta. I'm beat." He stood slowly and stretched. "I think I'll turn in. You care which bedroom you get?"

"No, either one is fine," Cari replied, disheartened.

"Goodnight. And thanks, Cari." Wilson gently took hold of her arms as he stood staring into her eyes.

"For what?" She gazed longingly back at him.

"The pep talk." Wilson smiled slightly, released his grip, and walked away. "Goodnight."

Cari blew out the candles.

"Good morning, sunshine. Sleep well?" Wilson asked her.

"No. Tossed and turned all night. You?"

"Been up most of the night planning."

"There's something I want to ask." She hesitated, looking at the floor. "Never mind. You'll think it silly."

"What is it? Out with it," Wilson said.

"I had this weird dream about Harrison."

"Harrison? I would have thought you were dreaming about Baroque." He turned away from her.

"No, be serious! I have a bad feeling this morning about the truck."

"About the truck?"

She nodded. "Is there any way we could get another vehicle to go to Atlanta today?"

"Jim has an old car out back. It looks bad but runs good."

"Would he mind if we borrowed it?" Cari asked.

"No. We'll leave the truck and if he shows up he'll know what I did."

"You must be good friends." *I wonder who this mystery man is?*

"Yes, we are. Okay, grab your stuff and let's hit the road. I want to get into Atlanta before dark. The only thing is, I have to find the keys."

Wilson searched through the cupboards and eventually found the keys, then left his in their place. It wasn't long before they were on the road again heading south.

"What's the plan now?" Cari asked.

"I know a lot of people in Atlanta and we have to find out who is loyal to me, then fish around for a name. These guys play rough so we have to be careful, especially when there's a lot of money involved."

"How do you plan to handle things after I'm gone?"

"You think I can't function without you, is that it? I did fine before you came along."

"No, that's not what—"

"Kidding!" he shouted triumphantly.

"Now you sound like me," Cari told him.

"No need to be insulting!"

"You're going to miss me when I'm gone." Cari smiled and nudged his arm.

"Can't wait to get rid of you."

"Get rid of me? What am I, trash to be thrown away?" she asked in mock indignation.

"Kidding!"

She smiled. "Okay, now you're annoying."

"You would be more convincing if you weren't smiling."

"Shut up!"

Detective Harrison was driving along the freeway when his phone rang.

"Harrison here... Hi Cap, what's up?... Somewhere in Tennessee... What?... How come no one found this before today?... A long paper trail, okay. So, James owns a cabin somewhere in Tennessee. Think he'll go there?... Okay, send me the location. I got GPS on this car. Maybe it's not far... I got to get off this interstate and program the GPS... Will do. Thanks, Cap."

Harrison pulled off at the next exit and punched the coordinates into the computer.

"Shit!" he exclaimed. "I'm less than forty miles from them! Maybe I'm no longer two steps behind." He felt a glimmer of hope.

"Turn left," the voice on the GPS instructed Harrison. "Your destination is two miles ahead on the right."

Harrison spotted the driveway and turned in. He was nervous with anticipation. Was this how it was going to end? He saw the truck beside the cabin and pulled up behind it to block the driveway. He sat for a minute, then got out and walked slowly around the vehicle. He peered in a cabin window but there was no movement. He wrapped on the door and tried the door knob but it was locked.

Harrison went around to the back of the cabin where he noticed fresh tire tracks. When examining them, he saw where the four tires had left impressions as though the vehicle had been sitting for some time.

"Damn!" he yelled. "Still two steps ahead! God damn it where are you James?"

This had become the most frustrating case of his long career. He pulled out his phone and dialed 911. Within twenty minutes uniformed officers and a detective were on scene.

"Detective Brian Peters," the detective introduced himself. "Tennessee State Police."

"Detective Harrison, Las Vegas."

"Long way from home, Detective," Peters said.

"Getting farther all the time. You familiar with the story?" Harrison asked.

"Yes. We had a tip they were headed this way. What's with this place?" Peters gestured to the house.

"Turns out James owns it. It was buried in some phony business he set up. Nothing illegal but made it difficult to find. My guys in Vegas came across it this morning and I was nearby heading to Atlanta. But the son of a bitch got away before I arrived. I think there was a car parked here because there are fresh tire tracks leading out. I would like to see inside."

"Going to take forever to get a warrant. Patrolman?" Peters called to one of the uniformed officers. "Check in those flower pots by the door for a key."

After a few minutes he yelled back, "Found it."

"Open the door then return to your car." Peters turned to Harrison, "The door appears to be open. We should investigate. There might have been a robbery, or someone inside could require assistance."

Harrison smirked. "Better safe than sorry."

They two men searched the cabin and found the truck keys but nothing else that would help Harrison.

"I'll check around to see if we can find out who was living here. Maybe the car was registered in their name," Detective Peters suggested.

"I'll leave you my cell number. Nothing for me to do here. I might as well continue on to Atlanta. Thanks for your help." Harrison shook his hand and went out the door.

"Good luck getting them," Peters called after him.

"Thanks. It seems luck is all I have. Bad luck."

Detective Harrison returned to his car.

"Where are we?" Cari asked rubbing the sleep from her eyes.

"Alabama, nearing the Talladega Mountains. We're about another hundred miles from Atlanta. Maybe three hours."

"What's that light on the dash?" Cari pointed to it.

"It's the check engine light. It's been on for a while." Wilson waved her off.

"Shouldn't you check the engine?"

Wilson shook his head. "It's probably a short or something in the wiring.

The car is fine. There's no need to worry unless the light starts flashing."

"Like it is now?" Cari informed him.

"Darn!"

"Watch the swearing! Are you going to check the engine? Is that why we're slowing down?" Cari wondered.

"We're slowing down because the car is dying. I'm going to pull off on the shoulder." Wilson glanced around for a place to park.

When they came to a stop he got out and opened the hood.

"Know anything about engines? In other words, did you learn anything about engines since our last breakdown?" Cari asked.

"Was this in your dream?" he asked while peering around under the hood.

"Shut up and fix the car."

"I can't fix it. We need to hitch." Wilson looked up and down the highway.

"Hitch to Atlanta?"

"We can find some place closer and get another car."

"You don't get it!" Cari pushed him.

"Get what?" He caught himself and stared at her.

"We are never getting to Crete! Or even Atlanta! And even if we do I can't get out of the country. It's over!" Cari sat on the side of the ditch beside the car.

"I sense a bit of negativity."

"Shut up!" she barked.

"Where is the girl who was all 'oh we're going to make it' last night?" Wilson stood looking down at her.

"Yeah well, that was last night. I now see things in the clear light of day and it SUCKS! Leave me here beside the road. You go on and save yourself."

"Don't be such a baby! Get up here this instant!" Wilson grabbed her arm.

"Fuck you!" She wrestled herself from his grip.

"Look, I had, wait, someone is coming. It's a van. Oh, you aren't going to believe this!" Wilson moved onto the road and waved at the approaching vehicle.

The van slowed and the passenger leaned out.

"Praise be the fishes in sandals!"

"You've got to be kidding!" Cari stood up. "The Man of God?"

"Praise be! It's a sign from above!" Wilson called out.

The giant painted face of Jesus began to move as the side door opened.

"We meet again," July called to them. "Need help?"

"Car broke down," Wilson said.

"Where you headed?" July asked.

"Atlanta."

"Us too. Big convention there this weekend, something to do with computers. All nerds but they got lots of cash. Plenty of young men to add to the congregation. Get in." July waved them in.

"Apparently Rose isn't going any farther so only I will–"

"Always joking around, this one," Cari said, coming around the front of the car.

"July, before we get in there's something I want you to know. We're not who we said we were. My name is Wilson James and this is Jessica Stone and we're on the run from the law. Well, she is. I'm just tagging along for the ride."

"Hey!" Cari glared at him.

"We know who you are. In fact, we knew the first time we picked you up. Everyone pretends to be something they're not, except for The Man of God. He's the only sane one amongst us. Get in. Don't worry, we don't judge. Our church is all inclusive." July patted the seat behind her.

As Wilson started to get in Cari grabbed his arm. "Ladies first."

"You're a lady now?" he asked in mock surprise.

Cari stuck her tongue out at him.

Wilson smiled and jumped in. July pulled the door closed and called to Ziggy, "All in, let's go."

"The cops stopped us in Oklahoma and were asking about you but no one said anything. I think we messed with them pretty good," July told them.

"The lions never lie with the bluebirds!" The Man of God added.

"Amen, brother," Wilson yelled out. "Thank you for that, but we have a big problem. Cari needs a passport to get out of the country and the guy I know in Atlanta who does it got himself killed. Would any of you know who might help us?"

"Can anybody help him?" July asked, looking around. "I wish we could but we don't travel in those circles," she added after a round of negative responses.

"We'll figure out something. Oh, there's one more thing I should tell you, we aren't married." Wilson could feel his face turning red.

July shrugged. "We have many in our congregation that are married and believe me, you two are in a better place than all of them. You just don't have the sense to realize it."

What does she mean by that? Wilson thought.

"We're going to stop up ahead. Ziggy knows a quiet place to camp for the night. We'll take you into Atlanta tomorrow if that's good for you?" July asked.

"Sounds perfect." Wilson said.

"What happened to the pink car?" Cat asked.

"It got spotted so we had to abandon Pinky," Cari informed her.

"Pinky? You named the car? That is so cool." Cat smiled.

The van slowed and they turned onto a narrow dirt road. Ziggy drove a few minutes then pulled into a clearing. July opened the door and everyone got out.

The little group set up a cook stove and started a campfire. They sat around the fire until all had finished eating.

"The lamb travels with the fishes," The Man of God spoke up.

"He wants you to go with him," July told Wilson.

"How do you do that?"

"It's a gift. He doesn't like to ask twice." She motioned for Wilson to leave.

"Sorry." Wilson followed The Man of God down the road until he looked back and decided they were far enough away from the rest.

"Here," he handed Wilson a small folded piece of paper.

"What's this? Looks like a phone number," Wilson said, staring at it in the fading twilight.

"When you get to Atlanta, call this number and tell the fellow that answers

The Man of God sent you. He'll get you what you need."

"I don't understand?"

"The passport for your lady along with anything else. He can do anything, for a price. And if they give you any trouble, tell 'em The Man of God will kick their sorry asses!"

"I don't know what to say." Wilson stared dumbfounded.

"Try thank you." He smiled.

"Of course, thank you. You don't have any idea how much this means to me."

"I know how much this means to you, but I wonder if you know." The Man of God placed his hand on Wilson's shoulder.

"I'm not sure what—"

"The ones most blind are those who choose not to see."

"Thanks for the advice. Mind if I ask you a question?"

"Shoot."

"Why the act?" Wilson asked.

"The crazy man never gets blamed, or asked to do anything. I ride around the country with three beautiful women. Why be sane?" He raised his arms toward the heavens.

"You don't have to worry about your secret, I will take it to my grave." Wilson put his hand over his heart.

"Good. I wouldn't want to have to put you there!" He stared menacingly at Wilson for a few seconds then burst out laughing. "We should return before they start talking about us."

"Praise be the ones that listen to the words of the bumblebee," The Man of God yelled out as they neared the group.

"Hallelujah!" Wilson responded.

Blankets were spread and the group turned in for the night.

"I'm beginning to like sleeping under the stars," Cari said.

"Wait till it rains."

"You're such a pessimist!"

Wilson leaned on one elbow. "Listen, I've got a connection in Atlanta for your papers. We're good to go. It won't be long before you're on a plane to Crete."

"Are you serious?" Cari sat up.

He nodded and gave her a half-hearted smile. "Better get some sleep. We've got a big day tomorrow."

As Wilson lay staring up at the stars, he thought, *what did he mean? Am I missing something? My relationships have been disasters. Besides, she isn't interested in me. All she does is insult and belittle me. She would prefer someone like Baroque!*

Almost there! Cari thought. *I'll put everything behind me and start new with Wilson. I mean, I will start over on my own! That's what I mean. I'll find another mark in Europe. Or I could stay in Greece until I find something better. Crete does sound nice.*

Detective Harrison received a call informing him they had tracked down the owner of the car James and Stone had taken from the cabin; that was the good news. The bad news was it had been found abandoned on the western edge of the Talladega forest in Alabama. It seemed to confirm that they were headed to Atlanta, but the trail was lost yet again. Harrison was becoming more frustrated with each passing day.

He met with authorities as soon as he arrived in Atlanta. James' and Stone's pictures were sent to the airport, train and bus stations, and every officer in the city had a copy with them as did taxi drivers. News stations were carrying their pictures and reporting on the story constantly. Harrison was growing more confident they wouldn't get away this time.

The van pulled up in front of a derelict motel in Atlanta, not far from the airport. July went in and got them a room, handed over the key, and they said tearful goodbyes.

"It's not as bad as I thought it would be." Cari tried to put a positive spin on the condition of the room. The drapes were shredded, stains of various sizes dotted the carpet, and a strong odor that was definitely not any cleaning product burned their nostrils.

"With any luck, we won't be here long," Wilson assured her.

It was just past 12:00 p.m.

Wilson's hands were shaking as he unfolded the piece of paper The Man of God had given him. He fumbled with the buttons on the phone and his stomach was full of butterflies as it rang. On the fifth ring a husky male voice answered.

"This is Bookman. I got this number from The Man of God. I need some merchandise. Can we meet?... There's a bar at the corner of Third and Melrose, know it?... Good. Three o'clock... Ball cap and whiskers, slim."

"Well?" Cari asked anxiously as he hung up the receiver.

"He'll be there. I got to go get some stuff. You lay low. Bolt the door and don't let anyone in," Wilson said.

"Not even you?"

He bent over and kissed her on the cheek, put on his cap, and left. "Won't be gone long."

That was strange, Cari thought, as she touched her cheek. *Definitely more than a friendly peck. But he doesn't seem interested in me. Am I missing something?*

Wilson returned in less than a half hour carrying a small bag. "Here, dye your hair again and apply some makeup. Be quick about it. We don't have much time."

"Red? Fuck! Why didn't you get blond?"

"Less conspicuous."

"Fine. So, what's the plan?" she asked.

"I need to talk to this guy first. Now color. We don't have much time."

When Cari emerged from the bathroom, Wilson exclaimed, "Holy hell!"

"Don't swear."

"You may not use makeup, but you did one great job with it. I would hardly recognize you. And with that red hair. Man, you look great. Not like yourself at all."

"What's that supposed to mean?" Cari stood, hands on hips glaring at him.

"No, I didn't mean it like that, it's—"

"Kidding!" and burst out laughing.

Wilson posed her and took a few pictures with a cheap camera he had bought. At 2:50 p.m. he hurried out of the room and down the street. It was nearly 3:00 when he entered the darkened bar that was practically empty. Wilson moved to the back and sat at a corner table where he could watch the door. He was getting nervous when the guy still hadn't shown by 3:20. Finally, a large bald man who had a long scar down his right cheek walked in and stood peering around the room. Wilson caught his eye and nodded. The man went over and sat down opposite.

"Bookman?" the man asked.

"Yes. You?"

"Francis. How do you come to know The Man of God?" He settled in a chair beside Wilson.

"Long story. He said you could supply me."

"What do you want?"

"Three passports and a girl."

"I ain't no pimp."

"Not that kind of girl." Wilson held up the camera and flashed the pictures of Cari. "I need a girl who looks like her, only with black hair."

"Could probably do that. It would take a few days." Francis replied, studying the image.

"I need one passport for this girl and two for the girl you supply. Two different names and also one return airline ticket to Bogota, Colombia and another to Athens, Greece. The girl must purchase the ticket to Bogota personally from a travel agent. The other needs to be purchased online so it can't be traced. And I need everything by tomorrow afternoon with flights both leaving tomorrow evening."

"Impossible! Will take at least a few days." Francis leaned back.

"Tomorrow. How much?" Wilson pressed him.

"By tomorrow? Ten. For ten I can probably do it by tomorrow. If I can find a girl. What happens to the girl in Bogota?"

"She vanishes when she steps off the plane then returns under another passport later."

"I can't make no promises." Francis shook his head.

"Ten plus another five if they fly out tomorrow night. And I need a driver to take my girl to the airport."

"All in advance." Francis held his hand out.

"Five now, five when you hand me the passport and ticket, and the balance when I know she's safe."

"Forget it!"

Wilson stood up and started to leave.

"Okay! You got the five?" the big man asked.

Wilson patted his pocket, then sat back down.

"I need this picture." Francis pointed at the picture.

"Keep the camera."

"Bogota for my girl. Athens for yours."

"That's it. And friend, if you screw me over..." Wilson glared at him, though inside he was a nervous wreck.

"Meet me here at 2:00 tomorrow afternoon," Francis said.

The big man got up and left. Wilson went in the bathroom and stared at himself in the mirror. "This is real! Suck on that, Baroque!" After he stopped shaking, he headed out for more supplies and returned to the room.

"You look like you saw a ghost," Cari observed when he came in the room.

"A big one. Got you some stuff." He dumped several items on the bed.

"Stuff?" Cari was gingerly pawing through the pile.

"A suitcase and purse. It will look suspicious if you show up at the check-in counter without luggage. And bought you some clothes from a secondhand store."

"Ahh, what's this?" Cari asked. She had looked in one of the bags and was holding a coil of rope and a roll of duct tape. "I'm not into the kinky stuff."

"That's not to tie you up, it's to tie me up."

"Again, not into the kinky stuff!"

"It won't look good when the police find me and I'm sitting around this room. If you kidnaped me you wouldn't do that. You are going to tie me up and gag me before you leave." Wilson indicated the material Cari held.

"In that case, I should have bought this tape days ago!"

"Still not funny."

"I got to admit, I'm really nervous," she said.

"So am I, but we're nearly there." He gently touched her arm.

"Care to elaborate on the plan?" Cari asked.

"For your part I should have a passport and ticket to Athens for you by tomorrow afternoon for a flight out later in the evening."

"Tomorrow? I'm leaving tomorrow?"

"Is this a problem?"

"No, it's just that I thought we would have more time..." She became quiet and sat on the bed.

"The sooner you leave the better. I don't expect Harrison is too far behind. Anyway, there will be someone to take you to the airport, then you're on your own to Athens. I'm going to arrange for a friend of mine to meet you at the airport and drive you to the Piraeus."

"What's that?" She stared at the floor.

"The port of Athens. He'll put you on a ferry to Crete that travels overnight and arrives early the next morning. Stephanos will meet you at the ferry. He's the shepherd on my place. He will take you home."

"Home?" She looked up at him.

"Your new home." He smiled.

"And what about you?" Cari asked.

"In the morning when the maid comes to make up the room she will find me tied up, call the police and then, well... But it doesn't matter because by that time you will be on Crete."

"It matters to me!" *Shit, I can't believe I said that!*

Wilson looked at her. *Am I missing something?* "Don't worry. I have the best lawyers and a fertile imagination."

"Fertile alright, bullshit! God, they're going to put you away forever and it's all my fault!" She ran her hands through her hair and paced the room.

"Look, I'm a big boy. I knew what I was getting into, I just didn't know I would—never mind. I knew what I was getting into. Don't feel guilty. And besides, it seemed like a good idea at the time! They're going to have to be pretty smart to outsmart me. I'm like a coyote, the trickster."

She came over and hugged him. "I hope you're right, coyote." *Stop it!* She pulled back. *I don't have feelings for him! It's pity. That's it! I feel sorry for him because they are probably going to lock him up. But I'll be free, that's what matters. Focus! Don't be a sap like with Ralph.*

"Ah, you okay?" he asked, looking down at her.

"Fine! Perfect! It's almost over. You'll soon be rid of me. That's what you want, right?"

"Ah, yes. I mean, I want to succeed. For the book. Yes, for the book." *Don't be a sap! Soon she'll be gone. Maybe she'll take off when she gets to Greece and I'll never see her again. It's for the best.*

They dined on yet another take-out dinner in their motel room.

"I won't miss this," she said, trying to force down more greasy fries.

"You'll like the food in Greece. A friend of mine used to go every year and always said it was to cleanse himself with their food and lifestyle. You'll like it there. Better try to get some sleep. I've got to call Athens but must wait until midnight."

"Isn't it risky calling there? They can check phone records. I have seen a few episodes of CSI."

"I still have the burner phone Chris gave me." Wilson pulled it from a pocket and caressed it. "After I make this call I'm going to break it into pieces and flush it down the toilet along with Jason Bourke's passport and driver's license."

"What about the bank card? Shouldn't you destroy that too?"

"I have plans for that."

Cari rolled her eyes. "Oh God, another plan."

"You were nicer when I first met you." He glanced at her and frowned.

"I was pointing a gun and attempting to mug you."

"Like I said..." He laughed.

"You're still not funny. I'm going to bed." Cari lay on the bed but tossed and turned.

Wilson couldn't relax either. He paced back and forth in the small room continuously checking his watch. He couldn't even enjoy an episode of CSI he came across on the TV. It would be a long night.

Cari had drifted in and out of sleep and thought she was dreaming when she heard a strange language coming from the bathroom. Wilson emerged.

"What was that?" she asked him, sitting up.

"Talking to my friend in Athens."

"Sounded weird."

"I was speaking Greek to him."

"You speak Greek? That is so cool. I'm still learning new things about you. Does your friend speak English?" Cari asked.

"No, but don't worry. He'll be waiting at the airport in Athens holding a sign that says Blondie."

"Oh, real funny." She frowned at him.

"He'll drive you to the port. You'll have to wait a while because the ferry doesn't leave until after 11:00 p.m. You can get a room and sleep on board. It arrives around 6:00 the next morning. My friend is contacting Stephanos and he'll have a sign that also says Blondie. As soon as I know your flight number I have to call him back with your arrival time," Wilson explained.

"How close do you think he is?" Cari asked.

"Who?"

"Harrison."

"It depends. If they somehow found the cabin and truck they know we left in a car. And if they find the owner, they have the license. And if they have that, they probably found the car, which would mean they have figured out we're headed to Atlanta. Which means they are going to be watching the airport closely."

"You're such a ray of sunshine!"

"But that's good."

"Good? Still a lunatic!" Cari shook her head.

"They are going to be looking for us, not you alone. And with your makeup and red hair, I believe you'll slip past them. And if not we have a decoy."

"A decoy?"

"A girl that looks like you and has black hair who is also going to be in the airport, but headed somewhere else. If she makes it through, you're golden. They will track her to South America and not even consider Europe. And if she's caught, it will distract them long enough for you to get out, like a magician's trick."

"I hate to admit this, but that sounds like a brilliant plan."

"As good as Baroque could have come up with?"

"Better! What time is it?"

Wilson stood a bit taller. "Just after 2:00 a.m. Twelve hours until I meet the guy again."

"Let's watch some TV. I may not see any English shows for a long time. Does Stephanos speak English?" Cari asked as she switched on the television.

"I don't know."

Wilson had nearly worn grooves in the carpet from pacing so much. Finally, it was time to head back to the bar.

"You need to be prepared to leave as soon as I get back," he told Cari.

"It won't take me long to get ready."

Wilson hurried along the street back to the bar. What would happen if Francis hadn't come through? He might have taken off with the five thousand Wilson had given him. Then what? Or they might have to wait longer. Wilson sat at the same table. A few minutes after 2:00 p.m. Francis came in and sat down.

"Get everything?" Wilson asked.

The man pulled out two brown envelopes and handed them to Wilson. He slid out the contents of one.

"Natalia Spencer," he read the name on the passport. "She looks like my girl. No question about that. Return ticket to Bogota. And this other one, Nancy Collins. Looks good."

Wilson replaced the material and opened the other. Looking at Cari's picture as a redhead he read the name, "Cynthia Matthew. And a return ticket to Athens. What's this?"

"Driver's license. Sometimes they ask for another ID. There's some shit going down in the city and they're watching the airport."

"Very thorough. I'll remember you in the future." Wilson smiled.

"Boss says the price is twenty five for everything."

Wilson frowned. "I don't like price increases after we make a deal."

"This was difficult. You don't like the terms I walk."

"Another ten now. The balance when I know she's safe. If she doesn't make it, no more."

"They won't like that." Francis leaned menacingly across the table.

"That's the way it is," Wilson said, staring him down.

"Got the ten?" he asked.

"A driver?" Wilson asked as he counted money under the table.

"Pick her up at 3:00 p.m. Where do I tell him?" He relaxed and leaned back.

"You know the No-tel Motel?"

"Yeah."

"Room 9. Here's the balance. We good?" Wilson handed him an envelope.

"We're good. Three o'clock. Tell her to be ready."

"Nice doing business with you." Wilson stood.

"I don't need to tell you what happens if that balance don't come. Even The Man of God can't help you."

"I always pay my debts."

"That's a good policy, Bookman." Francis got up and walked out.

Wilson slid the passport, driver's license, and ticket in his pocket and went to the door. As he was about to step out a police cruiser was coming down the street. He stepped back in the bar where he could watch it drive past then hurried back to the motel.

"We're good to go!" Wilson told her, a big smile of relief on his face. "Here, a new name to learn."

"Cynthia Matthew," Cari read the passport.

"I can call you Sin. Appropriate, don't you think?" Wilson chuckled.

"Ha, ha. This looks good." She continued to study the documents.

He looked at his watch. "Get ready. The car will be here at 3:00 to take you to the airport."

"You called a taxi?" Cari looked up at him.

"To risky. This is a private car service."

"How private?"

"Even they don't know they're a car service." Wilson winked.

"That makes me feel better," she said sarcastically.

"Your flight leaves at 6:45 p.m.," Wilson informed her.

"Tonight?"

"That's right. By tomorrow morning you'll be in Crete."

"What's the driver's license for?" She held it up.

"Second ID for insurance. I need to shave and you have to tie me up. You ready?"

"Going to put on some makeup."

Wilson took out the scissors he had purchased and began cutting off his beard. *Won't be needing this anymore.*

After Wilson had finished he swept the whiskers into a pile on the bureau. Next, he called Athens, informed his friend of Cari's arrival time, and then broke up the phone. He went through the room to make sure everything incriminating was gone and his adrenaline was flowing when Cari came out of the bathroom.

"Here, this is all I have left on me," Wilson told her as he held out a roll of cash. "You'll need some money. You can change it to Euros in Athens."

"I will pay you back everything, including the twenty," she said, accepting the money.

"All you have to do now is tie me to this chair. I put it in front of the TV. It's going to be morning before they find me."

"Are you sure about this? It seems a bit, ah, extreme. And a really stupid idea!"

"We went over this. It has to be done. Come on, start tying, and don't leave the knots loose. They can't think I did it to myself." Wilson seated himself, hands behind the chair.

A fucking lunatic, she thought. *But he's my lunatic. Stop it! It's almost over and then I'm done with him!*

"Ow! That's too tight!" he complained.

"Don't be a baby!" *He is kinda pathetic. He needs someone like me to look after him. If he ever makes it to Greece.*

"But you're cutting off my circulation!" He moved his hands in a vain attempt to loosen the rope.

"Alright, I'll loosen them a bit. You're such a baby." *I suppose I could hang out in Crete for a while and wait for him. He might be worth it. As long as he never figures out the truth.*

"Now put a piece of duct tape over my mouth," he instructed her after she finished tying him to the chair.

She hesitated. "You think this is a good idea?"

"They'll ask why I didn't yell. You need to put on the tape."

"Okay," she replied, shaking her head. "I hope you know what you're doing."

"Trust me, I have a plan."

Cari cut a piece of tape and stood in front of him. Before she placed it over his mouth she leaned down and moved close. Their lips were nearly touching when there was a knock at the door.

"That's the driver. You need to go!" he told her.

"Yes, okay, it's just I wanted to say–"

"Put on the tape and get out of here!" Wilson ordered.

He knocked again. Cari stuck the tape over Wilson's mouth and went to the door.

"Who is it," she called through the door.

"Driver."

She opened the door against the chain.

"You the package?" the driver asked.

"Yes. I'll get my suitcase."

"Need help?"

"No." She closed the door and went back to Wilson. "I want–"

"Ummm." He motioned toward the door.

She took his head in her hands, leaned down, and kissed him on the forehead. Then she placed her head on his. Finally, she moved away, turned on the TV, grabbed her purse and suitcase, closed the lights, and went out shutting the door behind.

When Cari approached the car, the driver opened the back door for her and she noticed a gun under his jacket. He closed the door as she settled in the seat.

I wonder if I'll ever see him again, she thought, and wiped a tear from her cheek.

Detective Harrison was on his way to the airport to join the many officers already watching for the pair. If they were going to try and fly out tonight he wanted to be there to put an end to their party. This was it! He could feel it! Tonight, he would have them! The net was tightening.

The ride to the airport was uneventful. The driver pulled into the departure area and stopped by the sign for Cari's airline, got out, and ran around to open the door. She stepped out, grabbed her suitcase, and thanked the driver. She was extremely nervous as she walked up to the auto-check-in. She set down her suitcase and dug out the passport.

Cynthia Matthew, she said over and over in her mind.

Cari placed the passport into the slot but nothing happened. She pulled it out, checked to be sure it was in the right way, and tried again. Still nothing.

Oh fuck, she thought, *the damn thing is no good!*

"Problem?" an attendant asked. Cari jumped and almost dropped the passport. "Sorry, didn't mean to startle you. Having a problem?"

"It doesn't seem to be working," Cari stuttered.

"We've been having trouble all afternoon with these machines. Come over to the counter and I'll check you in. You have a ticket?"

"Yes, it's, ah..." She was digging in her purse.

"Don't worry, I only need your passport."

Cari followed her to the counter. Her mouth was so dry she could barely speak. The woman took her passport.

"Any checked luggage?"

"One bag," Cari replied.

"Place it there," she told her and pointed to the side of her station.

Cari set the case beside the counter. That was when she noticed the flyer taped to the side of the next station; her and Wilson's pictures were on it.

"Here's your boarding pass, miss. Miss?"

"What? Oh, sorry." Cari straightened up and took the document.

"You had better go directly to security. There's something going on today and it takes longer than normal to get through." The attendant indicated the direction.

"Thanks"

Cari collected her passport and boarding pass and went in the direction of security. She couldn't think. She wished Wilson was with her. She noticed many police in the halls of the terminal and more at security. Entering the line, she stood, looked down and tried to act calm. Out of the corner of her eye she could see pairs of police officers walking amongst the passengers and asking for their identification. She realized it wasn't random when they approached a man who looked vaguely similar to Wilson.

"Passport and boarding pass!" an officer ordered Cari. She jumped again. "Sorry miss, didn't mean to frighten you."

"It's alright officer," she whispered

"Passport and boarding pass, please," he repeated.

"Oh, yes." Cari handed both to him and he glanced at them then passed them on to his partner.

"Do you have another ID?"

"Ah, I have a driver's license."

"May I see it?"

"Of course." Cari dug into her purse and pulled out the license. Her hand was shaking.

"Cynthia Matthew. What do you do for a living?"

"I'm a writer."

Cari could see his partner comparing her passport photo to her real picture on the printed flyer.

"And the purpose of your trip?" the officer asked.

"Vacation."

"Where are you going?"

"Athens."

"Know anyone there?"

"No, I've never been. I hear it's nice."

"Couldn't say. Enjoy your vacation," he said, and handed her back her papers.

Her heart was beating so fast she could barely breathe and thought her legs would give out at any moment. She moved robotically as the line inched forward.

"Passport and boarding pass, miss. Miss?"

"Oh, sorry, here." Cari handed them over.

The woman scanned both and gave them back. "Next!" she called.

Cari moved to the x-ray scanner and placed her things in a basket.

"Take your shoes off," one of the security guards told her.

She placed them in another basket and moved through the metal detector. Then she saw him. Detective Harrison was talking to a security guard beyond the metal detectors and directly in front of her. She couldn't breathe.

"You're clear, miss. Move ahead, please."

Stop staring at him! Cari berated herself and lowered her gaze.

She grabbed her bag and walked past him.

"Miss! Oh miss! Wait!" someone called to her from behind.

Cari froze.

"Your shoes." The attendant smiled as she handed them to her.

"Thank you," Cari replied.

Harrison was standing so close to her she could hear him talking to the guard. Cari had to force herself to move forward. Walking in her sock-feet she stopped next to a post and hurriedly put her shoes back on, not daring to turn back and see where he was. After, she walked as casually as she could toward her gate. Suddenly she heard the "beep, beep" of one of the personnel carriers coming behind her and stepped out of the way. She turned her back to the carrier. Out of the corner of her eye she could see the white shock of Harrison's hair as he disappeared down the corridor. Looking up she saw a sign for the toilets and rushed in to one of the stalls and threw up.

Once she felt better, she continued along the corridor. It seemed police were everywhere. She found her gate, sat down, and glanced at the clock. Less than an hour before boarding. She went to a stand at the edge of the waiting room and bought some water and a magazine and sat pretending to read. A pair of officers were strolling amongst the passengers. She attempted to focus on the magazine as they advanced toward her.

"Excuse me, could we see your papers?" one of the officers asked Cari.

"Certainly, officer." Cari kept her head down as she searched for them in her purse. "Here they are." She started to hand them over but dropped them. "Oh, I'm sorry!"

"No problem, miss. I got 'em," the officer replied as she picked them up. Her partner held the flyer of her and Wilson. They looked at both then at her. "Traveling alone?"

"Yes."

"Thank you. Enjoy your flight," the officer said as she handed back the papers.

"Thank you," Cari replied, and thought she was going to be sick again.

Wilson's nose itched but there was little he could do about it. Cari had tied the ropes fairly tight, but he didn't want to say anything a second time. *At least I don't have to listen to her berating me. Or praising Baroque! Wait until he reads my novel. Then he'll know what good writing is! He's such a hack! I miss her.*

"Welcome to Toon Time TV. At this time, we're proud to present a Willikers marathon. Nothing but Willikers episodes for the next twenty hours!" the television blared.

Nooo! Wilson screamed to himself. *Not the Willikers! Anything but them! Anything! Fuck no! Oh, oh, I'm starting to sound like her!*

"Seen anything yet?" Detective Harrison asked the guard behind the metal detector.

"Nothing, Detective. You think they will try to get through here tonight?"

"I wish I knew." He shrugged.

"Are they traveling together?"

"As far as we know. They have stuck together the whole way and it seems likely they'll remain together." Harrison scanned the passing faces.

"This is the Wilson James that created the Willikers?" the guard asked.

"Same one."

"What caused him to go bad?"

"Wish I knew." Harrison perked up when he spied a man with similar features to Wilson, then sighed upon realizing it wasn't him.

"Here's your ride, Detective. You can check all the gates now." The guard was indicating a personnel carrier stopped a few feet away.

"Thanks." He left the guard and approached his ride.

Detective Harrison brushed past a red-haired woman who was leaning on a post putting on her shoes, and then got on the carrier. The driver pulled out and headed down the corridor.

I don't know why it is, Harrison thought, *but I have a feeling I'm close.*

The knock on the door startled Wilson awake.

"Housekeeping," a woman's voice called from outside the door.

I wonder if it's daylight, he thought.

Another knock. "Housekeeping!"

Wilson heard a key in the lock and the door opened. The woman switched on the light, saw Wilson, screamed, backed out, and slammed the door shut!

"Ummm," he mumbled.

Several minutes went by before he heard the key in the lock again. When the door opened this time, there were two women. The older one went over to Wilson and motioned toward the tape.

"Want me to pull it off?" she shouted.

"Mmmm," he nodded.

She grasped one corner. "Ready?" still shouting.

He nodded, she pulled.

"Owww! Sweet Jesus that hurt!" The combination of the tape and newly shaven skin made it much worse than he had anticipated.

"Oh mia!" The woman crossed herself several times. "I'm sorry!"

"It's okay! I'm fine. Not a baby at all! And you can stop shouting. There's nothing over my ears!"

"What?"

"Nothing. Listen carefully, I am Wilson James the author. I was kidnaped in Las Vegas by Jessica Stone who left me like this last night. Call the police immediately!"

"The police?" the woman asked.

"Yes, right away."

The two women looked at one another, shrugged, and headed for the door.

"Could you untie me? I really have to–," the door slammed shut, "pee!"

"Okay, probably should have gone before she tied me up." Wilson glanced around the room and struggled against the ropes, to no avail.

About fifteen minutes later the door opened once more and another woman came in. She wore a name tag that read "manager."

"Good morning, sir." She was smiling.

"Good morning. I'm Wilson James the author and–"

"The Wilson James who created the Willikers?" she asked.

"Yes, and I have–"

"My grandchildren love your books. Except for the last two. What stinkers!" She waved her hand in front of her nose.

"Yes, thank you for reminding me. Listen, could you call–"

240

"I gave one for Christmas last year. She started to read it then threw it out in the yard. I think the dog buried it. And those are expensive!" She rubbed her finger and thumb together in front of Wilson's face.

"My apologies. Could you call the police?" he asked again.

"Do you really want me to do that, Mr. James? Because we find at least one a week like this."

"What are you talking about?"

"My girls, they find men tied up like this. You see, a man comes here with a young lady as his 'date.' She says it would be better for him if she tied him up first, then she robs him and leaves. But most of the time the man is naked." She was shaking her head.

"No, no, no! It was nothing like that! No date! I was kidnaped in Vegas and tied up so the woman could make her getaway. Please, call the police!"

"Okay, Mr. James, I will call. But I hope you know what this is going to mean to your reputation, you being a children's author and all. Even though you're no good now. I will call." The manager headed for the door.

"Thank you. And could you please untie me because I really have to–" the door slammed shut, "PEE!"

Another episode of the Willikers began.

"Oh, come on! This must be the third time you've shown this episode! Give me a break!" he shouted at the TV. "Definitely did not think this through!"

It was a half hour before the door opened again and a uniformed police officer came in.

"Oh, thank God, officer. I'm Wilson James and–"

"Wait! You're Wilson James? The author?"

"Yes, could you–"

"Every cop in the city is looking for you! And I found you! This is my lucky day." The officer grabbed Wilson by the shoulders and was beaming. "Excuse me, I got to call this in. Don't go anywhere." He ran for the door.

"Could you untie me? I really have to–" the door slammed shut, "pee. Definitely did not think this through! Could you at least change the TV channel?"

he yelled at the closed door.

It was another hour before a detective arrived at the room.

"Mr. James, I presume?" he asked when he entered.

"That's right. Could you–"

"I'm Detective Ehrenberg. A lot of people are looking for you." He stood staring down at Wilson.

"Could you please untie me? I really have to pee." Wilson was squirming on the chair as much as the ropes allowed.

The detective walked around Wilson looking at the ropes.

"Sure, why not. She did this to you? That Stone woman?"

"Yes."

"Know where she went?" He knelt down and began unfastening the ropes.

"No idea."

"There you go," the detective said after untying him.

Wilson jumped up and rushed to the counter, grabbed the remote, and changed the TV channel. Then he hurried into the bathroom. When he returned to the chair and sat down, the detective shut the room door and pulled up another chair directly in front of Wilson.

"Between you and me, you haven't committed any offences in Atlanta. I'm not sure what you did in Las Vegas, but it would not look good on me, or the department, if we arrested a beloved, okay, formally beloved, children's author who made Atlanta his home for many years. And it would save me a lot of paperwork. But there is a Detective Harrison from the Vegas police who is very interested in you. Here's the deal; if you talk to him, and return to Vegas without a fight, I won't charge you with anything. But you got to promise not to run again."

"I haven't done anything wrong here, or in Vegas, or anywhere else. I have no problem returning to Vegas if Detective Harrison so desires. And you have my word, I will not go anywhere. At the moment, I have no papers and no money. It will take me some time to contact my lawyer and get things back to normal. If the department could put me up in a hotel for a few days, I'm sure when this is over, I could find a large donation for the policeman's brotherhood.

And pay back the charges for the hotel."

The detective smiled. "I'll have an officer drive you."

"Thank you. Your kindness will not be forgotten." Wilson continued to rub his sore wrists.

"Ah, perhaps we shouldn't mention this to Detective Harrison. Seems like a high strung fellow."

"It's between us." Wilson winked.

"I'll get that ride for you."

There was a knock on the door. Wilson went over and opened it.

"Detective Harrison, what a pleasant surprise. Please, come in."

"Mr. James, thank you." Harrison came in and looked around the posh suite. "Not exactly the type of digs I expected to see you in."

"Something with bars, perhaps?"

Harrison glared at him. "Don't get too comfortable, Mr. James."

"Please, sit. Would you like a drink?" he asked.

"No, thank you. Where is she?" Harrison settled onto the couch.

"You refer to Jessica, Ms. Stone."

"Quit the bullshit, James. You're wanted for aiding and abetting. And don't give me that kidnaped shit. I heard how they found you bound. Cute trick but I ain't buying." He wagged his finger at Wilson.

"You want the story, is that it?" Wilson sat across from him.

"I want the truth and you in prison for a very long time." Harrison scowled.

"At least we agree on the first point. This is what happened. Do you want to record it?"

"I'll keep notes." Harrison pulled out a pad and pen.

"Very well. Miles Jacoby hired a hitman to eliminate Brentwood. He had planned this, but when Ms. Stone showed up, he saw an opportunity. He knew she was desperate and he offered her a lot of money to let him 'frame' her for the murder. He would get her out of the country and you would believe she had

243

committed the murder and he was off the hook. He would take over the company and be very rich."

"Really? And where do you fit in?" Harrison was skeptical.

"Wrong place, wrong time. I met Ms. Stone one evening and felt sorry for her. She saw me as a patsy, followed me back to the hotel, and forced me to help her. I still felt sorry for her, and half believed she was innocent, but the real reason I went along was purely selfish."

"Let me guess."

"Oh no, Detective, not what you're thinking. I saw this as an opportunity to research a book. I stayed with her as a reporter." Wilson admired how calm and collected he was keeping himself as he spun the tale.

"You went along for the story? You expect me to believe that?" He stared at Wilson, trying to intimidate him.

"It's the truth." He raised his right hand.

"It's a load of bullshit. You come back to Vegas with me and we'll let the judicial system decide if you're guilty or not." Harrison stood abruptly.

"But there's something else. Wonder where she got the money to travel cross country?"

"The thought crossed my mind."

Wilson stood and went over to a desk, opened a drawer, picked up something, and handed it to the detective.

"It's a bank card in the name of Jason Bourke. What's this about? Who's Jason Bourke?" Harrison inquired.

"Miles Jacoby. He gave her this card and the pin number. Apparently, from what I could deduce, this is some kind of secret account he had. Trace that card and I am willing to bet it leads to Jacoby. You've spent your time following false scents, a decoy. Trace this card and it will lead you to the real killer. I mean, Jacoby didn't pull the trigger, but those types never do, am I right?" Wilson folded his arms and leaned on the corner of the desk.

"How did you get the card?"

"We had been using it, and she often sent me for the cash, but I knew you would never believe what happened, or have any evidence on Jacoby. Last night when she was in the bathroom I swiped the card and stuck it in the bottom of my shoe just before she tied me up."

"And why did she tie you up?" He moved close to Wilson.

"I don't think she ever completely trusted me and wanted to make her getaway before I could go to the cops." Wilson stood his ground.

"Know where she went?" Harrison asked.

"No, but I did see the name on her fake passport."

"Really? And that would be?"

"Natalia Spencer. I only caught a glimpse of it but I'm positive that's the name she was traveling under. Check departing passengers from two nights ago to see if I'm telling the truth."

"What was that name?"

"Natalia Spencer."

The detective wrote it down. "Mind if I use your phone?"

"By all means, Detective. I'll be in the other room."

"Don't run off."

Wilson smiled and left. He could hear a muffled conversation in the other room. When the detective hung up the phone, he returned.

"Everything okay?" Wilson asked.

"It seems some officers questioned a dark haired woman fitting the description of Stone two nights ago at the airport, but she seemed to check out, and they were positive she wasn't Stone. They think she was going to Colombia."

"Colombia? No extradition treaty, if I'm correct. Tough break. When are we going back to Vegas? I have to wait a while because I no longer have any identification papers, but my lawyer is working on it. Speaking of lawyers, should I have one meet me at the airport in Vegas?"

"You sit tight and don't wander off anywhere. I need to return and sort through this first. But don't go anywhere!"

"I won't. I have a book to write. And Detective?"

"What is it?"

"No hard feelings?" Wilson was is a cheery mood.

"Once you're behind bars, they'll be no hard feelings. Until then..."

The detective went to the door. Wilson opened it for him and bowed slightly. Harrison stopped abruptly and turned back to Wilson.

"I damn well better come off good in that book, for your sake, James!" he growled. With that Detective Harrison departed.

Wilson sat in a restaurant in the small town of Kato Gouves on the north shore of Crete. A light breeze was blowing across the Mediterranean Sea, causing the ripples to sparkle like stars in the night sky. He had just arrived on the island and stopped in at one of his favorite places for lunch. Nearly a year had passed since that last night together in Atlanta. Detective Harrison had continued digging into Miles Jacoby, but had not been able to connect him to the account of Jason Bourke. Under further questioning, the 'witness' who had identified Jessica running from Brentwood's room, admitted to being paid, but would not reveal by whom. With Brentwood's company held in legal limbo, and all assets frozen, Jacoby had sought protection by the police from the mobsters to whom he owed large gambling debts. In exchange, he had agreed to become an informant and enter the witness protection program. Wilson was never charged with any crime.

Jessica had sent a large anonymous donation to a gas station in a small town in Texas, and could well afford it because she had increased Wilson's wealth by a considerable amount. She had decided to remain on Crete, at least until she could find a better mark.

And the book? Wilson had finally drawn up the courage to sit down and write it, thanks mostly to Jessica, who had given him the confidence. A newfound confidence he was in Crete to capitalize on.

Wilson heard the whine of a motor scooter coming along the road that ran between the restaurant and the beach. It stopped in front of the restaurant and the driver parked in the road.

Must be a Greek, Wilson thought.

The driver got off and removed her helmet. Shoulder length blond hair rolled out. Her back was to Wilson as she placed the helmet on the seat, but he knew. She turned around and there was no mistaking that smile. Wilson stood and stepped out the side door.

"Never know who you'll run into on Crete, eh Blondie?"

Cari walked up to him and stood momentarily staring into his eyes. Without a word she grabbed him and planted a kiss on his lips. The world seemed to pause, nothing existing but her lips on his. Wilson wrapped his arms around her and kissed her back with an intensity he had never experienced before in his life.

The End

Postscript

Baby-Boy decided to go legit and leave the forged papers business. He purchased a trucking company that he now uses to smuggle drugs in from Mexico. Rattler is still looking out for Federales. She got another dog. Agnes continues to drive people around northeastern New Mexico to supplement her disability pension and recently married husband number eight. "Eight's the charm!" she stated.

Wilson sent a substantial check to his cousin Chris to repair the old house. Chris promptly purchased large quantities of beer, marijuana, and sides of pork. The party lasted several days and was dedicated, appropriately and rightly so, to Wilson. July, Cat, Moonstone, Ziggy, and The Man of God continue to spread the word of the church of the, well, you know what it is, as they travel around the country. Detective Harrison delayed his retirement by a year to continue working on the murder of Ralph Brentwood. The case remains open. Wilson sent him an advance signed copy of the book that he dedicated to Cari (a name she made up).

The book was well reviewed but sales were slow, eclipsed by the latest action thriller by John Baroque. It didn't matter to Wilson because his new Willikers book shot up the bestseller lists, and pushed Baroque's out of top spot, due to the introduction of a new character; Harrison, the white-haired goat-like creature. "Suck on that, Baroque!" Wilson was quoted in an influential newspaper. He sent a copy of the book to Detective Harrison, who was not amused. But his grandchildren loved it!

And finally, in case you missed the significance of that "kiss" at the end, Wilson and Cari were married in a small ceremony on Crete, a place they decided to make their permanent home. Cari spends her free time writing a novel about a dork and an ex-con on the run. Wilson can't understand why Cari replaced him in the story.

As a wedding gift, Wilson bought Cari the complete series on DVD of the crime drama *CSI.* Just in case!

Now this is the fucking end! (Author's note: sorry about that, Cari wrote it. She has promised to cut back on the swearing after the baby is born. Apparently, they found a barn on Crete!)

Post-postscript

The person who killed Ralph Brentwood was (continued on the next page)

Made in the USA
Middletown, DE
10 January 2019